DESTINY IS YOURS

BOOK 2 IN THE LIFE IS YOURS TRILOGY

ABIGAIL YARDIMCI

Soft Rebel
PUBLISHING

Dedicated to Mustafa - the shadow who inevitably finds my light

———

*"The only zen you can find on
the tops of mountains is the zen
you bring up there."*
Robert M Pirsig

CONTENTS

How This Book Works   vii

Prologue   1
1. Respite   5
2. Shit Class Hotel   8
3. Experiments In The Art Of Living   14
4. Make Contact   21
5. Look-A-Like Day   38
6. Moments of God   59
7. Dalyan   87
8. Polishing   102
9. Tiny Dot   112
10. Language of the Heart   120
11. The Coffee   124
12. Tipping Point   136
13. The Rock in the Sea   146
14. The Pure Path   152
15. Surprise   162
16. Game Plan   168
17. Cold Shoulder   176
18. Ten Years' Time   183
19. A Wish   190
20. Cappadocia   198
21. The Balloon Ride   202
22. See What Happens   212
23. The Return   222
24. A Thousand Times Before   227
25. Someone Random   234
26. Lucky   241
27. Mesut's Birthday   247
28. Melis   261

29. Packing Up   271
30. İnşallah   277
31. New Direction   282
     Epilogue   286

     More by Abigail Yardımcı   291
     Acknowledgements   293
     About the Author   297

HOW THIS BOOK WORKS

In 2006 I had the most unexpected, tumultuous and life-altering year.

I'll never forget it. And that's why I wrote about it in three parts, of which this book, 'Destiny Is Yours', is the second.

Through exploring my own lived experience, I decided to capture the year through the eyes of a fictitious character. I called her 'Jess' quite simply because when I was a young slip of a girl I thought Jessica was the most glamorous name ever and couldn't understand why my parents hadn't seen fit to give me it.

So once I had the character of Jess conjured up, I realised what I really needed her for was to create a bit of distance between me and the story. I needed a gap where I could understand more deeply what I'd been through and let all the juicy stuff come up. It meant I could exercise a bit of artistic license with the order of things, I could merge characters where there were too many to keep track of, and change names out of respect for people who might recognise themselves in the pages.

I hope you enjoy the story because, like the other books in the trilogy, the majority of it happened exactly like that: incredible people showing up and blowing my mind with their timing, their authenticity and their undeniable part in helping me find my way.

The rest of it is yummy fiction that I hope you relish in your own way.

Now let's go spend a month in Turkey . . .

PROLOGUE

I'm stomping down the street yet again. Fury in every footstep. The sweet peas clinging to the stone wall by the post office curl away from me in pastel swirls. Shy. Careful.

"Jessie!" He shouts from way back over the concrete hill. "I was only jokin' lass. Howay and eat yer chips love. There's nowt wrong wi' being a fatty."

Hate, hate, hate him. He's not even the one supposed to be looking after me and my brother. He's extra. He tags along. Decorative, he likes to say.

Well he can go and decorate somewhere else.

It's okay though. I know exactly where I'm going. Even if my eyes are hot and full so everything's blurry. And I'm not breaking any rules either. Sandra always says, "No further than the crossroads at the bottom of the hill else yer mam'll 'av me guts for garters. You bairns and yer adventures. They'll be the death of me."

"Nah, she'd never make it back up the hill a roly-poly like 'er! Just chuck 'er in the back yard Sandra pet, we can watch 'er bounce around a bit. Come on. We'll invite the neighbours!" His laughter streaks through the house like a black whip.

Making it back up the hill is the last thing on my mind right now. I just want to get to the edge of the crossroads so I can find the things I'm looking for. The things that tease the lump from my throat and lull the bubbling in my chest. I can't believe Sandra has let him into our house again.

A fresh blanket of wind throws itself at me as I turn the corner of the sandstone terrace. I'm big enough now that it doesn't knock me off my feet anymore. Instead I walk right into it with my head held up high, not caring that a coat would have been a good idea. No doubt he would have had something to say about the way I struggle into my Minnie Mouse bomber jacket, as it is a bit small. So there really was no point even trying.

I look downwards to where the sandy brick meets the flat, grey pavement. Bursts of green. Puffs of white. They're waiting for me. It's just the right time of year for it. Or the wrong time as my Mam would say.

I stoop down and pick just one at the base of the stem. An instant oily tang fills my nostrils. I stand back up to face the valley. Looking out over the green and yellow hills that dip and curve against a sky so blue it beams, I wonder why the council have not come and put benches here. Nobody but me seems to know it but this really is the best view in the village. Not even the end-terrace houses have windows on this side. I'm only seven and even I can see what a very big opportunity they've missed.

The memories of Sandra's chunky chips on a plate, his yellow teeth grinning and nicotine fingers prodding at my belly start to fade as I brush the edge of the dandelion clock against my cheek. The softest, lightest touch calms my beating heart and I might be wrong but it seems the wind has settled down too. For a moment.

I get ready for my ritual. Because I've figured out that's what this is now: a ritual. We learned about them at school and I know it's all about doing things in a certain order to make people feel proud and better and true. So here I am. Ready for all of that.

I hold the fluffy flower right in front of my face, so close I can see all the important parts – black seeds puncturing the spongy centre, wispy white wands that spill out into starbursts of flossy white. Most kids my age do the whole clock thing. One o'clock, blow. Two o'clock, blow. I can't see the point myself. I prefer my way. Even if I found it because of something – or someone – so awful.

Who can I think of? I know. That old lady in the corner shop this morning. The one who didn't have enough pennies for her favourite tea bags. I wish for her more money and more teabags. Blow.

Now my teacher at school says her dad is sick so she has to take some time off. I wish for her that he gets better soon. And for him. Blow.

The lame cat that keeps sneaking in our kitchen looking for food. I wish for him a happy, cosy home with lots of delicious food (maybe ours?). Blow.

My best friend Kelly who wishes her dad would come home. Blow. My brother's friend who doesn't have shoes that fit him. Blow. My Dad who hates his job and wants to change it. Blow. Sandra's rubbish taste in men. Blow. All the poor, hungry children in the world whose pictures I see on the telly but I don't know how to reach. Blow.

As I think and blow, think and blow, I watch the starry bursts of white allow themselves to be picked up and carried away by totally invisible forces. Whether they drift or whether they soar, I like the way they invite themselves without saying sorry, into the wild. The white magic of my wishes is out there now. Nothing anyone can do about it. So I keep going.

When I've wished all I can for everyone I can think of, I

remember to pick one last dandelion for myself. I stand up straight and fill my lungs with air.

A new Minnie Mouse jacket. Blow. The sun to shine every day. Blow. The shop to stock more Cola Cubes. Blow. To be allowed to watch Get Fresh on a Saturday morning. Blow. For Sandra to find a new boyfriend. Blow. My mam to find a new babysitter. Blow. For him to be gone when I get home. Blow.

The dandelion is spent so I drop the last stalk and just stand there, watching my magic do its work.

And it will. I know it will.

1

RESPITE

Lindy didn't have to wait for long before Jess returned to their glowing beach alcove, where they'd been sitting comfortably and cosily for a little while now.

She watched as Jess scuffed through the silvery sand, the sleeves of her purple hoodie rolled up, silver bracelet jangling and blonde waves bobbing around her face. She was clutching an already opened bottle of red wine, two glasses and a paper bag.

"The bloke at the traditional Turkish place opened the bottle for me and said I could have the glasses as long as I return them later. He gave me a proper wink and a nudge but, you know, best to ignore that."

Jess laughed, threw herself down next to the fire and flattened out a patch of damp sand. She planted the base of the glasses firmly and Lindy reached to pour the wine, watching it flow freely under the glimmering moonlight, just like the dark, rolling waves only feet away from them. It made that wonderful glug-glug sound of the first pour.

"Thanks Jess. This is so what I need."

"No probs. Turkish wine isn't always up to much but I've had this one before and it's alright. And wait till you taste this."

Jess unwrapped a small selection of sticky-looking, flaky pastry cakes, all decorated with nuts, seeds and dried fruit and scented with cinnamon.

"Baklava. It's not exactly a bumper bar of Dairy Milk but it'll do."

Jess set the cakes down between them both and Lindy reached for a particularly delicious looking glazed pastry triangle drenched in honey and crushed pistachios. She sank her teeth into it and enjoyed a sudden shot of sweetness that made her shiver. That aromatic honey, pastry as fine as flower petals and a solid, earthy bite to the nuts . . . She'd never fancied it when her mum had shoved it under her nose before now, but tonight things were different. She could feel it in her bones, in the cool whisper of the sea breeze.

Tonight there was a new story beginning to unfold.

Lindy wondered where her parents would be now. No doubt they'd be shacked up at their favourite Brits-abroad dive, taking it in turns to roll their eyes and despair at what they were going to do with their wayward daughter. It was New Year's Eve, after all and they would be expecting her to get in touch before midnight at least. Lindy checked her phone. There was time yet.

And let's face it, 2006 hadn't exactly been kind to her. She remembered how she'd felt earlier that evening, just before she'd met Jess, when she'd been wandering aimlessly on the beach with only tears for company. She'd felt that familiar sense of dread claw at her and try to pull her so far down so that she might very well become part of the mass of wet sand she was walking on, part of the cold, dark depths of the ocean below. Even here, in the perfectly nice holiday resort her parents had managed to drag her to, away from everything at home that was shit and awful, she hadn't been able to find respite.

That was, until she'd spotted Jess's fire in the alcove.

It was as if all of this had been waiting for her. The alcove, the fire, the wine, Jess and her story of heartbreak and pain, magic and hope. She momentarily considered looking around for hidden cameras, for her parents crouching behind a rock with Derren Brown or somebody equally dodgy, only to reveal she'd actually been hypnotised into all of this. But there were no hidden cameras here.

Just some strange coincidence that she was, at last, choosing to embrace.

"Come on then, what happened next? How was the second holiday in Turkey?" Lindy was ready to find out what Jess had done with her huge slice of time back in Turkey. Frittering a whole month away just to ponder the meaning of life seemed like a mental thing to do when you had a failed relationship to mourn, not to mention a business that was crashing and burning in a big way. But having heard the reasoning behind it all, Lindy was totally on Jess's side.

Sometimes you just had to say fuck it.

"Well, it was so much more than a holiday that's for certain. Where can I start? I know. Let me tell you about Shit Class Hotel." Jess took an impressive mouthful of wine and wiped her mouth with the cuff of her jumper. She leaned back into the rock and planted the base of her glass in the sand again, fingers tracing along the rim and her blue eyes alive.

Lindy leaned back too and wondered what kind of story could possibly start with a shit class hotel.

2

SHIT CLASS HOTEL

Thanks to our incredibly cheap flight tickets, we arrived at Bodrum airport at some unearthly hour. My newly-mended heart beat so fast I had to take a couple of deep breaths as we passed through customs. *It's okay sweetie,* I told it, *we're in this together.*

Gillie's gangster-style love interest, Demir, had offered to pick us up from the airport, having badgered her since our last holiday with constant texting. When we tumbled out of the airport into the dry heat of the night, we saw Demir standing there, in an exact replica of the image we'd joyfully anticipated: pointy black shoes gleamed to within an inch of their life, pressed chinos, hair sculpted into a glistening, razor-like point and a soppy smile on his face that contradicted all of the coiffing efforts he had made.

"Hello girls." He said. "Welcome back my country."

He air-kissed me on both cheeks and fixed a rushed, determined kiss straight on Gillie's mouth before whisking us away in his car.

We drove the couple of hours to İpeklikum, Gillie in the front chatting to Demir, and me in the back watching this new world go by. This really was the first moment I'd had to myself in quite some time.

Things had been so busy at home what with all the holiday preparations and making sure our community arts business, Firebelly, would survive until we got back. Now that I was here, in the back of this bizarre man's car, with the warm wind whipping through the open window and the unfamiliar night landscape whizzing past, I could finally appreciate the weirdness of what I'd done.

There was something comforting about arriving in İpeklikum. I recognised some of the lamp-lit streets, restaurants and shops as we drove into the resort.

How funny, I thought, *that a place you've only known for a week in your entire life can coax you back into contentment so very easily.*

Demir stopped outside our home for the month: First Class Hotel. And it looked okay. Maybe not first class exactly, but it looked clean and bright and it would do.

Demir sauntered inside and arranged for the porter to take our bags and show us up to our room. Then he waited obediently in the car as Gillie quite rightly instructed him.

Lacking the natural hospitality of Demir, our porter literally chucked our bags in the corridor leading to our room and shoved the key in my hand saying, "Only one key, okay?" He then dashed back downstairs to continue watching some Turkish equivalent of Eastenders on the dusty flat screen in reception. Gillie and I were far too excited to be pissed off with him and squeezed ourselves into the little corridor so we could shut the door behind us.

Gillie climbed over our haphazardly hurled bags and chirped, "Come on Jess, our room must be just through here . . . oh."

A world of disappointment was in that 'oh'.

"What is it Gillie?" I asked as I scaled the bags myself and half tripped over to where she was standing. Then I saw it. The corridor that led into our room? It wasn't a corridor. It was the room. And gone was the promise of *'two ample-sized single beds'* as outlined in the brochure, more like *'one tiny double bed designed for pixies'*.

And somehow, though god only knows how, they'd managed to squeeze in a match box sized bedside table, two single red lightbulbs hanging on shoestring wires, and a series of little alcoves built into the wall which we presumed to be the equivalent of a wardrobe.

"Bloody hell, a few days in here and it'll look like an award-winning art installation ."

Gillie slumped down on the bed, knocking her knees on the scarily close facing wall. "Oh but look at this. What do you suppose they were thinking?" Gillie giggled and pointed at the corner of the bed where somebody had quite clearly spent the best part of an afternoon folding every towel, flannel and paper tissue into shapes which resembled perky little swans.

"Hah. You can't have access to basic necessities in this hotel, but you can dry your arse on a towel shaped like a swan!"

Gillie flung herself backwards and laughed up at the ceiling, a mixture of genuine amusement, despair and sleepiness. I then proceeded to give her a running commentary of our new temporary home. "And you will see madam, that if you place one foot, quite literally, in front of the other you can amble down this side of the room to an opening fashioned not with a traditional door, oh no, but with a 1950's synthetic folding mechanism which allows you to access a wonderfully . . . erm . . ."

I wedged myself into the bathroom and continued from inside, "A wonderfully condensed bathroom arrangement with the added design feature of sink, shower and toilet all being no more than five centimetres apart. I think you'll find it a very convenient assemblage to rival any other bathroom setting."

I could hear Gillie from the other side of the paper-thin wall. "Stop Jess, you're killing me!"

"But it doesn't stop there. Once you've twisted yourself away from the bathroom's multiple attractions . . ." I popped myself out and lurched to the opposite side of the room, "you'll notice that the room has the obligatory holiday feature of a south-facing balcony. It is disguised behind this rather fetching heavy tweed style curtain. But, if you pull it back . . ." I heaved the grotesque, dusty curtain with all my might to reveal our last scrap of hope, a balcony with a sea view, "You will reveal this marvelous single French door which opens – wait for it – inwards! So you can bash the well-located bed every time you wish to go outdoors. And you will no doubt be delighted to find that you can actually fit your entire set of toes onto the balcony floor! As for the sea view, if you look hard enough you will discover a chink of rippling ocean can be seen between the two fifteen-story hotels which are not more than fifty yards across the road. It has been known that sunlight can even find its way into this apartment through that very same gap on a completely cloudless day."

I turned round and beamed at Gillie, "Well, I think that concludes the tour of your luxury new dwelling in Shit Class Hotel!"

"Yey for Shit Class Hotel!" Gillie cheered. "Thank you tour guide. Now let's get changed and get out of this place. I want a beer!"

———

Half an hour later we'd been driven to our old haunt from just a couple of months back, Beerbelly. And were enjoying a beer, as planned, under the stars.

We'd arrived to find the legendary, long-haired cocktail-maker Mesut and cringey ladies' man 'Bad Boy' lounging in a thick cloud of cigarette smoke, watching 'Kill Bill' on the super-sized TV. We flinched a bit when Demir demanded that we be served immediately, especially when the boys protested that it was too late to be serving customers now.

The whole confrontation was delivered in quick, angry Turkish, but Gillie reckoned Demir had pointed out if Bad Boy could have a scantily clad Essex girl wrapped around him then surely Mesut could be freed up to make a couple of drinks. So Mesut stormed off to the bar, head hung so low that his long black hair blocked out any angry retorts he might be making, and returned seconds later with several bottles of ice cold Efes lager.

Long story short, we were finally here with our beers and the stars. Bad Boy had obligingly disappeared with his clinging Essex girl, Mesut had slumped in a definite huff, back in front of his movie, and Demir started to recount the story (though god knows how it turned into an actual story), of our tiny little box room.

"So now," Demir said in fits of giggles, "Jess is calling it *Shit Class Hotel*! Do you get it Mesut? Shit Class Hotel!" Mesut kept his eyes on the screen but tipped his head slightly and kind of snorted which I assumed was his version of a chuckle, whilst Demir hurled himself back into his chair and bit a cushion to curb his own hysteria.

Gillie and I exchanged glances. Okay, maybe we had to learn a thing or two about the sense of humour over here, because suddenly I had become an award-winning comedian.

And that was the thing, I suppose, that we wanted to get out of this trip. We could become anything we wanted. We could let people think whatever they liked. Nobody knew us, nobody had ties to us, or expectations of us. We could live one long month of blissful, harmonic, euphoric anonymity.

I stretched my legs out onto the table despite a withering glance from Mesut; smiled at Gillie and Demir engaging in an already predictable game of flirtation; leaned back and took a long, cool gulp of beer.

Yup. This was going to be a damn good month.

3

EXPERIMENTS IN THE ART OF LIVING

When I woke up the air was thick and hot.

My eyes were still closed, my head was fuzzy, my body still heavy in slumber. Images floated around my consciousness – a bright white crescent moon in a dark indigo sky; pointy black shoes; a cold glass bottle topped with white froth; sand dripping through my fingers; dangling white fairy lights, or were they stars? I noticed a tingle in my left arm and shifted to relieve the blood flow, stretching both arms upwards, turning onto my back and pointing my toes as far as they could go.

"Ouch! That's my hair you're pulling!" Gillie squeaked, and bam, I was back to Shit Class reality.

"I think we managed the night quite well, all things considered." I said, untangling Gillie's hair from between my fingers and thus freeing her from her contorted position in a crumpled zig-zag across the bed.

"Yeah, kind of. But Jess, why do you have to be so damn tall?"

"Family flaw." I said, and literally rolled out of bed into the bathroom. I needed to introduce my skin to soap and water again. "Just going to check out the shower, then we can go for breakfast."

"Okay. Jess? Does a cocktail count as breakfast?"

I smiled and spoke loudly above the spray of water against cold, cracked tiles. "On this holiday Gillie – fuck yes!"

———

Later that day we were lazing on cushioned basket seats in a beach-side bar, slowly sipping our breakfast.

We hadn't seen or spoken to anyone yet, apart from Demir and the guys at Beerbelly, our porter and the barman here. We were pleasantly sinking into anonymity, blending into the world of tourists very nicely and didn't plan to emerge from it for quite some time, if at all.

There was, however, the small question of whether or not I was going to see the famous Ekrem again.

Ah, Ekrem. A smile teased my lips as I lay back in my basket-chair and let the giant, lumbering vision of him settle in my mind. He'd been a giant ball of cologne-drenched fun last time I'd been here just a couple of months ago, notwithstanding rickety sun-loungers and dark, deserted hotel balconies. He too, had sent me a few naughty texts since I'd returned home which I'd responded to with amusement and not much else to be honest. I'd actually quite liked the idea of never seeing him again and writing him off as my first ever holiday fling. But, hey, would it really harm anyone to revisit that particular episode?

Probably not.

Anyway, for the moment we had something more important to think about. As we swung gently in our seats, glasses in hand, there, on the table between us was a large white envelope. And it was all down to Gillie's recent ex. Marcus.

It was the envelope he'd given me, literally just before we'd left for the airport, and now it felt like he'd followed me here.

"*I made this for you the other night. Loads of thought went into it so I hope you like it. I think – or hope – it will fit perfectly into your holiday. Although it may take a bit of an open mind . . .*" I could remember his grin as clear as day. He was totally up to something.

"It's probably just a travel guide or something. Maybe he found some random information on Turkey online and thought you'd be interested?" Gillie said. "He's always glued to that bloody computer."

"Then why ask me to wait until I got here to open it? And why would I need to keep an open mind? That just doesn't make sense."

Gillie shrugged and slurped up the last of her cocktail. She immediately stuck her empty glass in the air, knowing that the doe-eyed, bare-chested barman would come flip-flopping her way to collect it. Which he did. Within seconds.

We kept staring at the envelope. I had a feeling that opening it was going to be like opening a can of rebellious worms. Damn Marcus and his surprise-springing ideas. Why did I have to go and make friends with him? It was much easier when him and Gillie had been a thing and I'd disliked the fibre of his being. 'Friends' had been a bad idea from the start. I pulled the envelope across the table towards me. I'd stuff it back into my bag and forget all about it. Maybe I'd tell Marcus it had got lost.

"What are you doing?" Gillie shrieked. "I know him and whatever's in there will be worth looking at. Just bloody well open it!"

I paused with the envelope clutched to my chest, my other hand holding open my beach bag with full intention of stuffing it away for good. But I could see that Gillie was about to bust a gut so I dropped my bag, grabbed my cocktail for some Dutch courage and thought *what the hell.* I ripped it open.

When I shook out the contents we found two identical sheets of A4 paper with some kind of official looking letter printed onto them, and six small sealed envelopes. Everything lay on the table for a milli-second before Gillie and I each snatched up one of the A4 letters and Gillie began to read out loud.

I listened and followed on my own copy.

CONTRACT

This contract is to certify that **Jess Parker** agrees to undertake '**Experiments in the Art of Living**'. This scheme is devised by **Marcus Lane.**

Jess Parker understands that she has been a shadow of her former self since splitting up with her ex-life-partner and co-business-owner, Jack. She now wants to make more of her dull and mundane life. She is willing to undertake each of the six experiments exactly as stated in the challenge envelopes enclosed, and realises that **Marcus Lane** cannot be held responsible for things that may happen to her if her life begins to get a little better.

This binding contract details a series of challenges that will give **Jess Parker** an insight into how life could be, rather than how it has been.

Jess Parker agrees to record everything relating to the challenges in diary and photographic form and undertake a de-brief session on her return to England. She agrees to meet with **Marcus Lane,** and pay for any and all drinks that may be consumed during the de-brief session.

During said session, **Marcus Lane** will also give feedback and confirm whether or not Jess Parker is, indeed a better person. If she has fulfilled the challenges to the required level, she will be awarded with a certificate that will confirm she is now well and truly alive (e.g. foundation level).

I agree to undertake all the challenges as written in the challenge envelopes.

Signed:
Date:

I agree that, even though it doesn't look it, this contract is genuine.

Signed:
Date:

I agree that the two signatures above are mine.

Signed:
Date:

```
This is what my signature looks like with my
other hand.
```

```
Signed:
Date:
```

"Oh. My. God." Gillie concluded.

"Indeed."

Just exactly what kind of a brain did Marcus possess? And how did he know me so well all of a sudden? I mean, I'd made an active effort over the years to not reveal any of myself to this man who I didn't trust even an inch.

Of course, I'd been out on many an evening with him, double-dates, weekends away, birthday parties, shopping trips, bonfire nights, Christmas get-togethers – as you do in an effort to be civil to your best mate's bloke. But I had always, always kept my distance from him. I'd been careful not to let him into my life in any meaningful way, in a bid to stay faithful to Gillie, who I knew, one day, would figure out that he wasn't right for her. So how the hell, with just a few simple words and a crazy idea like this, had Marcus hit a very tender nerve when he wasn't even in the same bloody country?

Maybe he was cleverer than I thought.

Maybe by staying so far away from him for all those years I'd actually revealed more of myself than I would have done if we'd got up close and personal. Maybe I'd shown more about who I was by what I hadn't done, than by what I had done. Could that possibly make sense? In these times, and in this tumultuous, riotous year, it seemed that it could.

Okay Marcus, okay. I'll take you up on it. I will do your crazy challenges – every single one of them. And I will do them with spirit. Because maybe you know better than I do what I need to get out of this trip.

"Right Gillie, that shithead ex of yours has got himself a deal." That second, Gillie's tender young thing of a barman flip-flopped over with her refreshed cocktail glass. As he leant forward to set the drink down on the table, I eyed a pen tucked in the waistband of his surf shorts. I whipped it out, smoothed the paper out on the table and swooped my hand down to sign on all four of the dotted lines.

"There you go Marcus. And let the records show that you started this."

4

MAKE CONTACT

It wasn't until the next day that I decided to open the first of the challenge envelopes.

I'd waited until now to launch into Marcus's crazy scheme because on the previous day Gillie and I had done nothing more than drink, lounge and be merry. We'd stayed away from all things familiar, opting instead to stay close to Shit Class Hotel and check out our local amenities.

On the plus side, those amenities consisted of a small secluded beach with shallow, turquoise waters and white sands; a handful of relaxed beachside bars; and a dramatic rocky cliff-side offering stunning sunsets. On the down side, we had hideously over-priced grocery shops; appalling dance music pounding out of every establishment by night; and more than our fair share of shabby, towering hotels blocking our every path. A little bit of heaven and a little bit of hell.

And, of course, I was drip-feeding myself my own little version of hell by having my usual body-image shit-fit.

Gillie knew nothing of this. It was a life-long habit, but I was ashamed to admit to her that all the bikini-clad bodies I was faced with, sent me into a raging storm of inhibition. In recent weeks, I'd realised that some of these inhibitions may have been made entirely worse by what I thought had been a wholesome relationship with my ex-fiancé, Jack. He'd always been so protective and coveting of my body, that I'd assumed it was just sweetness in abundance. Looking back, I could now perhaps see that seven years of encouraging me to wear baggy clothes, assuring me I'd look good even in a bin bag, was anything but sweet. Jack's dominion over my wardrobe now had my skin crawling at the idea of showing it some sunshine.

And even though all of the bodies around me were worlds apart – round bodies, flat bodies, smooth bodies, tanned bodies, bodies that strutted and bodies that bounced, bodies that flowed and bodies that flounced – it didn't matter. Whether they fit into the senseless skinny-ass conventions flaunted by magazines or not, I still found something in them that was better than what I had.

What was it about putting on a bikini that did this to me? I'd done so much work over this year so far, on the kind of person I wanted to be. On how to rise way above my insecurities. I *knew* I was so much more than my pasty skin, my straggly hair, my chubby rolls, my dimpled thighs. I *knew* I was much more than my body. I *knew* I was lucky to have a body that worked and did everything I needed it to do. But those two pieces of fabric that were supposed to cling to my boobs and bum and make me feel like a tropical beach babe had me feeling anything but.

So I decided to do away with the bikini for now (who said I had to like wearing one anyway?) and rely on my good old swimming cozzie and artfully draped towels. I just hoped that these were merely early-holiday jitters and that I'd ease into beach babe mode the longer I stayed in İpeklikum. Yes, I was working with a lifetime of body-related inhibition but surely, now that Jack was nowhere near me or my wardrobe, this was the time to let it slowly slip away?

And Marcus's challenges would make for the perfect distraction.

So, we were sitting by the Shit Class pool when I opened the first envelope. It was after lunchtime and we'd just had a nice long dip in the pool – which, incidentally, was not Shit Class at all and was apparently the envy of many a hotel in İpeklikum, so at least we'd got something right. I tore open the envelope, pulled out a small slip of paper and read out loud.

Challenge 1 – Make Contact

Touch at least 30 people today.

NB: Marcus Lane does not condone the sexual touching of strangers. To do it and get away with it is a highly specialised skill and must not be attempted by amateurs.

"No sexual touching? Boring!" said Gillie as she took the slip of paper from my hands to read it again.

"Obviously, the man's got no understanding of where we are. It'll be simple to touch thirty people in one day here. But let's get real, it's totally going to be at least a teeny bit risque." I was referring, of course to the fact that you only had to walk ten yards down the street before some manicured hunk of a man quite literally grabbed you and tried to get you into their dining / drinking / dancing establishment. "Well at least it's an easy one to get me started."

So with our new-found challenge to complete, and this juicy opportunity to see what my body could do other than disappoint me, we dashed up to our little box room, got slightly glammed up, and ventured out into the main town of İpekllikum.

We were only half-way into town when I'd already managed to touch five people, all of them eager young gents, trying to usher me into their restaurants. I aimed to keep the contact gentle and humorous. Perhaps a little hand shake or a playful nudge. But once or twice these men were a bit too insistent for my liking. I wasn't particularly taken with having my waist gripped or a sweaty arm slung round my shoulder for an entire conversation.

Gillie, however, was quite the pro and reveled in all the attention, no matter how questionable it might have been. So when she was chatting with an especially attentive young fellow with yellow shorts, I slipped into the café he was so passionately promoting: 'The Four Seasons'.

As soon as I strode in, Gillie's yellow shorts man deserted her and tripped over himself to show me through to the private beach bar at the back of the restaurant. This little haven was marked out with broad orange parasols trimmed with pink tassels, and white plastic sun loungers which looked rickety enough to bring back instant memories of my night on a hotel balcony with Ekrem only weeks before. I ordered myself a diet coke (enough of the cocktails for now) and chose a sun lounger right at the edge of the sea. If I let my feet dangle, I'd be able to dip them into the shallow lapping waves. Nice.

I couldn't quite believe it but there was nobody else around. Not a soul on this gorgeous little private patch of beach. I made a silent vow to myself that if I ever did a holiday in the sun again, it would most definitely be towards the end of the tourist season. I mean, this was bliss.

Something I hadn't thought much about since arriving in Turkey was my trusty old notebook. I'd had it with me all the time but it hadn't quite made it out of my bag yet, even though it had served me so well these past few months, whilst I navigated one hell of a heartbreak. And now, I decided, it was the perfect place to file all of Marcus's challenge stuff, and make notes about how I was getting on.

So, I wrote across a new blank page:

Feeling crap about wearing a bikini so dumped that idea and opened Marcus's first challenge

Touched five people walking from Shit Class into town. All men. This is too easy. These men want to be touched . . . physical contact is their chosen language!

At that moment a shadow crossed the page and I looked up to see Gillie standing over me.

She was the picture of holiday glam. Designer bag flung over one shoulder, purple kaftan casually draped off the other, jewelled flip-flops in hand and huge, oversize sunglasses drawing back her copper-toned hair. And she wasn't alone. She had five – count them, five – male specimens standing right behind her laden with trays of fresh fruit, mixed nuts and cock-tails. Did this girl have no shame?

"Gillie? What are you doing? I ordered a diet coke."

"I know. They told me. What were you thinking?"

Before I could even protest, the male entourage had dragged over a sun lounger for Gillie, set down our platters on a small table and had arranged themselves in slave-like poses at our feet. Our feet!

Even Gillie must have felt a tad too Cleopatra-like because

she patted the edge of our loungers and they all jumped to sit next to us rather than below us. Which was marginally better.

One of the entourage leaned forward and took both mine and Gillie's hands in his. He had large, tilted oval eyes as deep and brown as pools of hot chocolate. His skin was deliciously dark and he was naked, as far as I could tell, except for a swathe of white fabric wrapped low on his tiny waist. He wasn't doing much to eradicate the ancient Egyptian fantasy which was rapidly growing in my mind.

"My name is Bob." He said.

Bob?

"This my place and to come here is okay all the time if you want." I think Gillie and I would have clapped our hands with glee at the cuteness of his stunted English (and the inappropriateness of his name) if he wasn't grasping them so very tightly. He looked at us with a perfectly crafted intensity.

"Anything you want, you can have."

And with that, he firmly kissed each one of our hands and took slightly too long over it if you ask me. At least that was another one for the book.

After Bob had introduced himself, he left the other four boys to look after us. I decided I was not going to be the passive challenge-doer, oh no, I was going to be the master of touching here thank you very much. So I initiated hand-shaking, shoulder-clapping and knee-patting before there was even the first sip of a cocktail. I realised, however, how quickly this was going to backfire on us when the boys suggested we all had our photos taken together. If there was ever an excuse for them to get up close and personal with us, then this was it.

Before we knew it one of them had grabbed my phone, and the others had piled onto us in an expertly arranged human bundle, with 'Bob' joining in when he heard the commotion. It was all muscly thighs, wandering hands and big, hopeful eyes.

And the heat! When you threw the heat of the day into the equation, it suddenly became very real and very clammy.

Yes, they were gorgeous young things, and maybe we were crazy not to go any further, but Gillie and I weren't quite ready to throw our keys in the bowl thank you very much. It was just too much for the second day in.

So there was no option but to feign heinous sunstroke. Within seconds we were clutching our tummies and threatening to vomit over our entourage which led them, surprisingly, to tend to the needs of the customers up in the restaurant. We took this opportunity to sneak out, remembering of course to leave money for our drinks and a healthy tip. We scampered down the street laughing wildly and quite literally wiping the sweat from our brows (and other places).

Once we were clear of the Four Seasons, we slowed our pace down to a stroll. We walked down a steep, cobbled hill which gave a wonderful view of the main tourist strip, the wide, sandy beach and the mountains and cliff edges beyond. Directly opposite us, but far away on the tip of the next holiday town, we could see a slowly rotating Ferris Wheel, pinprick lights of green, red, orange and blue turning, turning and inviting the early evening to settle. The sky had turned from vivid blue to dusky purple and a bright white crescent moon was beginning to smile down. The air was notably cooler and a gentle breeze floated effortlessly along the pathway.

As we walked slowly along, we noticed that families, couples and groups of friends were steadily joining the strip, either chatting animatedly or walking quietly. This was the land of the holiday night out, and now we had to decide what to do with ours.

"Let's go to English Rose" said Gillie.

"Hmmm . . . I don't know Gillie. Ekrem might be there." I said.

"Of course he'll be there. That's the whole point. You want to see him again, don't you?"

"I suppose so. I mean, he was nice."

"Nice? Jess, he was a god. Come on, we're going." Gillie linked my arm and quickened our pace amongst the growing tourist throng. I decided to submit to her demands. I mean, look at the facts: I was hungry, I was thirsty, and I was curious. What harm could it do?

On the way to English Rose, I continued 'Making Contact' by trying it out on some people who were altogether less Turkish. I clasped a little boy's hand when he picked up my strategically dropped sunglasses; I accidentally-on-purpose bumped into a young couple, causing them to stop a growing argument in its tracks; I noticed and stroked a tattoo of a black puma on the arm of a strapping skinhead bloke; and when I saw a beautifully large, curly-haired lady all done up in a sparkling black basque, I touched her on the shoulder and told her how fabulous she looked (and made an extra special effort to really mean the compliment without inwardly comparing her body to mine – result).

When we got to English Rose it looked exactly the same as I remembered. I had to keep reminding myself that it was only a few weeks since we'd been here really, and not a millennium. The guy at the door greeted us eagerly with further kisses and handshakes, introducing himself as Keith (*Keith?*) and said of course he remembered us, how could he forget two such "*beautious ladies*"?

We were shown to our table and welcomed with immediate glasses of wine, napkins flipped onto our laps and menus placed in our hands. Half of me wanted to hide behind the menu and not go through the nail-biting process of looking for Ekrem, and half of me wanted to seek him out immediately.

But what else were best friends for? Whilst I skulked

behind the menu, Gillie gave a running commentary. "Right, I can see pretty much everyone else we met last time, but I can't see Ekrem . . . maybe he's on a break. Oh, hang on . . . there's a tall guy over at the bar, he's got his back to us, he's loading drinks onto a tray. That could be him. Come on, turn round."

"Okay Gillie. Whatever. Let's just order our food."

"He's turning round, just checking the last item on his notepad . . . now he's really turning round. Yep! It's him Jess! It's Ekrem. Phwoar. I forgot he looked like *that*. He's coming over here, he's definitely coming this way. Oh god, he might pass without seeing us. Shall I get his attention?" Before I could say absolutely no frigging way, Gillie had her hand in the air and a big, wide smile on her face. "He's seen me! He's coming over!" I watched Gillie play out a silent conversation with Ekrem where she pointed at me excitedly and then brought her finger to her lips in a miniature shushing gesture, then mouthed at him, *"she's right here."*

God, how old were we?

It was then I felt a large, soft pair of hands cover my eyes and I could smell that familiar spicy scent. I heard a voice. "Guess who?"

"Oooh, I don't know. Elvis Presley?"

And with that he flicked his hands away and fell to his knees in one swift movement. He chuckled and took my hand to kiss it. "No, is just me. Your Ekrem."

I have to say he looked absolutely delicious. His skin was even darker, due to a whole summer of work in the sun, his eyes were bright and his smile was as warm as can be. He was all dolled up in his crisp white shirt, slim red tie and black trousers. He had a white tea towel thrown predictably over one arm and was the picture of five star restaurant service.

It was once I'd taken in his appearance that I realised every female customer in the entire place was looking our way. Out of jealousy or amusement or what I don't know, but it felt a bit weird.

"Get up, you dope." I said and stood up to give him a proper hug.

Gillie and I enjoyed a delicious meal of stuffed vine leaves, assorted salads and rice which was interspersed with comments like, "So, you have boyfriend now, or not?"; "I think that you now grow more beautiful"; and advances such as following me sneakily into the toilet cubicle. A hotel balcony by moonlight was one thing, but a toilet cubicle was quite another. You have to draw the line somewhere.

But, I have to admit, it did feel nice to be desired again. Exactly how genuine that desire was, was perhaps something to consider, but I didn't want to think about that right now. All I knew was that it felt good and that's why, before leaving, I agreed to see Ekrem after he finished work that night. Gillie was happy. As far as she was concerned, it was mission accomplished.

By the time we traced the familiar route over to Beerbelly bar, the sky was dark and smooth. The majority of holiday-goers had finished their evening meals and were either strolling back to their hotels to put tired kiddies to bed, or zapping from bar to bar, soaking up karaoke and alcohol.

We were glad for our own little sanctuary in Beerbelly.

The first half hour at Beerbelly was spent convincing Demir that no, we hadn't been avoiding him and yes, we were going to stay in Beerbelly all night so he could fawn over Gillie. He had it bad for her and who could blame him? She was gorgeous. I watched her strut across the bar floor, enthusiastically re-introducing herself to people she remembered from our last visit. She had transformed her beach kaftan by tying a strip of jewelled green ribbon around her waist and trading her earlier denim hot-pants for a pair of white, tailored linen trousers.

Her jewelled flip-flops peaked out from under the trouser hems, displaying an impressive range of toe rings on her dainty little toes. It was almost like Gillie had put on her holiday costume and assumed a different character. I'd never really seen her looking so flamboyant. I wondered briefly why she shied away from any attention at our work when she was obviously capable of taking it in her stride. Well, maybe this trip would be good for her and show her just what potential she had.

While Gillie flounced about, I got up to speed with my 'Making Contact' challenge by re-acquainting myself with all the bar's usual characters.

Bad Boy, minus the Essex girl, slumped himself down in the chair next to me after crashing my drink down on the table. I remembered the over-sized track-suit bottoms, loose white vest and scuffed-up trainers from last time. His glare was marginally less intimidating and you could see those angelic features if you looked close enough.

"You see me with girl the other night?"

I had no idea if he was demanding or asking so I just nodded.

"Yes. You see me with girl. She not good. She not good for me." And he launched into telling me about Amy, the Essex girl, who was apparently breaking his heart.

They'd been on-off for years (which alarmed me because she didn't look old enough to have been having any kind of a relationship for years), and were currently going through a difficult patch. As far as I could tell, that patch involved her enjoying her holiday and her youth by going out to nightclubs every night, whilst Bad Boy was stuck 'working' in Beerbelly. So I offered Bad Boy my shoulder to cry – or sneer – on, whilst conveniently ticking another one off my 'Make Contact' list.

Later, whilst I was sat with Gillie, Demir and Bad Boy, we were visited by Esad, the owner of Beerbelly. If I remembered rightly, he was the cousin of Demir and the older brother of Bad Boy. The family ties around here were immense. Anyway, he practically leaped over to us from his spot on the dance floor, where he'd been throwing shapes all night. He was dressed as if it was mid-winter, including a beanie hat and a neckerchief. What in god's name could possess someone to dress like that if they intended to dance in a hot, sticky climate?

"Ah, girls. I think you could not stay away from Beerbelly! We too good for you, isn't it?" And before we could answer, he started dancing in the little bit of floor space between all of our feet.

Well, with my 'Make Contact' head on, I saw an opportunity here. Plus, I'd guzzled a fair amount of Chardonnay, fuelling me with the nerve to jump up, grab Esad by his sweaty hand and lead him onto the dance floor. As the inexplicably intense Turkish hip-hop music kicked in, I took every opportunity I could to touch Esad in a craftily-choreographed way. Shoulder-clashing, bum-bumping and thigh-slapping all made an appearance in our little routine. Gillie fell about laughing. Bad Boy looked mortified. And Demir stared in open-mouthed confusion. This clearly wasn't in the realms of his good humour.

But it was apparently in the realms of humouring all the hip teenaged girls currently hanging out in Beerbelly. After Esad and I had performed the shoulder-clashing, bum-bumping and thigh-slapping routine a good few times, all of them got up and started to copy it. They didn't make the copying obvious, of course. They were far more understated and cool. But those were definitely our moves. I couldn't believe it! Since when do moody, with-it teens copy the ridiculously random moves of their elders?

And when I retired to my seat, I watched in amazement as the girls were joined by equally moody Turkish boys who also adopted the moves as if they'd been the in-thing all along. My bit-of-a-joke dance moves were now being matched effortlessly to the sultry music streaming out of the bar. Now that's something you do not see every day.

Or possibly ever again.

Once two o'clock had come and gone, Beerbelly's tunes died down to a slow, rhythmical chill-out groove and Gillie and I once again found ourselves sitting in a cloud of smoke with the boys. Bad Boy was waiting for Amy to return from her escapades; Demir had locked up Mega Tour and now had his legs propped up in Gillie's lap; Esad had fallen asleep in a chair, legs and arms splayed out as if he'd landed there from a great height; and Mesut was wiping down the empty tables.

There were only two lots of customers left in Beerbelly apart from us: three Birmingham girls perched round the last dregs of a fish bowl; and an extremely drunken old couple bafflingly accompanied by a giant Alsatian dog.

I was waiting for Ekrem. Gillie and I had agreed that we could separate on the condition that we would meet back at Shit Class later. I was vaguely nervous but mostly just willing to accept whatever the night still had to throw at me. As I waited, I was leafing through my notebook and reading the notes I'd made about all the people I'd touched that day. Only thing was, I had only made it to twenty-nine and the challenge specifically stated that I must touch thirty people.

I looked around me for a potential victim. I'd managed physical contact with everybody I was sitting with apart from Gillie, and that would just be cheating. I glanced over to the Brummy girls and then at the drowsy couple and their beast-dog.

Nope. Didn't fancy making contact with any of them.

Then a shadow invaded my thoughts. Mesut threw down his cloth on our table and sat down opposite me. He pulled a packet of cigarettes out of his pocket and propped one in his open mouth. When he placed his palm outwards, Bad Boy chucked a lighter into it and in a flash Mesut lit his cigarette, leaned back into his chair and tilted his head to look up at the sky. Smoke was trailing upwards in thin, curling wisps. Now here was a man who looked like he did not want to be touched in any way, shape or form.

But Marcus had not used the word 'challenge' for nothing.

"Hard night Mesut?" I asked.

He stayed in that position, with his head tilted back for quite some time. Eventually, he lifted his hand to his mouth and took another long, slow drag on his cigarette, which seemed to last at least the count of twenty, showing absolutely no indication he'd heard me. As he exhaled, his chest sank and the smoke continued its slow climb into the black night.

I was just considering cutting my losses and slipping away to the loo when he looked in my direction suddenly as if to assess who, exactly, was talking to him. Then he leaned back again and said, "Something like that."

Not knowing what else to say, I came out with, "You've got really nice hair." Oh god. The words *I carried a watermelon* echoed cringingly through my mind.

There was a pause as he inhaled deeply on his cigarette again, and time seemed to slow even more.

Then it caught up again as he exhaled fully and sat up straight in his chair to look at me. "I know."

"Yes. Yes of course you do." I mumbled. I couldn't believe this man. Who says 'I know' when they are given a compliment? I decided to ignore it and get on with the challenge at hand.

"Let me have a look at it," I said as I jumped up and dashed behind him to touch his hair. I could feel him flinch as I bunched his hair into my hand, then let it drip out again in long, falling strands. It really was as black as night.

"I'm going to plait it, okay?"

By this point, all the boys and Gillie had turned to stare.

What, had they never seen anyone touch Mesut before? He wasn't a museum artefact.

Mesut looked back at them, glanced up in my direction and then threw his arms up briefly as if to say, *I give in*. He leaned back once again, stared at the wall in front of us and continued to drag on his cigarette. I felt a very small sense of accomplishment, although god knows why, and cheerfully continued to plait his hair. Gillie whipped out her phone and took a photo of person number thirty.

There you go Marcus. Experiments in the Art of Living is well and truly underway.

———

Much later that night or, more accurately, into the very early morning, I was lying among crumpled sheets next to a sleeping Ekrem.

True to his word, he'd come to Beerbelly when he'd finished work and whisked me off to the beach where we'd sat kissing for a very long time. I really hadn't intended to end up in bed with him. Honest.

But he went on and on about wanting my first night with him to be special blah, blah, blah, and I just went along with it.

So, I followed him to his friend's hotel which he could conveniently rent by the hour, then followed him through his seduction technique of sitting me out on the balcony under the stars and telling me how much he had missed me. I let him carry me – yes, carry me – to the bed and undress me slowly. I let him switch on the bedside lamp which was nothing other than a single red – yes, red again – lightbulb so he could '*see into my eyes better*'. I mean, it was possibly the corniest sex experience I'd ever had but I traipsed through it just to see what it would be like. And what was it like? It was fine. Not as good as last time, but not as bad as it could have been. Okay for a repeat episode.

Whilst Ekrem lay sleeping I recalled the last twenty-four hours or so. It had certainly been an eventful day and I had only just started to scratch the surface of this holiday world. I grabbed my notebook which was still in my bag and scribbled down a few highlights from the day, using the slutty red light-bulb to see what I was doing:

Discovered that Shit Class pool is NOT shit class at all

Battled body image demons for the bazillionth time

Spent a few blissful moments alone at Four Seasons

Got in a hot tangle with five almost-naked men

Stopped couple fighting by bashing into them in the street

Started dance craze for hip British girls

Invaded personal space of moody barman

Had corny sex with man who is practical stranger

And, as I reviewed my little list of weird accomplishments, I wrote down three key words to summarise what feelings went with all of this:

COURAGE

INDULGENCE

VIGOUR

And this, I knew, was not a bad day's work on a trip that was going to be about personal discovery. With that in mind, I snapped shut my notebook, pulled my clothes back on and nudged Ekrem to wake up.

Time to get back to Gillie.

5

LOOK-A-LIKE DAY

Challenge 2 — Look-a-Like Day

Find your doppleganger

It was a couple of days later by the time I'd opened this challenge. I didn't want to do one every day. Better to spread them out and make them last.

We'd had a couple of heavenly days which had consisted chiefly of swimming, sunbathing, reading, chatting and frequenting Beerbelly (my bikini still hadn't made an outing but I was beginning to care less about this). And I had a nagging feeling that I was losing time. Wasn't I supposed to work out what I wanted from this trip? Lounging about was all well and good but was it getting me anywhere? I didn't think so. But how do you break a holiday pattern, when you don't know what you want to break into? That's when I decided it was time to see what Marcus had in store for me next.

So when Gillie read Challenge Two out loud from our sunny spot on the main beach, I thought she might be having me on.

"He's joking, isn't he? We're in a Muslim Country! I haven't got a chance in hell of finding someone who looks like me!"

Gillie swept one beautifully bronzed arm outwards and gestured towards the beach. "Jess, just look around you. There are hundreds of Westerners here. You'll be able to take your pick of fair-skinned, leggy blondes."

We both looked around and took in the scene before us. Now I have never been one for stereotyping, but this was the Brits Abroad club if ever I'd seen it. I couldn't see one person who didn't have skin that either folded into brown, leathery wrinkles or looked fit to burst if I were to prod it with a fork.

"Yeah, thanks Gillie. I can see I'll have a tough time choosing between all these people who so closely resemble me."

"Don't worry, we'll do it. We'll just make sure we look absolutely everywhere." Just then Gillie's phone chirped from her handbag. She found it, flipped it open and strolled down in the direction of the shore, floppy sunhat and silver sarong rippling in the breeze.

I knew she was getting out of earshot from me. I knew because this pattern had been repeated a few times since we'd been here. At first I'd thought it was Demir, calling her up whenever she wasn't at Beerbelly. But his communications came in quick-fire rounds of text messages. And these Gillie always showed me:

You coming to see me now please

I wait for you long time.

Why you not tell me you on beach?

It was obvious that Demir had a complex network of undercover agents to report to him where Gillie was at any one time.

And they weren't even an item. Gillie had flirted with him, yes, but she hadn't even gone so far as kissed him. I assumed she was keeping her distance because of her new-found connection with lovely Oliver, a bloke we met on a business course back home, and who had unwittingly become my own personal life coach after I split with Jack. She wasn't exactly committed to him either but I think we both knew he was a safer bet.

Whatever Gillie was doing, I thought she might be playing with fire.

And the phone calls were obviously something Gillie wanted to keep to herself. I was curious, of course, but I knew she'd tell me when she was ready.

Whilst Gillie was off having her secret conversation I thought further about why on earth I was here. The last thing I wanted to do was go home at the end of the month with zero emotional progress. I wanted something big to happen. I wanted to discover something or reveal something or unearth something. I wanted some magic to happen. And I wasn't talking about the dodgy-hotel-sex-with-a-single-red-light-bulb-type of magic. I was talking about real, soulful magic that makes a difference to the rest of your life. But where the hell do you find that in a commercial holiday resort?

I was looking in my bag for a mint to distract me from my troubling thoughts when I came across the scruffy little paperback Oliver had generously given me before I'd left. 'The Alchemist'. I'd almost forgotten about it. Perhaps it had some answers, or could at least distract me from worrying that I'd never find out the purpose of life.

I flipped it open and began to read.

———

A little while later and my new best friend was a shepherd boy called Santiago.

He was on a quest to discover the meaning of a dream and he was bumping into all manner of folk along the way, as you do when you're the lead character in an internationally best-selling novel. These people included a beautiful daughter of a merchant, a dodgy fortune-telling gypsy woman and an old man who was in disguise and was really a mighty king. I was well into it already and didn't particularly want to put the book down when Gillie suggested packing up our stuff and getting some lunch. But it was almost the hottest part of the day and I didn't fancy sizzling to a cinder along with the rest of the Brits Abroad either.

So, having bumped into Ekrem during our slow amble back onto the main promenade, we found shade in English Rose. "Come my girls. Let us find lunch and coolness for you." And lunch and coolness we did have.

Ekrem's boys dragged a heavy-looking upright fan over to our shady table and switched it on full blast. We were brought ample cool drinks in tall, chinking glasses and lots of little plates of salad, rice, bread and dips. Ekrem was busy with customers because, as ever, English Rose was packed to the rafters. Whilst I found his company amusing, it was nice to be left alone even just for a little while. Gillie and I had got to that point on holiday, where you've exhausted all the excited chat and are able to rest in that gorgeous, comfortable silence only very good friends can share.

Although the restaurant was busy, activity was at a minimum, and it felt like the volume was turned down low. People lounged in chairs with sunglasses masking eyes that were probably at least half-closed; children sat and swung their legs slowly, loosely, giggling at waiters who made jokes with them. I wondered precisely how many people here, no matter where in the world they were from, knew exactly what their lives were supposed to mean.

Were they looking for some kind of magic to happen? Did they already have it? Or were they happy with a Pina-colada and a nice table with a sea view?

Just before I'd started reading The Alchemist, I'd suspected I'd perhaps become a tad egocentric. Everything that had happened to me that year, what with Jack's sudden rejection of our seven-year relationship and running straight into the arms of a local pub landlady, our business failing catastrophically and the pretty swift removal of a rug from beneath my feet, had given me nothing to concentrate on but myself.

Me and my beliefs. Me and my values. Me and my relationships. Me and my past and me and my future.

And look at me now. Here I was in a place miles from home, giving myself the opportunity to do a bit more thinking about me.

But after reading just a few chapters of Oliver's little book, I'd come across at least four or five passages that really seemed switched on. The shepherd boy Santiago had listened to what the King had to say about his *destiny*. But he didn't know what *destiny* really was. Ditto. I didn't know if the word had ever even crossed my lips. You can't exactly go round asking what happened on Eastenders last night, which pub do you fancy going to and, oh yeah, how's your destiny going? So what was it with that word? Was it pretentious beyond belief or was it seriously misunderstood?

Whichever it was, the King explained it like this: *'It's what you have always wanted to accomplish. Everyone, when they are young, knows what their destiny is.'* Now I still didn't have a clue how to slip the word into a run-of-the-mill conversation, but I was turning that statement over and over in my head.

Everyone, when they are young, knows what their destiny is.

Is that what I needed out of this trip? To discover my true destiny? Oh, to go back in time and talk to my seven-year-old self.

"Jess, look, look!" Gillie snapped me out of my trance. "Look at that little girl!" Gillie was pointing further down the promenade at a couple strolling hand-in-hand and a gorgeously chubby little girl darting around them, rattling a plastic bucket and spade. Not only did she have short blonde hair, impossibly fair skin, freckles on her nose and big blue eyes, but she was also wearing a pink skirt and yellow vest top combo scarily similar to my own.

And she was probably aged about seven.

As much as I was taken with the urge to rush up to her and say, *"Hello Mini-Me, any chance you can let me in on my destiny? There's a Cornetto in it for you"*, common sense prevailed and I just sat and watched the little girl skip about like she owned the street. I remembered that twirly-skirt move and that carefree swing of a plastic bucket. A lump rose in my throat as I wondered how long it had been since I'd felt that uninhibited.

Gillie shot me an impatient look and tutted. "Well, if you're not going to rise to the challenge, I bloody well will." And she strutted off towards the family with a huge beaming smile.

I sank back into my chair and hid behind the plethora of mini umbrellas that were adorning my lemonade in the hope that Gillie would seem like a lone loon as opposed to one with a sidekick. It was only seconds though, before she reappeared at my side with the little girl holding her hand.

"Jess, this is Samantha." Samantha looked at me with a wide grin and that lump in my throat pretty much melted. "I've explained to Samantha's parents that she looks just like your niece back home and that you'd love to have a photo of the two of you to show her. Okay?"

"Erm, yes. Exactly. I mean, okay."

I hadn't expected to find someone who even faintly resembled me, let alone a seven-year-old who could have jumped straight out of one of my mother's dusty old photo albums. With absolutely no qualms, Samantha jumped up onto my knee and grabbed two mini umbrellas out of my drink. She slid one into her own hair and then one into mine which did absolutely nothing to deter the emotion swirling in my chest.

"Yeah," she said. "That looks pretty. Ready!" She turned and faced the phone Gillie was holding up and smiled a massive smile.

Snap, the photo was taken, I swallowed back a pool of inexplicable tears and 'Find Your Doppleganger' was complete with the rest of the day to spare.

———

As Gillie and I walked towards Beerbelly that night, we noticed a strange phenomenon sweeping the resort of İpeklikum.

And no, it wasn't the making of paper napkin roses for giggling girls. That was old news. Nor was it men with tea towels on their heads smashing open clay pots of steaming stew emulating ancient Arabic tradition. It wasn't even random sparklers stuffed into drinks, cakes, or anything else they could possibly be stuffed into.

It was a dance.

As almost every establishment in İpeklikum had its fair share of god-awful music, it also had its fair share of oiled-up, scantily clad young men. And on this particular night, no matter what music was playing in each bar or restaurant, these fine young specimens all seemed to be throwing the same moves. So we stopped to watch. Naturally.

We stood there with our jaws dropped not because of the

tangible gorgeousness of the male dance troupe before us, but because this dance seemed eerily familiar.

The dance was made up of three repetitive moves. Shoulder-clashing. Bum-bumping. Thigh-slapping.

"Erm, Jess . . . do you, like, recognise those moves?" Gillie whispered to me, hardly daring to say it out loud.

"I believe I fucking do." I replied and we turned to face each other, smiles gradually taking shape.

My dance moves with Esad! They were my dance moves performed only forty-eight hours before! Marcus's challenge had swept İpeklikum and now everyone was 'making contact'!

"Holy crap on a tap. Jess, what have you started?" Gillie gasped as we made our way down the promenade and saw the dance either starting or finishing in virtually every bar. Maybe *this* was my destiny. Maybe I was destined to be a world renowned choreographer!

As we walked up the steps into Beerbelly, we saw that it was no different here. There was a group of teenagers in the centre of the bar, clashing and bashing together like there was no tomorrow. Looking around, there were even mums and dads, grandmas and granddads sitting at their tables, doing a bizarre sitting-down version of the dance: shimmying their shoulders together when the beat came in, shuffling their bottoms on the seat cushions along with the chorus.

"Gillie, Look! It's contagious!"

"Bloody hell, this is mental. Someone properly with-it has obviously picked up on your little routine otherwise there's no way it could have spread through the bars so quickly."

"Are you suggesting I am not with-it enough to have initiated that myself ?" I asked, having a celebrity strop as we dropped down into some empty sofas. But Gillie was too busy staring up at the dancers to notice my hilarious pouting.

"Err, Jess. I think we may have found the perpetrator." She

nodded in the direction of the dancers and at first I saw nothing, or no-one, out of the ordinary. Just a group of teenaged girls who weren't even getting the thigh-slapping right for god's sake. But then the rubbish thigh-slapping girls drew back and I saw the subject of their distraction. Oh.

"He's . . . amazing" murmured Gillie.

"He's . . . incredible . . ." I added.

We watched a slinky, streamlined young man flip his limbs and twist his torso with a quality that was unfathomably smooth. Most people need to pout or frown or at least wear designer gear to look cool, but this guy was smiling from ear to ear as his gloriously tanned body rolled into every move.

"He's . . . . beautiful . . ." Gillie continued.

"He's . . . astounding." I agreed.

He had a creative energy that had cast a spell on my silly dance so that it appeared to be complex, cool and sexy. He was somehow warm and elusive as he hyped up the moves towards the end of the song, and everyone around him stood aside. His body flipped and bopped through the final chorus, as he effortlessly clashed and bashed into the waiting bums and thighs of his admirers.

Oh my god. I had created that.

"He's . . ."

"Seventeen years old." Demir's voice shattered our infatuation. How long had he been sitting next to us?

"What?!" Gillie and I spluttered.

"Seventeen. And he my cousin. Kadafi. He come to help me with holiday season."

"He's certainly helping me with my holiday season." Gillie said, under her breath. "Well," she now boomed, "how nice for your cousin to come and help you out."

"Yes. He will work hard," said Demir as he pawed at Gillie for her hand. She happily gave it to him and they sat entwined on the sofa, but I knew she was still reeling from the seventeen-year-old dance phenomenon.

I looked over to the space where the apparition had occurred and saw that it was empty now. The music had changed to a much more tasteful chill-out tune and the volume was a whole lot lower. Kadafi was nowhere to be seen; Mesut was behind the bar obsessively polishing shot glasses; Bad Boy was slouched gangster-style on a sofa draped with yet more adoring young women, Amy strangely absent; and Esad was snoozing, randomly in the darkness of Village Corner. Hardly your Beefsteak pub standards.

I was just pondering how I might get an actual glass of wine when my phone buzzed with a text message. Ekrem.

You meet me tonight when work finish. 2am.

Two in the morning? Bit late for a hot date, wasn't it? Could I really keep this up for a month? It was fun being with Ekrem but could I actually be bothered?

With a big gulp of sea air and a swift memory of Ekrem's positively engulfing embraces, I decided that yes, I could indeed be bothered and texted back a proposition:

Yes, but you meet me. At Beerbelly.

I had to call the shots at least a little.

I looked up from my mobile and saw Gillie, still tangled up with Demir who was shouting something over to the bar, and she was wearing a fixed grin and an incessant wink as if to say, *'You go girl!'* She didn't miss a trick.

I returned her bizarre sign language with a drinking gesture followed by a very Mediterranean shrug of the shoulders which was meant to be interpreted as *'where the hell are our drinks?'*

And that's when Kadafi entered our lives. As well as a white wine spritzer and a Pinacolada. He set them down on a tray on the table between our sofas with an actual flourish which extended effortlessly into a sweeping bow. Gillie and I looked at each other for a milli-second and almost laughed out loud. Demir saved the day.

"Girls, this my little cousin, Kadafi. He help you with anything you need."

"Yes Mrs Ladies, I will. You are Demir's friends so you are also mine." And he tossed back his head, stood completely upright, clicked his heels together and flicked his hands behind his back. He looked like an English butler waiting for instruction. His English was almost butler standard.

"Nice to meet you Kadafi. I'm . . ."

"Mrs Jess. I know," he said, taking my hand and shaking it vigorously with both of his. "And you are Mrs Gillie. Thank you for being here both of you." And in a weird instant he stopped that stiff, upright stance and practically somersaulted over to my sofa and landed next to me. He continued the conversation with a round of loose, flamboyant gestures that punctuated every single sentence.

"You like dancing, yes? I love dancing. I do it all the time. Tonight we do new dance. Very hot in all the nightclubs right now."

Gillie and I exchanged a smirk.

"I go to all bars and restaurants to promote Demir's tour business and they all want to know new dance. They say they will send Demir new tour customers every day if I show them dance. They don't know I just learned it yesterday from English girls! Hah!"

"Hah!" We returned.

"And you are both loving İpeklikum, yes? Isn't it bloody marvelous?" He threw his brown, stringy arms out to indicate the bloody marvelousness of our surroundings. Then he flipped them back and slapped his own knees so hard it made my eyes sting. But still, that gorgeous smile remained and he said, "It's very different from my village. You would not believe we were in the same world never mind same country!"

"What do you mean Kadafi? It can't be that different." Gillie pondered.

"Ah, Mrs Gillie, it's bloody marvelous in a different way and really my mum should be telling you because she, now she, is champion storyteller." He edged closer to me and bent forwards so that Gillie had to lean in to hear. Demir had left long ago and Kadafi seemed somewhat looser still, now that he was gone. "In my village they call her . . . The Oracle. Hah! Everybody gathers to hear her gossip each week!"

He rolled about on the sofa, laughing at his own joke and clutching his non-existent tummy at the sheer hilarity of it all. Then he used my arm to pull himself back up and grasped onto my shoulder as if I was hauling him out of deep water so he could breathe fresh air.

"Phew! I tell you, my dad does not know what he will do with her. He is very important man and it's not good for his reputation!"

And over the course of the evening, even though Kadafi was summoned away for short intervals to help Demir in the Mega Tour office, we found out all about his life. He was indeed seventeen and on a summer break from college. He was from a village on the outskirts of a south eastern city called Diyarbakır, which was famous for its Kurdish culture, Armenian ancestry, historical folklore and – most importantly – gigantic watermelons.

His dad was mayor – or some Kurdish equivalent – and therefore highly respected in the local community. This meant Kadafi and his thirteen siblings (yes, thirteen) had to be respectful and sensible at all times. He hooted with laughter as he told me about the times he'd shamed his father with clownish antics: going to school in disguise; rolling in mud and terrifying a gang of little girls; transcribing his mum's best-known stories and selling hand-written magazines to villagers.

"Hah!" He said. "Can you imagine a volcano rising up in a man? That was my dad every time!"

And even though we knew only a slither of information about Kadafi, his family and background, we could totally appreciate how he'd manage to charm his way out of such situations. He was ridiculously likeable. You'd have to forgive him in an instant.

By now he was practically sitting on my knee and, unlike the Cleopatra's male harem we'd experienced only days before, I didn't feel his proximity was at all sleazy. This was a genuinely enthusiastic boy who had a passion for life you don't see in many people. Somehow, as he'd got older, he hadn't had one iota of zest squeezed out of him, like many of us do. His gusto was still going strong and his favourite activity – aside from dancing – was clearly interacting with others. He devoured it.

And bloody hell, this was refreshing! Gillie and I adored each other's company but here we were lapping up the words of this young man. It made such a change from many of the other Turkish men we'd met.

Number one, he was not trying to get us to spend money.

Number two, he did not complain about how hard his life was.

Number three, he certainly was not trying to get us into bed.

Number four, he smiled and he meant it.

"But now Mrs Gillie and Mrs Jess, although I am helping my cousin for a short time, what I really want . . ." He paused and looked around. The bar was beginning to slow down because it was getting late. Empty chairs and tables. Discarded straws and burned-out sparklers. We leaned closer in to him. ". . . is to follow my destiny."

I gasped loudly and a chill shot down my spine. Gillie stared at me, probably thinking I was making fun of him or something.

But far from it.

"Always I try to follow it but sometimes it is hard. Sometimes people want my help and I have to do it if it is my duty. But I know I will get to it in the end."

Was this some kind of joke? Never in my life had I participated in a conversation involving the word 'destiny', let alone read about it in a book, yet here it was, clear as a bell, the focal point of a conversation with a random seventeen year old from a far flung Kurdish village.

What the fuck?

"And what is your, erm, destiny, Kadafi?" Gillie asked.

"Hah! It is my secret Mrs Gillie. I will tell you when I reach it." Kadafi smiled and crashed joyfully backwards into the sofa which wobbled precariously and for one dreadful second I thought I was going to topple back to a head-smashing incident which would have severely damaged any chances I ever had of finding out Kadafi's destiny, never mind my own.

But no. We were saved at the last minute by a shadow that came swooping in and gripped the sofa, propelling it back to its upright position.

"Nice one Mesut. I didn't fancy visiting a Turkish hospital tonight." Said Gillie.

Mesut dipped his head in brief acknowledgement before turning to Kadafi and blasting some irate words his way. His hands still gripped the back of the sofa and had caught a couple of hairs on my head so I couldn't move without pointing it out. I weighed up the consequences and decided to wait until he moved his hand before I could release myself from the inelegant twist my neck was in. Luckily, that came seconds later when – shockingly to both Gillie and I – Mesut joined us for a break before last orders. Would wonders never cease?

Obviously not, because the next words spoken were, "Kadafi say you talk about destiny. I wonder what you think?"

We resembled baffled fish for a moment as our mouths opened and closed in honest attempts to contribute something. I spluttered, "Well, obviously, it's all, erm, very important."

I swear Mesut narrowed his eyes. It was hard to tell due to the shadow he was sitting in and the streams of black hair.

"I just want to be happy." Gillie said and saved me. "It's simple really. Whatever makes me happy, I hope I can find the courage to do it."

"Exactly!" whooped Kadafi. "Finding the courage to follow the goodness. Follow the goodness Mrs Gillie – always!" He slapped his knee inexplicably hard yet again. "That's what it's all about."

"I think not," said Mesut. "You have to find it first. You have to find it. Courage, and maybe goodness, come later."

"What do you mean you have to find it? We all know why we are on this earth!" Kadafi was triumphant.

"No Kadafi. You know it. Everybody not like you." Mesut spoke nonchalantly, the only tone he seemed to have apart from something just shy of fury. "Somebody people take long time to find it. Somebody people not want to find it. Somebody people not even think about it. Ever."

Somebody people (namely Gillie and I) were starting to wonder how we'd found ourselves caught up in this conversation. And what was 'it' exactly? Were we still talking about destiny?

"Mesut abi," Kadafi replied (We later found out that 'abi' was meant to show respect to a man older than yourself, meaning something like 'big brother'). "Maybe people lose themselves as they grow. They start to get nervous and worry that people will not like them. They worry that they will look weak or stupid if they search for something nobody else understands."

Mesut tapped his cigarette lighter on the glass-topped table in a steady rhythm in keeping with the slow, chill-out music now playing in the bar. Tap . . . tap . . . tap . . ."I never worrying about that one." He said.

"Of course not Mesut abi! You are one of a kind!" Kadafi slapped his hands together in sheer delight that he'd unearthed a specimen such as Mesut. "But it is sad, isn't it? That so many people might lose themselves as they grow. They lose their God and themselves."

"Is sad for them," Mesut replied. "Not for me."

This sent Kadafi off into another round of spirited slapping and whooping.

"I don't know anything about God." I said with a new-found courage because I was determined to be a part of this. "But I do agree with Kadafi. It's sad if people don't ever question who they are or why they're here. They will never find out that there's more to life than, say, having expensive things or looking fashionable."

"Why?" Mesut asked. He continued to tap that lighter in the same slow rhythm. Tap . . . tap . . . tap . . .

What did he mean why? Wasn't it bloody obvious? Oh fuck, what now? "Well, because, well . . . because they are only satisfying the very surface of their soul, aren't they? There's nothing deeper. They're not listening to a deeper language."

Kadafi and Gillie looked at me like a frog had just hopped out of my mouth, and I instantly felt ridiculous talking about the soul when we were sat here drinking cocktails on a girlie holiday. Wasn't it all supposed to be about sand, sea and sex? I was just thinking of something hilarious to say when Mesut gave his cigarette lighter a final tap on the table and said "A deeper language. A language of the heart."

It made my own heart skip a beat. "Yes. Exactly." I said, which I hoped would conclude the whole thing for now and we could all get back to having expensive things and looking fashionable. But then Demir popped into our little circle of sofa-induced chat, positioned himself in Gillie's happy embrace, and got a quick update on the topic of conversation from Kadafi. And that was that. Demir took over.

Demir was not quite as open-minded with his philosophies but he still clearly enjoyed discussing something other than discount tour prices and the conversation moved on apace. We covered life-altering questions such as: Can something still be beautiful if you have no desire for it? Can God create a stone which God cannot hold? And, Kadafi's wonderstruck contribution: Does God dance?

I was finally warming to the conversation and contributing just as much as anyone else, when I felt those familiar fingers tickle the back of my neck. Ekrem. One look up at the crisp crescent arc of the white moon told me it was time to go.

After Gillie and I had sorted arrangements for later, I slinked off with Ekrem, leaving Kadafi and Demir to shut up shop, and Mesut went back to polishing his shot glasses. At the bottom of Beerbelly's steps, I paused for a second and looked back up at the place. It looked dark and cool and prickled with white lights.

For a moment, I felt it pulse with energy. A pulse that went through my heart. What was it about that place?

"Aşkım?" Ekrem gently turned me round and pulled my hand into his, walking us off away from Beerbelly.

"What does that mean?" I asked. "Ashkum?"

"It mean 'my love'. I like it for you. Aşkım." He laughed and pulled me in closer for a hug which I was glad for because two in the morning brought a definite chill in the air. Not sure I was glad of the Turkish endearment though. I was torn between thinking he might well be taking the piss and thinking it was most definitely not appropriate for a mere holiday shag. I'd let it slide for now.

We walked along the promenade and talked about the day. I told Ekrem about the little girl Samantha, who had been my double and lo and behold, it turned out he knew her and her parents well. He also knew all about the new dance craze. Apparently everybody was calling it the 'Tokat Dance', which meant the 'Slap Dance'. Marcus would be proud.

Ekrem told me about his day too. The millions of hours he'd worked, the complaints he'd dealt with, the trouble his boss had given him. Apparently his boss wasn't very happy he had brought me into the restaurant and made it obvious we were seeing each other. "He say I stop other girls from coming to restaurant. He say if they want me I should let them. He say I have to make them happy."

"What does he mean, happy?"

"He think I should do anything they want. If they have money to spend in restaurant, he say, I will get my reward."

I was aware of how pimp-like this made his boss and how gigolo-like it made Ekrem but I couldn't help but wonder, "And you're not pleased with this arrangement?"

"Jess, I be honest with you. I do this job now every summer for eight years. First few years is amazing. I have any girl I want and then she go home. Simple." You had to give him credit for his honesty. "But now is different. I not choose them. They choose me. And not just girls. Old women too. They all come to restaurant on big group holiday and they sit with menus and I know they are not choosing food, they are choosing us. And when they decide you, you cannot get away."

"Because?"

"Because boss is in corner watching and he make sure you do everything to please them. He want them come back every night and order many food and drink. Boss want to see us go home with them to really keep them happy and you know what that means." I did the maths. "And if I don't do it, I don't get money. Is normal. If I don't get money I don't go back law school and I can't send any money to family. I am fucking prostitute. Not waiter."

"Oh." I was a bit shocked. I mean, I wasn't stupid and I could see that the majority of holiday flings were at least a little business-related, but I'd never heard it put like this before. And I'd always assumed that it was done with the full enthusiasm of the waiter / barman / pool attendant. It seemed I was not the only one who had lost their way.

As I gave Ekrem a reassuring squeeze, a group of girls tottered past, giving me looks to kill and shouting to Ekrem in their best flirtatious whine, "Hello Eric!"

"See my mean?" he said and gave them a courteous smile back.

"Eric? That's not your name. Why do they call you that?"

"Is my English name."

"Why do you need an English name?"

He sighed, took my hand again and we kept on walking. "Many English people will not say Turkish names. Is too difficult for them. So we all have English name."

"Why did you tell me your Turkish name then?"

"Because I see you different. You not stupid Jess."

And suddenly it all fell into place. Bob from the Four Seasons and Keith at the door of English Rose. Jesus, was it really that difficult for a British person to stop and listen properly to a Turkish name? I couldn't believe the twisted logic of the holiday industry meant that we were allowed to visit a foreign place and then have the native people actually assume different names, and even personas, to satisfy our needs.

What with this and the now obvious male prostitution

circuit quite clearly operating around İpeklikum, I was beginning to have my suspicions about this resort. Maybe this was why nobody ever stayed for more than a couple of weeks. Because that's when the shine started to rub off.

So there we were, two confused souls wandering hand-in-hand down a street, wondering how we'd ever come to be hand-in-hand at all. Each from a vastly different background, speaking vastly different languages, thinking vastly different things. But were we? Didn't we both want to sort our lives out? Didn't we both want some answers? Something told me we weren't going to get them from each other and I was tired. Proper tired.

So, I insisted Ekrem walk me back to Shit Class and leave me there.

Later on I sat propped up in bed, waiting for Gillie to come back and wrote in my book by the light of the red light bulb. I couldn't be bothered to write anything with any format or sense. Just random thoughts that came to me from the day. Written down as I almost meditated my way through my recent memories . . .

Can God create a stone which God cannot hold?

Samantha . . . my 7 year old doppelganger . . . why did I get so emotional?

You know your destiny when you are a child

Mesut polishing shot glasses, a shadow, a cloud

Kadafi the clown . . . follow the goodness

Tokat dance craze, Kadafi is the dance master

Ekrem's sad face

Cigarette lighter on the table . . . tap, tap, tap

I know my destiny . . . I know it, I know it, I know it, I know it, tap, tap, tap

My heart's language. I know it, I know it, tap, tap, tap

6

MOMENTS OF GOD

And so the pattern of our days seemed to take on a somewhat predictable but nevertheless bloody lovely format.

We never rose in time to sample the delights of a Shit Class breakfast. We figured we probably weren't missing out on much. Instead we opted to wake slowly, chew fruit and nuts, drink orange juice, read our books, drift in and out of naps, and people-watch from our balcony.

Gillie had taken to going on a late morning stroll each day. Usually we'd run out of orange juice and she'd volunteer to nip out for it so I could languish in the not-so-luxurious surroundings of our room alone (or at least get dressed without swerving to avoid said room-mate). But I knew her little game. It gave her a chance to continue her mysterious phone conversations. She'd always leave with the aid of her phone and I'd see her as I peered down from the balcony, crossing the street and walking down a quiet avenue whilst she chatted.

I asked myself yet again, who the heck was she talking to? How could she possibly afford all these phone calls? Why oh why couldn't she tell me, her best friend, what was going on?

I wasn't quite at the point of feeling hurt, but I did wonder what law of physics exactly, prevented her from telling one little secret to a friend whose life had been laid out bare in front of her for the last six months. I mean fair's fair.

More often than not, I'd forget about all that and leap onto the bed to get through more of The Alchemist. I was totally taken by this book. It seemed that my life was running a parallel road to the shepherd boy Santiago. Okay, so I didn't have a herd of sheep that I'd given up to go and find treasure near the pyramids in Ancient Egypt. And I wasn't robbed of all my money in an African marketplace whilst admiring a bejewelled sword. And I very much doubt he gave a shit what he looked like in a bikini.

But . . . I *was* wondering what my destiny was, I *was* looking at other people and wondering if they were near or far to theirs, and I *was* doubting that I would ever get to experience true happiness in life if I didn't find my way sooner or later. Surely those were three good reasons to keep reading.

We'd often go down to the pool once Gillie returned from her secretive escapades and after a little dip (and to avoid getting all obsessive about my oil drum waist or definite lack of thigh gap) I'd dive straight back into the world of The Alchemist. It seemed that nothing was more important than reading this book with a sweet, milky coffee and sunshine for company. I'd get so wrapped up in it that Gillie would have to remind me to re-apply sun cream, to turn over and to wear a hat. I swear I'd have spent the rest of the holiday on a Turkish hospital ward if Gillie hadn't been there to save me from second degree burns. Not big and not clever, I know.

My notebook was making more and more appearances too. This made me feel slightly more in tune with myself. The more I wrote down observations, recorded characters we met and mused on holiday happenings, the more I felt I might be getting somewhere. I wrote down quotes from The Alchemist as and when they jumped out at me. As I wrote each one down, I'd contemplate them both as part of the story and as a stand-alone thought.

Whoever you are or whatever it is that you do, when you REALLY want something, it's because that desire originated in the soul of the universe. It's your mission on earth.

To realise one's destiny is a person's only real obligation.

The secret of happiness is to see all the marvels of the world, and never to forget the drops of oil on the spoon.

Some of them were so beautiful, my eyes actually tingled with tears. I'm not joking. They made me *feel* something, and that was no mean feat when you consider one massive part of my brain had to block out the 'tunes' which blared out of the pool-side bar every single day. Whigfield's 'Saturday Night' and the Venga Boys' 'Sex on the Beach' were strangely not conducive to the introspective quest for personal discovery.

On this particular day I was just reflecting on the concept that the universe contains a powerful force that wants me to realise my destiny when a seemingly equally powerful force pounded out the lyrics: *All of da girl with da sexy body, old a punny, anny nanny, air make me see, jump and check out and wiggle your belly.*

Before I knew it I was at the bar, stamping my feet, banging the spine of my book on the counter and yelling at a dwarfish Turkish man behind it, 'Punny, anny, nanny'? What does that even mean?! Please, for the love of God and of what is supposed to be your beautiful, welcoming, hospitable nation, please CHANGE THE BLOODY MUSIC!!"

Everything stopped. I mean, even the music. I didn't dare breathe. The tiny man looked up at me from the depths of the shade behind the bar, his chunky finger poised over the 'stop' button on the CD player and I swear his bottom lip trembled beneath his ample black moustache. I held his gaze, too stubborn to apologise for my attack yet too embarrassed to even move a muscle knowing that everyone around the pool – Gillie most of all – was watching me.

My left foot was still raised in mid-stamp and my precious book's spine was splattered into a puddle of something unspeakable on the bar's surface. That's when the man's gaze dropped. To my book. His eyes widened, his hand moved away from the CD player and he grabbed the book (thus losing my place, but we won't dwell on that) and he held it up in the air shouting, "Aha! Simyacı! Şimdi anladım!"

He seemed positively ecstatic and started to flick through the book, making smacking noises with his lips as if it was the most delicious thing he'd ever seen. Then he kissed it! He brought it up to his huge moustachioed lips and he kissed it multiple times.

As if that wasn't enough, he then stretched it over to me and pressed it to *my* lips! He bashed it against my mouth repeatedly before finally pushing it back into my hands, swooping down and disappearing behind the bar.

And just when I had the courage to glance back at Gillie who was sitting on the pool edge, eyes squinting and mouth agape, there was an almighty clatter of plastic. The man had turned out a huge box of CDs onto the floor behind the bar and was crouching down like a leprechaun with his treasure.

Why in the world I, and everybody else on the poolside, had been victim to the evils of the Venga Boys when there was a whole plethora of musical possibility behind there I will never know.

I was honestly, truly about to apologise for my behaviour when the little man jumped impishly to his feet, chucked the Venga Boys CD swiftly over his shoulder, slapped a new mystery CD into the player and grabbed my hand, purposefully. I was aware of how silly a nearly six foot tall blonde would look dancing with a tiny Turkish dwarf around a swimming pool, so I was about to protest when I realised he only wanted me for my index finger.

He wanted it for the majestic deed of pressing 'play'.

I did the deed, snapped my hand back and he breathed a huge sigh of relief, mopping some very real or entirely fake, I'm not sure, sweat from his brow.

I was dismissed from the bar and walked slowly, slowly back to my empty sun lounger. People were still staring. One little lad's chocolate ice cream had melted entirely down his arm and he hadn't even noticed. Neither had his mother. We were all waiting for the CD to kick in. And when it did, when those first chilled-out tones, tinkles of chimes and rumbles of drums lolled slowly into being, I think it is safe to say that everyone relaxed back into their day.

Gillie became unfrozen. I found the place in my book again. The fresh wipes came out of the mother's handbag and the little boy cried for a new ice cream.

All was well with the world.

———

A few hours later, when the early evening sun was smothering İpeklikum in lolling red ribbons of light, Kadafi was entertaining us in the Mega Tour office with hot apple tea served in little tulip-shaped glasses.

Demir had dashed out to rescue a group of tourists who'd fallen victim to a broken-down mini bus on their return journey from Ephesus, and Kadafi had taken over at the office. If you could call it taking over. He lounged on the cream leather sofa next to Demir's desk whilst we spun childishly on some battered executive chairs, avidly arguing a point with him. "But Kadafi," Gillie protested, "the younger girls outside might fancy you, but we don't. We're far too mature. Aren't we Jess?"

We were discussing this because we'd spent the best part of the afternoon sitting on a bench on the promenade, pretending to marvel at the twinkling sea, when really we were marveling at Kadafi's way with the general public. His primary task was to hand out leaflets in the sweltering sun to any willing passers-by. Now we'd been here long enough to learn that most people assigned to this job were hard pressed to get tourists to take one leaflet let alone stop and chat about the service offered.

But Kadafi was another breed. He seemed able to rid himself of a pile of five hundred flyers in the space of two hours without even dumping any in the nearest litter bin. Five hundred! That's more than four per minute and that's a lot of hard selling.

Or so you'd think.

Because nothing seemed easier in the world to Kadafi then getting people to stop and take notice. The world and his brother wanted a moment with this boy. Mega Tour and Beer-belly were perfectly partnered so that any adoring girlies (or boys for that matter) attracted by Kadafi's expert leaflet-distrib-uting techniques were able to enjoy a long, cold cocktail whilst signing themselves up for a whole programme of Mega Tour excursions. A business match made in heaven.

But what was different about Kadafi's charm was the pure effortlessness of it. Either that or we were sucked in good and proper. Sure, we'd seen Ekrem in action, with his lumbering, giantish appeal that attracted all sorts of people to English Rose. But Ekrem had perfected that craft over eight years. Kadafi, however, in his joyous blur of tanned limbs, wide brown eyes and jester-like energy was undeniably attractive in all senses of the word. People drifted towards him. This was something he had probably experienced his whole life. He'd most likely boogied on out of the womb seventeen years ago and knocked all the midwives for six. He couldn't help it. And this, we were coming to realise, he was perfectly aware of.

"Let me put it like this Mrs Ladies." Kadafi explained, tipping his head beautifully backwards over the edge of the couch, as if conversing with the gods. "It doesn't matter how old you are. You are both twenty-eight, yes? Or nearly thirty. Let's just say thirty. If you were seventeen . . . like me . . ." a pause, whilst he collected his thoughts, compiled his line of reasoning. "You would want me."

Okay, we could go with that. He was probably right.

"But, you are not seventeen. At all. So . . . if I was thirty . . . like you . . ." another pause. He turned to look at us, examined any tell-tale signs on our faces, inspected the tipped forward, entirely engrossed position our bodies were held in, shrugged and said . . . "you would want me."

He smacked his lips together, shrugged and held out his hands palm upwards. That was that. Not a flicker of flirtation. Not a slither of seduction. Subject closed.

And a bloody good job because at that precise moment, Demir swooped into the office fresh from his trapped tourist crisis, looking fit to combust. He smashed his briefcase down on the desk, actually stamped his pointy-toed shoes on the tiled floor and turned to stare at Kadafi who had whipped himself up into a standing position because the leisurely lounging on the sofa suddenly didn't quite seem to cut it. And neither did our juvenile spinning on executive chairs, so we quietly, ever so quietly, tip-toed (in our flip-flops, which was not easy) out of the office and closed the sliding door gently behind us.

"Shit," Gillie whispered, looking worried. "Not sure I like that particular side of Demir."

"I know," I said as we sat down at the nearest available table in Beerbelly. "I think his hair even got a little bit rumpled."

"And I think I noticed a scuff-mark on his shoe."

"Do you think we should go in there and, erm, do something?" We looked towards the door. It was actually shaking due to the volume at which Demir was shouting and the blinds had been pulled right down.

God, please god, don't let Kadafi's charm fail him now.

Mesut appeared silently at our sides. He was wearing a Harry Potter t-shirt with the sleeves ripped off and light blue jeans covered in holes. Since when could anyone rock that look? He seemed completely non-plussed by any crisis Mega Tour might be undergoing and wore an expression which basically said *'are you going to order a drink or what?'* Well, what else could we do? "Two white wine spritzers please." Gillie whooped.

And yet another night in Beerbelly began.

———

Now let's get this straight. I loved Beerbelly.

I didn't particularly want to go to any other bar and be bothered by the hordes of lecherous waiters. I loved that Beerbelly's entrance was adorned by signs advertising quiz nights and pool tournaments and karaoke competitions that never seemed to materialise. Somehow, in this bar, people had the space to be who they wanted to be. To do what they wanted to do.

Bad Boy only bothered girls that hung off his every word, Esad was in his own bizarre rave-dancing zone regardless of the music, and Mesut, well Mesut clearly preferred his own company.

And tonight I preferred mine. It felt that if I was equipped with a notebook, a pen and my copy of The Alchemist (which I was) then I didn't really need or want much else. Okay, so the soft night air and overhead stars helped things along. I was sorted.

Gillie was, by this time, discovering a new career as an agony aunt as she sat by the bar with Demir, listening acutely to every detail of his day. From what I could pick up from our mutually timed trips to the loo, Demir had reimbursed the whole group of tourists returning from Ephesus to compensate them for the inconvenience of the mini-bus breakdown. They had not appreciated being stranded on the side of a hot, dusty road in the middle of nowhere with no water supply or operating air-con. They had bled him dry with demands for their money back or otherwise promises to report him to the travel authorities.

Poor Demir. He'd made a massive financial loss, which might just seem unfortunate to you or I, but to him it was the difference between sending money to his family or letting them go hungry. But I don't suppose anybody on the mini-bus would have thought of that. Extra cocktails for them tonight.

Rightly or wrongly I was letting Gillie deal with the fall-out of this one. I made my space in Village Corner amongst the shimmering, patchwork cushions and got comfy. I'd nicked a tea light off the bar and set it down on the low wooden table in front of me.

There was something soothing about being in a totally public space, where people were conversing, laughing, drinking and dancing whilst I sat in a kind of hidey-hole away from it all. Still able to see it, smell it, reach out and touch it if I wanted to, but safe from it. If I'd done this in a pub back at home I would have instantly been dubbed a freak. But here not only was it acceptable, it wasn't even noticed.

So I'd been reading more of The Alchemist, jotting a few more things down and generally having some time to think. Right now I was doing nothing in particular, other than letting the background noise drift effortlessly in and out of my meditative space and staring at the flickering tea light. I remember wondering if this was what meditation was like. I'd never really tried it properly although was aware of the potential benefits.

Did it count if I was sitting with my feet up on a table in the corner of a busy bar as opposed to in the Lotus position on a cushion in an Indian ashram? Did a white wine spritzer at my side cancel out any meditative efforts I might be making? Was the fact that I was allowing these thoughts to invade this experience stopping it from reaching any real levels of divinity?

And could I be any further up my own arse?

I made myself smile and perhaps that was meditation enough.

A couple of gulps of spritzer later, I decided to do something naughty. Gillie would bloody kill me, but tough. I decided to open one of Marcus's challenges. Alone. The setting, the timing, the atmosphere all seemed too perfect not to. After all, he'd meant them for me, hadn't he?

I ripped open the third challenge and this is what I read:

Challenge 3 — Live in the Now

Allow yourself to experience Moments of God.

And that's when I thought Marcus might really have lost the plot.

Moments of God? I don't think I'd ever heard him utter a reference to the great creator other than a casual form of blasphemy which we're all guilty of from time to time. Moments of God? Had he suddenly converted to Christianity? Or any other religion for that matter, without thinking to mention it? I thought not.

I looked at the challenge title. 'Live in the Now.' Okay, I could get on board with that. I'd learned about it before – mindful living, paying attention to the moment, not worrying about past or future. I'd even experienced a bit of it thanks to Oliver during a chance meeting at a coffee shop and the little tricks he'd taught me, like the orangey-yellow happiness meditation. Was Marcus trying to get me to do more of that?

But why bring god into it? He knew I wasn't religious. Please tell me this whole challenge series wasn't some ridiculous attempt to get me to buy into something I wasn't interested in. If Marcus knew me at all, and I think he did, he would know this would turn me right off.

Mesut crossed the room at that moment and we glanced at each other for a second through the dark, filmy drapes hung around Village Corner. For someone who I assumed to be a self-obsessed weirdo, his eyes were completely calm and unassuming. Clear. He looked clear. Of what I'm not sure. I suppose that for someone who was managing a busy beachside bar pretty much all on his own, he still seemed to have space around him. And I don't mean physical space. Space that gave him a calmness. A peace. A stillness. A God?

I mean, as far as I knew, Mesut was Muslim. Maybe not a particularly devout Muslim, given his regular proximity to alcohol, but the way he spoke and behaved suggested somebody who gave his time to a god of some type. He gave an impression that amidst any chaos of everyday life, he was able to tap into a deeper sense of being. Could that sense qualify as a 'god'? Did Marcus also know how to tap into this? Was it something I could even begin to identify with?

I knew instantly that it was. After all, I'd had that bizarre episode kneeling on my kitchen floor, in the heights of trauma not long after Jack had left earlier this year, when my tear had fallen and shone back at me with an iridescent hope. The glow of the tear had created a space around the unbearable tangle of thoughts I'd been having about the loss of Jack and had spoken to me in the moment.

You're home. Don't worry because you're home.

Somehow, out of the simplicity of a tear, something very deep inside of me had clicked into the now. And I knew that was all I had to deal with. The present moment. Nothing more was expected of me.

Had that been a 'Moment of God'? It certainly felt like one. Fuck, did Marcus want me to have more of those? Because I'd been through a hell of a time to get there and wanted to avoid living in constant heartache if at all possible. If there was a god, or a divine creative energy, or a soul of the universe (as The Alchemist put it), then surely there was a bloody good chance I could find those moments without first feeling utter devastation. It was only fair.

In my state of introspection or meditation or whatever it was, I gradually became aware that the atmosphere around me was changing. The music had ended abruptly and I could hear the chinking of glasses and people saying goodnight. Esad poked his head through a gap in the curtains, fag hanging out of his mouth, woolly hat pulled down tightly over his head and sweat glistening across his entire face.

"Jess." He said. "You not dance with me tonight."

"No. I'm happy in here thanks Esad

He shrugged in a way that made me think of Kadafi earlier in the day, simply said, "Life is yours" and disappeared.

Life is yours. He'd said that the first time I'd visited İpeklikum just months ago and I'd been so taken with the phrase I had a.) created a kind of artwork from the words in my notebook and b.) had a soul-stirring revelation when I'd re-read it, that changed the course of things pretty swiftly. It was more or less how I'd ended up on this holiday. I loved that. Maybe that phrase also showed the difference between living in the now and living in a complicated weave of past and future. Life was mine.

The distinct lack of music must have made Gillie wonder where I was because she came hurtling into Village Corner like a mad thing. "Oh. Thank god you're here Jess. I'm sorry, I got so caught up in Demir's problems that I forgot where you said you'd be. I thought maybe you'd gone off with Ekrem or something." She plummeted down next to me, extinguishing the tea light on her way down. "Are you seeing him tonight?"

"Ekrem? I've no idea. Haven't really thought about it."

"Haven't thought about it? Are you mental? He's well into you. Get it while you can Jess, 'cos when we get back we return to the non-existent charm of British blokes."

"And that's what you're doing with Demir, are you? Getting your fix while you can."

"I'm not doing anything with Demir." I raised an eyebrow. She raised one back. "Really, I'm not . . . okay, so I'm getting an ego boost at best. I don't intend to actually *do* anything with him. We're just spending time together and I'm enjoying all the charm and shit."

"And he's well aware that charm is all he's going to get to exercise, is he?" I suddenly felt a bit worried for Gillie. We didn't actually know Demir at all, and those holiday horror stories in trashy women's magazines must be based on some kind of truth.

"Absolutely. He's having fun too you know. He says I'm different to the usual holidaymakers."

"Right . . . and that doesn't sound clichéd in the slightest."

"Oh relax." Gillie waved off my comments. "Everything's cool. Anyway, I'm going to go to his apartment tonight 'cos he's too tired and stressed to hang around here. He needs looking after. I'm worried about you though, you've been on your lonesome all night. Are you okay?"

"Couldn't be better."

"Well, I can't leave you all alone. I need to know you're being looked after. Why don't you get in touch with Ekrem?" I made a face. I just didn't fancy Ekrem's company tonight. And life was mine. "Okay, well, here's the perfect person to keep an eye on you."

Mesut, completely unaware of the role he was about to land himself, walked into Village Corner and rested on a low, round cushion opposite us. He snapped open his lighter, lit his signature cigarette and inhaled deeply.

"You'll look after Jess, won't you Mesut?"

"Look after?" He enquired, with a frown.

"Shut up Gillie," I pleaded. "I can take care of myself." For all we knew, Mesut could have a million and one girls lined up to leap on him now that he'd finished work.

Gillie completely ignored me. "You'll keep her company Mesut. She needs some company while I'm gone. With Demir."

Mesut's frown cleared. "I think she know what she need. Not you."

I had to stifle a giggle. It goes without saying that I love Gillie dearly but Mesut had said this without an ounce of cruelty. He was stating the facts as he saw them.

"Well . . . whatever." Gillie said, standing to leave but

looking flustered. "I'll just, erm, go and Jess, you call me if you need me."

"Fine." I said, and clutching her hand even though she was making her way to exit swiftly through the drapes, I gently pulled her down towards me. "And you call me if you need me. Be careful." I kissed her on the cheek. She paused and smiled for a second, knowing that all was well between us. Then made that swift exit which, presumably, was to get out of Mesut's way as fast as humanly possible.

Over the course over the next few hours I found out some interesting stuff. I found out that all of the boys slept at the bar each night even though they had perfectly good beds in various workers' digs around the resort. That Bad Boy was in a right state because Essex girl, Amy had arranged for her entire family to come out and join her in İpeklikum as a 'surprise', meaning an abrupt halt to any other little romances he might have on the go. I found out that Ekrem did not particularly like it when I turned down his offer of a session in yet another red-lightbulb-lit hotel room (*You not know your mind if you not come with me.*) And, most enjoyably, I learned that Village Corner turned into a luxury cinema complex after two o'clock in the morning.

Curtains were pulled back, cushions were rearranged and the large screen usually reserved for sports channels and MTV was dragged round to face everybody. And tonight's showing was Lethal Weapon with well-dodgy Turkish dubbing. Okay, so I wasn't exactly offered access to the remote control but what was I? Royalty?

By now I'd moved way past wine spritzers and was enjoying milky coffees and long, cool mineral waters. Mesut and Bad Boy had decided I was now so much a part of the establishment I was perfectly capable of nipping behind the bar and getting my own drinks. That was fine with me.

I was enjoying lolling about on the cushions, marvelling at

the voluminous qualities of Mel Gibson's hair and observing the way the boys reacted to the movie. They constantly chatted about the action as it unfolded, giving the film a commentary I wasn't sure it needed. They pointed and nodded and sometimes aggressively disagreed over some crucial point in the plot. But then they'd just settled straight back into a cloud of cigarette smoke and a deep, reclined position amongst the cushions, like a sticky cluster of honeycomb nestling easily in together.

The end of the movie passed me by unnoticed as I was busy scribbling in my notebook about the day's antics.

Dwarfish Turkish man swapping The Venga Boys for traditional Turkish music as a result of my little tantrum . . . Does he know about The Alchemist? I think so.

Kadafi . . . If we were 17, we'd want him . . . If he was 30, we'd want him!

Demir's drama is Gillie's comfort. Needing to be needed. What about Oliver?

Marcus – Has he gone barmy? Moments of GOD?!

The diamond glow in my tear . . . a moment of God? Are they only found in unbearable times? Do we need drama to find the peaceful space around our thoughts?

I was also completely oblivious to the fact that Bad Boy had upped and left to meet Amy, Esad had fallen asleep with the woolly hat pulled down over his eyes and Mesut was sprawled out across the cushioned floor, looking up and out of the open window at the black night sky. It was so quiet, you could only just hear the lapping of waves on the deserted shore. İpeklikum was finally asleep.

"Movie's finished, then?" I volunteered, just in case I was the only one who'd noticed.

"Mmm." Was all I got in reply.

I followed Mesut's gaze and saw a startling amount of stars so white and bright they looked like sugar crystals scattered on a vast black cloth. "Incredible." I breathed.

"Not really." Mesut said. "I see it too many times." I wondered how anyone could see a sky as beautiful as that too many times. "Is silly."

"Silly?" And then the penny dropped. "Ah, right. The *movie's* silly. Well yes I suppose it is."

He tilted his head back slightly to look at me and I saw that same clarity I'd seen before as he'd passed the drapes and looked in on me. "You thinking I mean sky? No. I am love sky. And is always best this time."

"Erm, Mesut. When do you sleep?"

"Just sometimes," he replied. "Just sometimes."

I noticed that I didn't feel tired at all right now, despite the fact I'd usually be falling apart at an hour like this. But I was high on holiday spirit and I hadn't been working a fourteen hour shift in a busy bar month-in-month-out. Mesut had. "I don't understand. Aren't you tired?"

"I not thinking like this, I am tired or not tired. Now I just thinking about this sky."

"And what do you think about this sky?" I was genuinely interested but Mesut tilted his head back again and gave me a look that made me think he was checking to see if I was taking the piss. Which, given the odds, I might well have been.

"I am thinking is beautiful. I am thinking is powerful. I am thinking is maybe like God."

At his words I took a sharp breath.

God? Was he having a Moment of God? I don't know how or why but the next words just streamed out of me like water from a tap.

"I remember about two years ago I was on a charity trek with my fiancé at the time, Jack. We'd signed up to go trekking in the Central Highlands of Vietnam to raise money for children with Cerebral Palsy. So we went to Vietnam and trekked miles and miles every day through jungle and wasteland, up mountains and through paddy fields – it was incredible. There were about sixty other English people there, all raising money for the same charity so you'd think there would be a lot of good feeling, a sense of unity.

"But it couldn't have been more different. A lot of people seemed to think it was a race. They wanted to prove they were fitter, faster and stronger. I remember thinking this was sad because, honestly, they weren't walking slowly enough to experience the landscape all around us. And I was more than happy to trail at the back of the group so I could really take the experience in. I didn't care how long it took me to do it.

"Some people were proper excited about the special equipment they'd bought for the trek. They showed off fancy hiking boots, posh rucksacks and expensive trekking poles. They talked all day about what they'd bought, how they'd spent hours trying to find it and how much it had cost them in the end. I really didn't give a shit! I wanted to talk about now. About the intense green floor of the paddy field we were passing. About the stark, blackened, spindly trees in the jungle during the dry season. About the heat and the air and the tribes and the villages.

"There was a particularly dramatic day when we got trapped in a jungle fire. It was scary and it was intense and nobody knew what to do. There seemed to be no way out. Instantly people started complaining about our Vietnamese guides. How could they have led us into this danger? Why weren't they doing something about it? But when I looked at the guides, some of them on elephant-back, they looked like they were doing plenty about it. They were talking, making plans, judging distances, checking time. The ones on elephants drove on ahead as it became obvious that they were in the safest position to do it. These people lived and breathed the jungle and I had faith they would know what to do.

"And they did. After several hours they had led us back to safety and into a remote tribal village where you could smell fish cooking on hot stones and hear children chatting excitedly from their hiding places as they watched us all troop into their homeland. I felt so humble to be there. They'd pitched tents for us on their land and they'd set up some sleeping bags in their communal village hall shack. The Brits had landed.

"And apparently, the Brits were in need of a wash. We were directed towards a little brick shower block with a male side and a female side and were told that if we hurried, the water would be hot. Hot! Hot water was not something any of us had encountered for days now. How could you in the middle of a jungle? I have to admit, I was excited, just as everyone else was at the prospect of a hot shower. I could have clean hair! I could momentarily soothe my trekking aches and pains. Hot water!

"So I was standing in this seemingly endless queue waiting for my turn and praying that the water would still be hot when I got to the front. The sky had long ago turned black and it was very, very cold. They don't tell you this about hot countries. No clouds equals no insulation. Add that to no sun and you've got a very cold night ahead.

"I was shivering and waiting and listening to the conversation around me:

"'Did you get a tent okay?'

"'Yes, I did. It's a bit shabby though.'

"'Did you get a pillow?'

"'No, can you believe it after all we've been through today?'

"'I know, I didn't get one either. And if there's no hot water left by the time I get to those showers I'll have something to say.'

"I wondered who, exactly, she would say something to. One of the women who'd cooked us a fish dinner? One of the children who'd pitched the tents?

"Then I started hearing things like: 'The ground my tent is on is so bumpy. I don't think I'm going to be able to sleep.' And more and more complaints about the food, the showers, the location, the guides, the cold, the heat, the routes. I genuinely couldn't believe what I was hearing. Did these people know what they'd signed up to? Did they even remember what they were doing it for? If they'd wanted five-star accommodation they could have bloody well found it somewhere far, far away from these very hospitable Vietnamese folk and even further away from me thank you very much.

"Then I saw it. I looked across the camp and I saw a little wooden shack almost hidden behind the trees. I'd noticed it because there was a candle burning inside of it making a soft, golden glow through the woven bamboo door. Earlier on somebody had mentioned there was another shower available but it was only cold water. Not something anybody fancied signing up for, queue or no queue.

"But do you know what? The prospect of cold water sounded fine to me if it meant I didn't have to listen to these people a moment longer. I hitched my rolled-up towel under my arm and tramped over towards the hut. And you've guessed it, nobody else was waiting.

"It was a good job the candle was there because otherwise it would have been completely dark. I undressed, flung my stuff over the top of the door and turned the little tap that was connected, by a plastic pipe to a huge barrel of water up above. The water poured, rather than sprayed, and soaked me instantly. It was so cold I couldn't breathe and it took me at least two or three minutes to acclimatise to the icy sensation.

"I was careful not to splash water onto the candle, and set about washing myself. It was achingly cold but I started to enjoy this moment of sanctuary, this moment of peace away from the trekking hordes. It was good to be alone. Just me and a candle and some icy water. The fact that I was naked seemed to add to the simplicity of the moment.

"Once I'd lathered my hair with soap, I tipped my head back to wash it all out. That was when it happened. It hadn't even occurred to me that the hut was roofless. But now it did. Because in front of my upturned face, was the most incredible sight I've ever seen. Stars. Billions of them. Each one as stunning and incredible as the one beside it and all dramatically thrown against the blackest expanse of sky.

"You hear clichés about twinkling carpets of stars and I'd obviously admired the beauty of a night sky before, but I'd never experienced anything like this. I felt light. Energised. Powerful. Enlightened. I felt that if I'd stretched onto my tip-toes my whole body would have continued lifting upwards until I became a part of the sky itself. I already was a part of it. Something in the spray of the water and bareness of my skin and the swathe of stars told me so. Looking back, if I've ever had a moment that was close to God, that was it."

Then it was quiet for a long, long time. I guess the memory needed some space to breathe. It must have been inspired by İpeklikum's own night sky and the way Mesut had referred to it. Beautiful. Powerful. Maybe like God.

And Marcus had unknowingly dragged this memory out of me too, with his stubborn talk of living in the now. And if I let that thought rest easy with me, that concept that a 'Moment of God' might mean a moment lived entirely in the present, a moment when you *feel* you are a part of the vast beauty of the universe without any thoughts about why or how or what the heck it might mean, then maybe it was possible to feel at one with God. Even if we haven't grown up believing in him or her or it. Even if we don't use the word 'God' and replace it with something else. Creation. Power. Presence. Peace.

Who cares? If it makes you feel the way I did on that night in my little hut in the middle of the Vietnamese jungle, or crouching on my kitchen floor inspecting a single tear, then I could go with it. I could definitely go with Moments of God.

But what about Mesut? What would he think of this peculiar outburst? Well, to be honest, he hadn't batted an eyelid. He lay there, on his cushions in exactly the same position he'd been in when I'd started. I might have thought he'd fallen asleep if he didn't still have his eyes open, still gazing up at the stars.

Finally he exhaled slowly as if he'd been holding his breath the whole time I'd been talking. "I think I know your mean." He sat up and looked at me without moving the thick ropes of black hair hanging over his face. "Is a moment God gave you. He give all of us but not everybody people notice it."

"Really? You think everybody can have these moments?"

"Tabi. Of course."

"Why don't some people notice it? Why don't I always notice it?"

"Everybody people too busy. With thoughts. With things. With life. You notice it once. Is good. You notice it more. Is better. You want coffee." He told me rather than asked then got up and moved over to the bar. A black shadow slinking across a dark floor. He flicked on the kettle and started washing a couple of mugs before waiting for my answer. I figured yet another coffee couldn't really hurt and joined him at the bar. I perched on one of the barstools and watched him prepare the drinks. This was another thing he could probably do in his sleep.

"Do you have moments like that Mesut? You know, like special moments when you feel good and strong. Like the world's speaking to you. It must be difficult because you work such long hours."

"Is not difficult if I am not thinking about it. If I am just me they come to me anyways. I am trying not to try."

I am trying not to try. I loved this. I loved that in my entire conversational history with this man (which was not vast, let's face it) that he used the simplest of language to convey his meaning. Okay, that was mainly down to his limited mastery of the English language, and my non-existent mastery of Turkish, but how unusual to speak to somebody in plain, simple terms. In my own everyday dealings with people from my own culture, words tended to become so complex, such an intricate network of hidden meanings and buried expectations.

And here was the chance to strip it right back. To get meaningful, satisfying communications without worrying about how I sounded, how I seemed. *I am trying not to try.* I knew exactly what Mesut meant by this.

"We have to allow them rather than try for them." I said. "Allow Moments of God."

He placed a steaming mug of coffee in front of me. Black, no sugar. Not how I take it but what the heck. "Something like that." He said and smiled. The first smile I'd seen on that dark, brooding face. It was broad, warm, sincere and glittered from behind the dark partition of his hair. And it suited him.

Though I'd keep that to myself for now.

———

Three black coffees and half a loaf of fresh bread later and I was sitting on the beach with Gillie, waiting for the sunrise.

She'd spent the entire night in the company of Demir, the details of which I had not asked for, whilst I'd been through the thrills and spills of a Turkish Lethal Weapon and late night chats with Mesut. We were both happy with our lot and now even happier to be sitting here on the cool sand together, waiting for the sun to make an appearance from behind the distant, ragged hilltops. We leant on each other for a little bit of extra warmth until the sun would come and spill back into our lives.

So it was all about being open. Allowing. Trying not to try. Marcus's 'Moments of God' weren't about thoughts or judgements or even God necessarily. They were about feelings. Overwhelming, all-encompassing, entirely soulful *feelings*. And then, I pondered, they were about length. Turning the moments into stages, passages of time and perhaps, one day, a way of living.

A memory suddenly pierced my ponderings. Dandelion clocks.

"Gillie? Did you ever have anything that, as a kid, made you feel well, you know, like soulful."

Gillie nudged her head into my shoulder and yawned. "What do you mean?"

"I mean, before life shit on you and made you a fully-grown adult, did you used to have things that you did when you were little that made you feel calmer? Better? Like, maybe, more in tune with yourself."

"Erm, yeah. Probably. I think so. Before my dad left he used to take me surfing. I liked that. And my mum's buttered crumpets afterwards were the best ever. Is that the kind of thing you mean?"

I nodded. "Those things would definitely count. I just think that perhaps, when we're kids we are way better at knowing what we need, do you know what I mean? I've just remembered that I used to love making wishes on dandelion clocks."

"Making wishes? I used to think they could tell the time."

"Yeah, I remember that too. But I loved holding the thought of a particular person in my head and wishing something for them that was, you know, kind and nice and might make life better for them. Then I'd take a deep breath and blow on the dandelion and imagine that when the little wispy bits were carried off into the wind that that was my contribution to the world. Madness, I know because actually what I was doing was spreading weeds around. But I loved it. It made me feel so much better."

"Better?"

"Yeah. You know how my mam and dad were journalists when me and Max were growing up?" Gillie nodded and snuggled further into my side. "So we had a babysitter who looked after us each day after school. Sandra. She was nice enough. But she had a fucking awful boyfriend for a while who, if I remember it right, wasn't very nice to her at all."

"And he was looking after you as well?"

"Well, that wasn't really part of the arrangement, but I suppose my parents didn't think anything of Sandra having her boyfriend there when they rocked up after a long shift at work. And, of course, he was always nice as pie to them. Anyway, I just remember him saying mean things to me and Sandra about our weight. He was always cool with Max but I guess he had, you know, being a male going for him. For the life of me I can't remember his name, but I remember the shit he said. He used to sit and watch Sandra eat to make sure she only had salad for dinner. On the days he wasn't there she used to send us down the shops to get her a few Mars Bars. Making up for lost time, I guess. And if she made chips for us – which was her go-to dish to be honest – he'd make her pile more onto Max's plate because he said I was fat enough as it was. 'Tubby little thing, aren't ya?' He used to say. 'Can't be feeding you up too much or that belly'll 'av somebody's eye oot.' He'd prod and push at my stomach and if I shed even one tear he'd do it even harder, sometimes with a fork. I remember that a few times he jabbed my tummy hard with his car keys. Sandra used to laugh at him at the same time as trying to get him to stop. It never really worked. Gillie. I was seven."

"Christ, Jess."

"I know, right? I think that's why I got a bit mushy when we met little Samantha yesterday. She was so much like me at that age, about the time he was, well, picking on me."

"Abuse Jess. It's called abuse."

I sighed deep and slow as Gillie's words settled. My whole body shivered. I whispered, "Total tosser."

"Quite." Gillie said. "Did you never tell your mum or dad?"

"I'm not sure that I really knew what he was doing was wrong. I knew from my mam's magazines and from movies and stuff that women were supposed to be thin. Sandra was always on a diet – except for the Mars Bars – and she always looked so bloody glamorous, so I just wanted to look like her. I did know that I didn't like being around him, regardless of whether or not what he was saying was okay so I'd try to leave the house whenever he was around. Looking back, I don't know what his fucking problem was. How can a grown man do that to a little girl? But that's why I asked you about whether you used to do anything that made you feel more soulful. I used to practically run out of my front door if he was on a roll, rage coursing through my bones, and I'd sprint down to where I knew the dandelions were. Then one by one I'd make my wishes and blow all the seeds off until I felt better."

"Sounds genius."

"But it was more than just feeling better. It was me getting back in touch with me. That man took me so far away from myself, into a place of such awful, crippling self-doubt, that I knew something had to be done. And back in the eighties nobody gave a damn if a kid went off playing by themselves for ages so off I went and found my dandelions and did the whole deep breathing thing and that was my way of coming back to myself."

Gillie sat up and looked at me. The rosy promise of sunshine suddenly highlighting the wispy twists of hair around her face. "Jess, do you have any idea how wise that was? Let's see now . . . in order to deal with Creepy Shithead Bloke, you a.) got yourself out into the fresh air, b.) immersed yourself in nature, c.) took deep, cleansing breaths, d.) focused on other people's wellbeing and e.) waited until your emotions calmed and passed. Do you have any idea how clever that is for a seven-year old?"

"I do now." I said.

"That's some mindful shit right there." Gillie laughed. "Even back then you were some kind of wellbeing guru."

"Hardly. But you're right. As kids we don't really think about it, do we? We just do what feels nice, good."

"We do." Gillie agreed. "And I can tell you something, I bet Creepy Shithead Bloke – wherever he is in the world – isn't anywhere near as enlightened as you are right now."

I laughed through some welcome tears. "You mean you don't think he'll have split up with his fiancé, ditched his business, exhausted his overdraft, run off to Turkey, got himself into some crazy set of challenges and be sitting on a random beach, caffeined up to the eyeballs with mascara halfway down his face?"

"He'd be fucking lucky if he was." Gillie said and suddenly threw her arms around my middle and squeezed hard. "Jess Parker I love your belly and it can put my eye out any time.

Tomorrow maybe we'll find you some dandelion clocks. That'll make you feel better."

"I already feel better." I gasped before collapsing onto the sand when Gillie let me go. "Your hugs will do that to me. And, well . . . this." I pointed out towards the far horizon to show Gillie what I meant. The sun was nearly here.

Gillie smiled and sighed and then lay her head on my shoulder again. We breathed deep together as that stretch of gold, and that stream of rose began to stroke the swelling waves with whispers of another warm day, of more discoveries and joys just for us.

And it was more than enough for me. It was more than enough for both of us.

7

DALYAN

It was time to get out of İpeklikum.

We didn't fancy a city break in the sweltering heat, and we'd already done the historical trip to Ephesus earlier in the year. We fancied something different and pretty and peaceful and fun.

So Dalyan it was. I'd never heard of it but Demir insisted Dalyan was the place to be. "Is quiet there girls. Is very beautiful. You will like." So we took the advice of the expert and found ourselves on a bumpy bus journey at an unspeakable hour in the morning.

We tried sleepily to chomp on delicious little rounds of bread shaped like bagels, which we'd bought freshly baked that morning, but it was not an easy task due to the numerous potholes marking the road to our destination. Plus the less than graceful gear shifts the bus driver seemed prone to. He was big and hairy and made a regular habit out of winking at Gillie and I via his rear view mirror, which was sometimes difficult to decipher on account of his huge, bushy eyebrows. But we got the general idea and made a mental note to let Demir know his coach driver was a bit of a sleaze.

We hadn't, however, been charged with assessing the performance of the coach driver. Instead Demir had asked us to observe and report on the overall performance of our tour guide. He was called Tarık and was fresh off a leisure and tourism course. Tarık was the son of a friend of a friend of a cousin and, typical of the majority of Demir's business dealings, was signed up as an employee purely on that basis. When we'd booked, Kadafi had explained the situation to us. "He pass the leisure and tourism papers, yes, but Mrs Jess, Mrs Gillie, the question is, will he bring Dalyan to life?"

Unfortunately for him, Tarık turned up to work unshaven, wearing a pair of cut-off jeans and a black t-shirt emblazoned with two stick-men in a seemingly obscene position. As we got on our pot-holed way, it became evident that Tarık had never used a microphone, and was not about to try and figure it out now, so instead he screamed at us above the rumblings of the bus, "We are going to Dalyan today. Is good. I am guide."

Luckily Gillie and I had come prepared and were able to read about the place in our travel book. The town of Dalyan was further south than İpeklikum and was well known because of its close proximity to Iztuzu Beach where endangered Loggerhead turtles laid their eggs. Therefore the beach was well protected and apparently very beautiful. The canals leading to the beach were over-looked by ancient Lycian rock tombs which folklore described as being the last resting places of the Kings of Kaunos.

What sounded like the most fun though, were the nearby thermal springs and mud baths. Apparently it was unheard of to visit Dalyan without bathing in large pools of mud alongside hundreds of other tourists and then baking yourself dry in the sun. The point of this seemed to be to get younger-looking skin which the guide book was quick to point out was not actually scientifically proven. So what? We were totally up for it.

We passed our guide book round the bus so everyone had a

chance to read about where we were going. Not usually required if your tour guide is worth his salt. However, Tarık seemed happy with his iPod and his back turned to his customers, cheerily oblivious to the eyebrow wiggles and wolf whistles the hairy driver was now throwing our way.

It took roughly three hours of driving across this unfathomably bumpy landscape and we arrived at the mud baths. Everybody got off the bus with whispered expressions of relief as well as many a crossed leg because toilet trips were long overdue. Tarık had to go and find out where the loos were, which inspired some gasps of disapproval and I wondered if Demir would end up giving refunds to a mob of angry tourists yet again.

Once everybody had visited the loo the mood seemed a bit cheerier and we all gathered around Tarık in a little café area to hear the plan of action. He cleared his throat and lifted his stubbly chin with an air of leadership. "You get in mud. You get out. You dry in sun. You get in thermal spring. You back on bus in two hours."

Then there was silence while we all waited for more. He'd realise in a minute that he'd missed a few things out. How did these mud baths originate? What were their properties? Where did we change? Where did we shower? What did we do with our stuff ? Was he going to take his iPod off? Had he brought a more tasteful t-shirt?

But no, Tarık was not going to realise in a minute that he'd missed a few things out. Instead he turned away from us all, stuck his headphones back on and put his feet up on a table with a can of Fanta by his side. Hairy Driver shuffled after him but not before sidling up to Gillie and I to say "Oooh . . . bikini time!" and making strange hand gestures around his chest and nether region just in case we didn't know how to actually wear a bikini.

"Yuk." Gillie said into his face and linked her arm through mine to march me off towards some plywood cubicles. "We'll figure it out for ourselves." Gillie said. "How hard can it be, getting covered in mud?"

It turned out it was very easy to get covered in mud, but also very smelly. This was something the travel book and Tarık (surprise, surprise) had failed to point out. The mud was rich in sulphur which gave it the aroma of rotten eggs. If you could, for a moment, ignore this overwhelming fact, then being in the mud felt fabulous. Like bathing in warm chocolate. If you lifted your hands they came out coated in thick sludgy stuff and it dripped off in gorgeously slow, thick drops. Gillie and I really went for it and smothered each other in the stuff, trying to master the art of breathing without our nostrils for the duration of the experience. It wasn't until we realised that Hairy Driver was watching the mutual smothering from his spot in the café, that we decided to vacate the mud.

Drying out in the sun was, to this day, one of the most bizarre experiences I've ever had. It wasn't going to qualify as a Moment of God, but it was certainly a moment of something. There was a vast platform built for the very purpose of mud-baking, upon which at least two hundred swim-suit clad people stood. The sun shone down upon these bodies, each one meticulously still whilst the thick, dark mud baked to a lighter grey crust, a fragile shell that would crack with the slightest movement. And something happened to the voices of these starkly still, statuesque people. Everybody was speaking in a hushed, awed whisper. As if speaking above a certain level would ruin the whole experience.

"Shall we go to the karaoke tonight?"

"Ooh, I fancy a beer now."

"I think I'm getting bunions from my flip-flops."

Gillie and I whispered about our crappy tour guide and our

lecherous bus driver but agreed that we were having a fabulous time anyway. Who needs a fancy hotel spa when you can stand mud-clad and baking in the sun with hundreds of living statues for company? It ticked all the boxes for me.

After a while, Gillie said, "Jess . . . can't oove ay owth."

"Uh?" I enquired, unable to form the word 'pardon' on account of the sudden tightness of crispy-caked mud around my lips.

"Can't oove ay owth!"

"Uh?!"

"Eurrgh! I said I can't move my mou-oowth!" Gillie had suddenly moved out of her frozen statue position and was now making weird, cranky movements with every moveable part she possessed. She cricked her head repeatedly from side to side, jarred her arms and legs into spectacular angles and did some kind of weird body popping act with her torso. "Ooooow! It hurts!" She squealed, now speaking perfectly but obviously in pain. Mud cracked off her in hard, flaky showers and fell all around her in a weirdly ceremonial circle.

"Ow, Gillie. You're ayking ee aff!"

"I don't care! I want this stuff off me. How do you get it off?"

"Ower!" I tried to tell her.

"What? Speak properly for god's sake!"

"Ower! O'er er." And in one swift robotic movement I spun round and pointed to the shower block only a few steps away from the drying arena. Gillie looked stunned beneath her cracked, peeling mud layer and I really thought for a moment that she might cry. "Et's go." I said and would have smiled encouragingly, or linked a friendly arm through hers, if it wouldn't have caused me immense pain to do so. Instead I did what everyone else seemed to be doing. I waddled stiffly over to the showers in careful, straight-legged steps. It was either that or the crazy mud-cracking dance Gillie had just invented. I don't think that even Kadafi could have saved that one.

After the showers we found our way into the deliciously warm thermal springs. If the mud didn't do it for you, then surely this was guaranteed to hit the spot. Warm, bubbly, non-stinky water to wallow in for as long as we pleased. Yes, it had to be shared with a group of tattooed men who boasted about how many kebabs they'd had last night and generated surplus bubbles wherever they soaked, but we could block all that out. Life was ours.

Well, it was kind of ours until Tarık tapped us on the shoulders and huffily informed us we were keeping the entire (hungry) coach-load of people waiting. "I say two hours. I think you can't count." So we tumbled onto the bus, still in our cozzies (much to Hairy Driver's delight) and wrapped in our towels, dragging our bags behind us. "I think they need more beauty time than everyone else." Tarık announced to our fellow tourists and that managed to get a few chuckles. So at least our tardiness was good for something.

It didn't take long to get into the town of Dalyan itself which was, as promised, incredibly pretty. There were no towering blocks, no imposing hotels, just cute little 'Pansiyons' dusted in peeling pinks, blues and whites, and covered in climbing purple flowers. The heart of the town was carved into with a wide, curving canal that gleamed gloriously in the afternoon sun and was sliced into by stacks of tall, swishing reeds. There were little cafés and restaurants dotted all the way along the road, some offering seating areas right by the canal and some a plain wooden platform where you could just sit and dangle your legs.

All of this was so sweet, so simple in its beauty that the sight across the canal was starkly dramatic in comparison.

The Lycian rock tombs were carved high up into towering cliff faces like a three dimensional page from a history book. It looked like the gods had perhaps reached down from the sky and carved them there only last night, whilst the locals were sleeping. The little shrine-like boxes were strangely tantalising tucked up there in the middle of the vast rock face. You could only imagine what it would be like to crawl inside, feel the black depths of their incision and peer out from behind the pillars and down onto the delicate sight of Dalyan.

The bus pulled up on a narrow road, behind some shops during a loud and intense exchange between Tarık and Hairy Driver. Hairy didn't want to stop there and was gesturing to go further along. Tarık was bashing his finger off his watch implying there wasn't the time to mess about and we heard Demir's name mentioned a few times. Tarık was obviously watching the clock in an effort to impress the new boss. Little did he know there were spies on board his first tour.

Tarık got his way in the end and we were herded off the bus and into – thank the lord – a restaurant right by the sparkling waters. All memories of the sulphur-ridden mud baths left me as my senses were filled with a zesty, blossoming scent that laced the air. Then I saw that virtually everywhere there were orange and lemon trees and it was as if the breeze was ever-so-finely brushing the surface of the fruits, releasing a scent you could never tire of. A smell that teased a smile from your lips.

As far as I was concerned, Dalyan had a lot going for it so far.

———

Later in the day, after a gorgeous lunch and a slow, drifting boat ride along the canal, we found ourselves at Dalyan Beach.

The beach was vast and much wider than that of İpeklikum with beautifully spaced out bamboo sunbeds each with its own raffia parasol. It looked like something from a Hawaiian travel brochure with honest-to-god diamond-white sand and turquoise water sparkling with violet hues. It was sadly lacking any Loggerhead turtles but we had learned from Tarık – yes, Tarık – that it was not the right season and incredibly rare to see them anyway.

Due to an incident on the boat, Tarık had earned himself a new level of respect from our coach party. The incident had involved a microphone and a piece of folded up paper taken begrudgingly from his pocket. He must have guessed, (or been instructed) that his tourists would be naturally curious about the Lycian rock tombs carved into the cliffs overlooking Dalyan. Ever the professional, he had come prepared . . . by ripping a page out of a travel book. He switched on the microphone and spoke slowly, carefully, examining every English word as he went:

"Dalyan rock tombs are resting place of Kings of Kaunos. They date back to 400BC and story is all around you in Dalyan. The ancient God, Miletos and his wife the Goddess, Eidothea, had twins, a son and a daughter. The son's name is Caunos, the daughter's name is Byblis. When the children have grown up, Byblis falls in love with Caunos and her love for her brother grows every day. She writes him a letter to express her love. Caunos is disgusted and feels hatred towards his sister. Because of this unacceptable love, Caunos leaves and Byblis is driven to madness. She tears up her clothes and jumps from a high rock. The nymphs take pity on her and turn her to a spring and her tears turn into a river. This is how we get the canals in Dalyan."

Tarık breathed a huge sigh from his epic efforts, folded the paper back up and put it in his pocket. There was a beat or two of awed silence then the sound of two hands clapping together. And then another person, and then another. Until everybody was applauding, whooping and cheering for the Crappest Tour Guide in the World Ever, and his efforts to denounce his title.

And now, recalling that little incident on the boat was causing Gillie and I much amusement. We stood waist-high in the quiet, gentle swells of the sea, looking onto the broad beach and giggled. "Aw, I thought he was going to burst with pride." Said Gillie. "He was well chuffed with himself."

"Until Demir hears how otherwise crap he is." I predicted. "He's gonna hit the roof when he finds out that was the only scrap of information we've had off him all day."

"Maybe we should go easy on our report then Jess. We don't want Demir's temperature rising too much."

"True. It might cause his flawless complexion to flush. Or perhaps his shirt will crease and therefore İpeklikum will spontaneously combust."

"İpeklikum?" Gillie asked incredulously, and I wondered if I'd overstepped the mark by joyously ripping the piss out of Demir. "Don't you mean the entire universe?" Yey! She was joining in. Good old Gillie.

"At least Kadafi will be there to ease the tension." I continued in my best impression of Kadafi. "'Demir abi, Let me lead your tours. I am by far the fairest in the land of İpeklikum. For anybody with a beating heart cannot resist my mystifying charm. They will come from lands afar to participate in my tours, learn the ancient myths that illustrate the history of our miraculous country and to catch a glimpse of me. Together cousin, we will make our fortune and live out our destiny! Forget Tarık. Choose me and follow the goodness. Follow the goodness!"

Gillie fell about laughing, clutching her cheeks. "That is so him! But what if Bad Boy had a go at doing the tour? That would be bloody hilarious!"

I hunched my shoulders and dropped my brow, gave my best moody look. "You thinking I am tour guide? Me not. Me different. Me not explain myself. Is very hard to understand me.

Just get on bus and don't look at me. Don't talk to me. Whatever I want I can do.'"

"Yeah." Gillie laughed. "He'd go down a storm. What about Esad? He's older and wiser, isn't he? He'd nail it." Gillie took a deep breath, composing herself for some genius performance of this older, wiser character. "'We–are–going–on–tour–we–are–going–on–tour–ge–et–on–the–bu–us–get–et–on–the–bu–us. Techno, techno, techno, techno!'" Brilliant! She was dancing as only Esad could, his very own techno style in a not very old or wise fashion but like a pilled-up, off-his-face, all-night clubber. It was perfect! It made me laugh so hard my sides hurt.

"Ouch! Gillie . . . I mean Esad . . . stop it!"

"'Okay–let's–stop–this–no–ow–okay–let's–stop–this–no–ow–but–let's–se–ee–Mesut–do–the–tou–our–let's–se–ee–Mesut–do–the–to–our. Techno techno, techno, techno, techno!'"

I had to pull my cheeks down with my hands to get rid of my insane smile and turn away from the bopping Gillie-Esad hybrid to get into the zone. Mesut. How did you get into the Mesut zone?

I slouched in a manner I thought might appear nonchalant. I hung my head down and pulled strips of my hair in front of my eyes. When I looked through them Gillie was ready and waiting. Here goes. "'You go to Dalyan. Is your choice. I go to Dalyan. Is my choice . . . somebody people like it, somebody people not. Not everybody people see what is in front of them. You see what is in front of you . . . is good.'"

"Yey!" Gillie yelped. "What about Ekrem? God, he'd charm the pants off those old ladies." She stood tall and puffed out her chest. "'I will give you tour you not forget. I will leave you wanting more. Even when tour is over I will come to you in your dreams and you will not be able to resist my massive hands to drive bus with and impressive height to create shadow where you can hide from sun. You need these things, you come on Ekrem's tour. You will not regret.'"

My hysteria died down during this depiction of Ekrem, because, let's face it, it had to stop somewhere. I couldn't keep up that madness all day. I'd lost it during the re-creation of Mesut anyway. Something had earthed me from the dizzy heights of laughter. Maybe it was recalling the dark, shadowy image of Mesut through the filmy curtains of Village Corner, the conversations we'd shared and the clarity of his eyes, the unquestionable space he had around him. How could you do an impression of him, as if he was a recognisable stereotype?

And so the impression of Ekrem was lost on me. Although I'm sure it was very accurate as Gillie seemed keener on him than I did these days. As we splashed back towards the shore to dry off, as we boarded the bus and began our pot-holed journey back to İpeklikum, as we merrily sang in Turkish gobbledygook along with the radio and our new pal Hairy Driver, I wondered what, exactly, I was going to do about that.

———

That night, I realised I'd never seen Ekrem dance. Until now.

As head waiter at English Rose, it seemed he had probably climbed the restaurant career ladder and been promoted above such tiresome tasks as dancing. Probably a good thing really, considering what I had in front of me right now.

When I'd got back from Dalyan he'd been waiting for me at Shit Class's reception area with a single red rose and a bar of chocolate. This had delighted Gillie beyond belief but somehow turned me cold. I wanted a shower, a bite to eat, maybe a nap, not a giant Turkish man expecting all manner of things from me.

So I'd gone along with his little plan simply because he (and

Gillie) had seemed so excited about it. He'd gotten the night off work (a very rare thing I was told) and wanted to treat me to a very special night out. "Because you are very special my Jess. You very special girl." Apparently not special enough for dinner though, because instead he whisked me off to a rooftop night-club in the centre of İpeklikum.

When we got there, the owner ushered us to a reserved table right on the top floor where we could sit and look out at the sea. Well, perhaps the table was reserved. Or perhaps Ekrem had a silent understanding with the owner that whenever he appeared with a girl on his arm he must be ushered to the most romantic table available. It was probably a business arrangement with all the waiters at English Rose. God, this place was turning me into a cynic.

And now we were doing what you do at nightclubs. We were dancing. Now, I think we've already confirmed that I am a pretty big fan of dancing. A few dance steps can go a long way to easing the spirit and loosening the mood. Strangely those rules did not seem to apply here. The very air around us seemed thick and tense so the dancing was never going to be much better than that. Ekrem kept grabbing me and planting kisses on my lips, chin and cheeks. He kept getting me to twirl under his giant arms and picking me up Dirty Dancing style. All things I would have adored aged thirteen but approaching thirty they just didn't cut it.

Our conversation didn't go much better, although Ekrem remained entirely oblivious to this. I have always had a pensioner's attitude to clubbing and have never been able to understand what leads people to actually attempt a conversation whilst in a nightclub. Dancing, yes. Drinking, yes. But talking? No way. I don't particularly want to spend a whole evening miming and calling on wild facial expressions to make a simple point. Nor do I want to pretend I can hear the person opposite me when all there seems to be in the world is the boom, boom of unforgivable trance music or the ugly thud of hip hop. What, I ask you, is fun about that?

And sorry Ekrem, but what is special about that? I thought I was a 'very special girl'.

I tried to push all of these thoughts aside as Ekrem pulled me back to our table and launched into an account of his life at the present moment.

He was still having a hard time at work, growing weary of the transactions he was expected to make with women of all ages both in and out of the restaurant. He was also dreading the coming winter because he was due to go to study his final year of law in a place called Erzurum. This place was in North Eastern Turkey and – contrary to the popular belief of a probable one hundred percent of British folk – some places in Turkey got very cold in the winter. Erzurum being one of them with temperatures plummeting to minus twelve degrees and snow for the majority of the year.

"I worried I get the depression. I worried because my friend went there last year to study same as me and he did not come back." He stared into his drink, sloshed it around a bit and looked like he was going to cry.

"What do you mean he didn't come back?" I tried to ask tactfully, which was practically impossible due to the aforementioned nightclub noise factors.

"He kill his self." He said abruptly. No gesticulations needed.

"Oh." Shit, now what? I held his hands because I didn't know what else to do. My skinny white fingers stroked his massive bronzed hands and that seemed to be enough for the moment. He shifted his gaze from his drink to my hands and, just when I thought he might shed a tear, that gaze moved upwards to my breasts.

His eyes rested there for a while and I felt certain that in a moment he would look away, feel embarrassed at having succumbed to his male ego at such a sensitive point in our conversation. But no. He licked his lips slowly. He grinned. He leaned even further forward to get a better view down my t-shirt, and talked directly to my cleavage. "But I am thinking Jess, there is a way I could feel better. Maybe you help me?" He slipped his hands out from underneath mine in slow-motion, held them up and cupped them in careful anticipation of the fondling he was about to perform.

I jumped up and away from my spot and stretched my arms up and out in an exaggerated yawn. "Well, Ekrem, I've had a lovely night but I'm tired now. Walk me home?" And his choice was instantly made for him as I jogged off down the steps, out onto the promenade and quickly began to close the distance between me and Shit Class as if my life depended on it.

And perhaps, in a funny way, it did.

———

Extricating myself from Ekrem's giant limbs outside Shit Class was no easy task.

He wasn't quite forceful enough to warrant a knee in the privates but he was getting there. He simply could not understand why I wouldn't invite him into my very empty hotel room (Gillie was under Demir's watch tonight). Finally I flung down his arms, jumped backwards and stared him in the face. "Ekrem. I have my period. And it is very, very heavy."

He slowly mouthed the words 'very, very heavy' and the light of realisation ignited his eyes.

"Oh. Right. Jess, you are boss then."

"Yes. Yes I am."

"Right. Well I see you tomorrow." He kissed my cheek and

started shuffling off down the road. Then he turned back looking hopeful and I thought for one insane moment he might try to talk me into a night of sexual favours. "You know Jess, is my birthday soon. Maybe we try our special night again?"

"Really? What date is it?"

"Twenty fifth. No forget, okay?"

"Okay Ekrem. I won't forget." Phew. Just a little old birthday? That was later, a good few days away at least. For now I was free to plod upstairs to my hotel broom cupboard and curl up with The Alchemist and my faithful old notebook.

Two things which I felt really, truly fitted the shape of this holiday even if Ekrem did not.

8

POLISHING

I was reading about the shepherd boy, Santiago again.

And yet again Beerbelly was my backdrop. It was that time in the afternoon when the sun is so strong it blisters everything it touches – paint on furniture, vinyl on signs, tarmac on the road. Gillie had gone off to the market with Demir and I'd opted to stay under a shady parasol at Beerbelly with only The Alchemist for company.

Santiago was seemingly wandering away from the path to his destiny. He'd stumbled across a crystal shop and had talked the owner into giving him a job. He was prioritising a sensible long-term financial plan in securing his new job rather than throwing caution to the wind and dashing off to the Egyptian pyramids as his dreams had instructed him. Let's face it, we've all chosen rational routes over crazy ones at certain points in our lives, haven't we?

I got the sense through this whole section about the crystal shop, that Santiago was not quite at peace with himself. He was selling lots of crystal, he was making good commission, he was going to buy more sheep and become a shepherd again. And his boss was well chuffed with him. What more could he possibly want? He even managed to get something out of the more tedious tasks such as spending hour upon hour polishing the crystal. He felt it cleansed his mind of 'negative thoughts'. A kind of therapy through his work.

I dropped the book face down on the table and leaned back to contemplate the whole crystal shop metaphor thing that was going on here. Why would Santiago have negative thoughts if he were happy working for the crystal merchant?

What was the problem if he was earning lots of cash and following his plan? Was it because a plan is different from destiny? Is a plan devised by the mind and destiny derived from the heart? Which is stronger? The head or the heart?

Right at the start of the book that mysterious king had advised Santiago of the importance of reading omens. That the world had all the answers if you were just open to seeing them. Well here I was, open as a book as they say. Bring on the omens.

I looked around Beerbelly but the bar was completely empty save for the crazy English girl devouring the weird book. The heat rippled across the table-tops and the heavy quiet clung to the air. In the shadowy depths of the bar I could make out Mesut, hunched over a stack of gleaming glasses, making them gleam even more with a soft, silent cloth swishing below his down-turned face and lengths of tar-black hair. My eyes slowly adjusted to the cocooned darkness he was wrapped in and I could make out the meticulous method he used to polish each glass.

Several swooping circles around the base; a lighter sweep around the rim; slow, sinking plunges inside the glass and long, deliberate strokes in repetitive parallel across the surface. Each glass was then ceremoniously placed on a dry, smoothed-out towel, making glossy rows that caught the light in brief, diamond splinters from the lazy disco ball spinning slowly above.

Mesut would pause after he'd placed each glass down on the

towel and look at his increasing collection of polished pieces. With a look of what? Satisfaction? Pride? Tiredness? Boredom?

Just when I remembered that Mesut was not an actual exhibition piece and tore my eyes away from his little polishing ritual, I got the sense that he now had his eyes on me. I'd picked up my book again and tried to find the sentence where I'd left off but already knew, with every single one of my senses, that he was walking over to me.

He set his tray of wet glasses down on the table in front of me, dropped down in the chair opposite and smiled.

Yes, smiled. He was getting better at that.

"You having a break?" I asked, gesturing towards the soft black cloth he was weaving between his fingers.

"A break? Well yes. But really I am liking cleaning the glass."

"You do? Wouldn't you rather be at the market or having a snooze like the rest of them?" I assumed that's where they all were.

"I am liking clean glass when everyone not here. It help me think if I need it. It help me lose my bad thoughts."

"Oh," I said feebly and clutched The Alchemist close to my chest. My heart had just thumped loudly and I didn't want Mesut to notice. To lose bad thoughts. That's why Santiago spent hours cleaning his crystal too.

Was the world chucking me an omen here?

"I think glass not only thing to get clean . . . my mind getting clean too. You understand?"

"Er, yes, I think so." God, I'd been thrown off track here and he didn't have a bloody clue. Calm it Jess, it's just a book and just a man. No big deal. "We all need something to remind us who we are. I like painting. That's my therapy."

Mesut nodded and stroked his chin against the cloth. "Therapy. Yes. And you like writing in your book, Jess. I see you with it all days. I am thinking you write and you get therapy. Yes?"

"Yes. Absolutely. It's kind of new for me but I love to write in my book. I don't show anybody, it's just for me.

"Is best way," Mesut said. "Is always best way." And I knew what he meant.

Then, with the blessing of the warm afternoon breeze and the distant whisper of the ocean, a kind of nod passed between us where I think we were kind of saying, *okay, let's get on with it then*. Mesut picked up his soft black cloth, a dripping wet glass and began to polish again, slowly and rhythmically. Knowing this was my cue to do my thing too, I turned back to my book. And I felt how wonderful it was to sit with Mesut like that.

Each of us just doing our chosen thing. Quiet. Involved. Separate but together.

Some time must have passed in that way because when I looked up from my book, the shadows had grown longer and were stretching over Mesut's finished tray of polished glasses. He was frowning and smoking and studying them intently. He fiddled absentmindedly with a bracelet he always wore on his left wrist. A silver rope strung with chunky, glossy spheres which he was flicking and clicking together in a rhythmical way.

He looked so serious I wondered if he'd managed to cleanse any negative thoughts at all or whether I should rush and fetch him a second batch of glasses.

But the next thing I knew a huge plastic bag of tomatoes and olives was dumped on the table, causing Mesut's glasses to shudder and chink. It was Gillie back from the market looking as flustered as ever and smothered in the scent of crushed spices. "Bloody hell, Jess, the market was stupidly hot! Demir's still there sorting out some business thingy." She collapsed into a seat and wafted herself with her sunhat.

"What have you been doing here all this time? Just sitting with your books again? Oh Jess."

She looked up at Mesut, clocked the tray of glasses and guessed he must be on duty. "Two glasses of something delicious please Mesut. Surprise us." Mesut gave a slow nod then something caught his eye out on the main street. He gave whatever it was a nano-second of attention then slunk away.

"Well you don't have to be bored anymore because guess who I found on my travels?"

"The Pied Piper?"

"Nope. Your gentle giant!"

"Sorry. Come again?"

"Ekrem you idiot!" She turned round and pointed out onto the street and sure enough, there he was, in his tanned, gigantic glory, being practically pinned down by a group of giggling girls. While he extricated himself from them, his eyes on me the entire time, I downed the drink Mesut had just placed in front of me. I had no idea what it was but it was strong. Good.

"Hello my love. I am here." Ekrem announced as he climbed the steps to Beerbelly. Then he stood at the top with his arms wide open, ready for me to fling myself into them, no doubt. Gillie nudged her head towards him, imploring me to do what he wanted, mouthing the words, 'but he's a god!' at me. Instead I managed to get away with the minimum. Ekrem got a kiss on the cheek and a brief hug before I pulled him over to sit down.

He was dressed ready to go to work. The crispest, most snow-white shirt with an even crisper jet-black waistcoat on top. He smelled as if he'd poured a bottle of aftershave over his entire body, and when I noticed his plastic bag filled with bottles of 'Black Heaven' from the market, I wondered if that was, in fact, a daily ritual of his. "My special girl. How is your day today? Why you spend time here? You can always sit in English Rose if you want it."

"I like it here Ekrem."

"Yes, yes, I know. But I do not know why." He leaned in close to me and took both of my hands and placed them dangerously high up his thighs. Gillie suddenly started inspecting her fingernails. "You meet me tonight after work. We will do something special together. Two o'clock. Yes?"

"No."

"No?"

"It's too late at night. Sorry."

"But I have seen you stay here also at that time and even later. Why not you come to me?"

"Because tonight I want an early night. I need to catch up on my sleep. Okay?"

It clearly wasn't okay because he stuck out his bottom lip and stamped his feet on the floor. How could anyone so huge look so childlike? "Well please come to me if you change your mind. And remember is my birthday soon. I know you and Gillie will be helping me celebrate. The twenty fifth. Yes?"

Gillie jumped in. "Of course we will Ekrem! We love an excuse for a party, don't we Jess?"

"Yeah, I suppose so. Come on Ekrem, you're going to be late for work."

As I walked him to the bottom of the steps, the giggling girls were still lingering on the corner of the promenade. The very early evening air closing in around them, inciting them to pounce on Ekrem as soon as I let him go. Nevertheless, he leaned in and planted a long, firm kiss on my lips. "My Jess. I do not know what to do with you."

"I don't think I'll be seeing you tonight Ekrem. I really do need to sleep."

"But I will see you soon. I will." He said firmly before taking a deep breath and walking off down to the promenade.

The girls hushed and swooped round to follow his long strides while I climbed back up the steps of Beerbelly.

———

That evening I discovered my holiday high was finally starting to wear off.

I was sitting in a kebab house with Gillie, hardly able to keep my eyes open while we waited for our dinner to arrive. I guess that's what staying up all night and watching sunrises will do to you eventually. And something else was bothering me too.

Gillie and I had wandered round the streets of İpeklikum before dinner, in a bid to get some air into our lungs and find somewhere new to dine. But we had the distinct impression we were being followed. And I don't mean followed by enthusiastic leaflet distributors like Kadafi. I mean really followed. By a strange woman.

This young woman had chinking bracelets, heavy make-up, strong perfume and seemed to be very taken with us. She'd started tailing us when we'd inevitably passed English Rose and when we'd stopped to check out a menu outside a cafe, she strode up to us and said, "Hello ladies." She was from London. Her accent was as strong as her tone. "Listen, I know y' don't know me, but I jus' wanna ask, is one of y' stepping out wi' that there Eric?"

We looked at her blankly.

"It's jus' that my mate Lisa, right, she's right keen on that Eric and she jus' thought she'd seen one of y' wi' him, yeah? She thinks 'e might be, y' know, like, 'The One' and she wants to make sure he's not messin' 'er about."

"Eric?" I said. "Neither of us knows anyone called Eric."

"Are y' sure?" She glared at us both through her heavy

eyeliner. "I don' want 'er gettin' 'urt. I know what these bastards are like."

"Honestly," Gillie said. "We don't know anyone called Eric. I'm sure your friend will be fine."

"Well, I'm just checkin'. Coz she thought she'd seen him wi' one of you two. But if y' say y' don't know him . . ."

"We don't." I said. "And neither of us is here for the men anyway. It's not that kind of holiday."

"Is that so? Right. 'Av a good night then ladies. Keep away from 'em bastards." And with that the girl walked off, leaving Gillie and I wondering what the heck that was all about.

In the cafe, I couldn't let it drop. "She was just so threatening Gillie. Not in what she said, just in the way she said it. It was as if she was looking for a chance to knock one of us out."

"I know, she was a bit dodge. But she was just looking out for a mate and it doesn't even matter anyway because we don't know anyone called Eric, do we?"

Then our waiter brought our food to the table. Hot, roasted vegetables with hummus and garlic wrapped in a warm, floury flatbread. With added spiced lamb for Gillie. It smelled divine and I suddenly realised how hungry I was. Gillie smiled up at the waiter. "Thank you . . . erm . . ."

"My name Kerim," said the waiter, "But all English they is calling me Keith."

"Okay, thanks Keith!" Kerim smiled graciously and ducked off. Gillie bit into her wrap but I dropped mine on the table as I realised what had happened. "Jess! I thought you were starving!"

"Oh Gillie, Eric! We do know an Eric."

"Will you stop going on about that? We bloody don't!"

"We bloody do, it's Ekrem. Eric is Ekrem. Ekrem is Eric. That's what all the English people call him."

The same realisation flickered across Gillie's face and her

eyes lit up with something like amusement. "Ekrem! That sly fox. Looks like he's playing you along with that other girl after all. Aw, Jess, do you want me to protect you?"

"Of course not. I couldn't give a flying flip about that cockney lass and her thirst for blood. But I don't want to be caught up in this stupid game. I'm supposed to be *pondering*, I'm supposed to be *clearing*. I'm supposed to be on a quest for immense personal discovery and I'm supposed to go home knowing what the fuck to do with the rest of my life. Gillie! How can I do that when I'm embroiled in some complex holiday sex triangle?"

Gillie shrugged. "Holiday sex triangle sounds good to me. Now come on. Can the quest for personal discovery wait until after our food?"

I ate my food, because I knew I needed it, but I couldn't ignore this. What had started as a bit of harmless fun had morphed into a typical holiday drama and a huge drag to my soul. It wasn't Ekrem's fault. It wasn't the tough cockney girl's fault. It wasn't even my fault. But if I wanted to be clear to focus on my inner journey I had to do something to change its course. I couldn't help but think of a line from The Alchemist which I had written repeatedly in my notebook:

There is only one way to learn. It is through ACTION.

I pictured my life as a map, and all of the actions I'd ever taken marked onto it like places of interest, paths, roads and landmarks. My education, friendships, relationships, jobs all marked with different contours to define their significance.

There was Firebelly, the arts education business I'd been

running for almost a decade, that Gillie and I were about to close down: it appeared as a rough-hewn track high across a mountainside. There was my whole past relationship with Jack as a city of love and loss with its towering buildings and stand-still traffic. And there was this 'thing' with Ekrem. A minute blemish. A tiny dot on the map of my life. I could handle a dot, couldn't I?

And I couldn't help but think of Mesut and the moments when he seemed to have that beautiful, indefinable, clear space around him. That he seemed so in touch with himself and the very moment he was in. I thought maybe even that concept was a bigger feature on the map of my life than Ekrem was.

Or maybe I just wanted it to be. And it wasn't going to happen with a random cockney girl hot on my heels and a Turkish waiter trying to get into my pants.

This had to stop.

9

TINY DOT

I couldn't get anywhere near Ekrem until after eleven that evening.

English Rose was as packed as ever and every single waiter was run off their feet. I waited at the bar, drinking lemonade after lemonade and feeling a strange mixture of nerves and assertion. The nerves caused a restriction in my throat, but the assertion I felt deep down in my belly and it was strong. I was glad to be doing this. It would finally clear the way for me. And Ekrem, surely, was not going to give a single shit.

I grabbed him on his ten-minute break and ushered him over to a bench on the promenade a short distance away from English Rose. Bless him. He clearly thought his luck was in. "Aşkım, Aşkım, we are going to have fun tonight. I am happy you change your mind."

"I haven't changed my mind, Ekrem." I took a deep breath and did my best serious face. "I don't want to see you anymore. You're lovely and the time I've had with you has been great, but this is where it ends. Go and choose one of your other girls please. The time with me is over."

There. Clear. Concise. Not cruel.

Ekrem smiled the warmest, widest smile and leaned in to me so I could smell that spicy scent of him. "Other girls? Aşkım, you know you are the only one."

"For fuck's sake, Ekrem, let's not even go there."

"No, really. I have changed my ways. You have changed my ways."

I had not been banking on this. "Ekrem. Take no for an answer. You know I didn't come to Turkey to find a boyfriend or even a fling. I am here for me and only me. Selfish as it is. I don't want to spend time with you anymore, I'm sorry."

"Jess, what has happened? We are too good together. I like you and, for first time, I not care what my boss think. Why you make me sad?"

"You are not sad, Ekrem. You just need to nurse your ego."

"Something has happened, hasn't it? Some girl has been speaking to you? Whoever she was, and whatever she say, it not true! I did not do it!"

Well, at least he knew how to cover all bases. "Ekrem, I really don't care what else you've done whilst you've been with me, and I don't need to know because right now you and me are no more. We do not spend time together anymore. Is that clear?"

He looked crushed. His giant posture softened and slumped. His wide smile faded and he looked away from me and towards the smooth, moonlit waves. "Okay. I understand. You really mean it. Friends, though, that is alright, yes?"

I stayed silent for a moment. I didn't want to get myself into anything at all with this man. But he wasn't a bad person. It wouldn't do any harm to part on good terms. "Of course, Ekrem, you're a good man." He looked back at me, smiled, and before I knew it he engulfed me in a hug. His signature, all-consuming hug.

"But Jess," he said, drawing back from me but not quite letting me go, "I have a feeling you will remember our nights together and . . ." he kept one hand behind my head and lowered his other onto my thigh, moving it ever so slowly upwards as he looked right into my eyes "you will come back to me and I will do all things for you . . ."

I slapped his hands away and jumped up from the bench. "For fuck's sake Ekrem, no means no! Jesus!" Part of me wanted to stalk off and be rid of him, but I felt that wouldn't represent the strength I was feeling inside. So I stood there, staring him down, the gentle giant of English Rose, and I would not budge before he did.

And that's when I saw that look flicker across his face. The pride. The damaged, bashed-in pride that he never usually had to endure during the course of a fling with the average tourist. He didn't have a clue what to do with it. He was a lost man right now. "Ekrem, go back to work. You have people waiting for you."

So he did. His boss was waiting at the doorway of the restaurant, watching him with his arms folded. And a gaggle of girls, rough cockney girl included, were practically hanging off the side of their outdoor table, watching Ekrem carefully to see what he would do next. I guessed the one with the flushed cheeks and the furious expression was the one who'd wanted me well away from 'that Eric'. Well now she could have him.

Ekrem finally stepped away from me and turned towards the restaurant. On the way in, he stopped to stroke the cheek of the furious girl who immediately relaxed and smiled as he probably said something insanely charming to her. Then Ekrem disappeared inside the busy restaurant, his boss hot on his heels.

Still rooted to the spot I took a huge gulp of fresh night air and breathed out luxuriously. Now I was done with all of that, I could move on. That tiny dot on the landscape of my life could remain tiny. Next there would be new horizons. But not before a bloody good night's sleep.

———

The next morning brought fresh eyes. Despite Gillie's demands to know every tiny little detail of what I'd said to Ekrem and why on earth I'd want to end a perfectly good holiday fling, I felt good. I felt good that I'd diverted a potentially complicated descent into a hellish holiday sex triangle. I just had to figure out what I wanted now. And that, Gillie insisted, could only be helped by opening another one of Marcus's envelopes.

So we did.

Challenge 4 — The Scribbler

Make your mark, quite literally, wherever you go today.

"Now what does he mean?" Whined Gillie. "These are getting more and more cryptic."

"I don't know what he means. But I guess we'll only find out by actually doing it."

"Okay then," said Gillie, who was applying lip gloss in the steamed up mirror of our tiny bathroom. And she swiftly wrote her name across the mirror with the tip of her finger. "Does he mean something like that?"

"Yes, I think he probably does." I said. "But surely, we're not allowed to do actual graffiti. We must have to find other ways to make our mark."

"Well, I'm sure we'll figure it out. Come on Jess. I'm meeting Demir and you know what he gets like if I'm late."

I followed Gillie along the sunny promenade to Beerbelly but at the last minute decided to double-back onto the beach. She could have her time with him and she could help him with whatever drama was unfolding in the Mega Tour office. I figured it was still early enough to enjoy the beach before the sun was too high in the sky.

And I had a date with The Alchemist.

The shepherd boy Santiago was nearing the end of his time in the crystal shop. He was ready to move on and had worked hard for over a year to buy a new flock of sheep and return to the life he knew best, as a shepherd. But there was something in his heart that was not happy with his decision. He'd worked so hard to make it happen, and had made a difference at the crystal shop, but it wasn't enough when there was a strange tugging at his heart telling him that was not, after all, his destiny.

He had two smooth stones which had been given to him at the beginning of the story by the mysterious King, which he'd forgotten about. They were called Urim and Thummim. One was black and one was white and they were supposed to help him make choices should he ever lose his way. He was to put them in his pocket and ask himself a question. If he then pulled out the black one, the answer was yes, if he pulled out the white one, the answer was no. I had a fleeting thought that I could do with an Urim and Thummim myself these days, but didn't suppose I could get them at the local shops round here. Shame.

Just then my phone buzzed with a text. It was Ekrem of all people.

I think you are missing me now. I know you are on beach. Why not come to English Rose?

I pressed delete. In time, his ego would pick itself up and the texts would stop.

Suddenly, in the ethos of Marcus's challenge that day, I decided to make my mark on the beach. I wandered down to the shore, picked up as many little stones and shells as I could hold in my hands and took them back up to my spot. I fancied a bit of creative time.

So, with children everywhere making sandcastles and digging holes, I, a grown woman, set about writing my name in the sand with stones and shells. When that was done, I made a circle around my name. When that was done, I created stars and moons. Then a few flowers. Then the date and the place and then I was satisfied. It looked pretty and I'd certainly made my mark. I took a quick photo to show Marcus when I got back home and headed back to Beerbelly to find Gillie.

I suddenly had a huge appetite and it was time for lunch.

———

After a delicious lunch at the corner kebab shop, Demir reluctantly gave Gillie up for the rest of the afternoon so we decided to have a shopping spree.

We never got time for this at home, what with working so hard on Firebelly and we didn't usually have the money either. But the exchange rate was looking good so we went off to spend a few Lira in some of the little boutiques up by the north end of the beach.

Gillie bought a gorgeous kaftan (yes, another one) which shimmered with tiny turquoise jewels when she held it up to inspect it. Then she was delighted when she found a bangle with matching jewels set into bright, polished, twists of silver. I bought a little palette of paints and some brushes. After my collage on the beach I thought I might get another creative impulse and it would be nice to have the paints as an option. My notebook could do with an illustration or two.

After shopping, Gillie and I treated ourselves to a light dinner of salad and roasted aubergine at a restaurant we'd never been to. It was set back from the main promenade, meaning we could relax away from the main throng of tourists and enjoy the quiet. Along with a beautifully chilled bottle of house white, we'd lulled ourselves into a calm, solitary state and didn't have to deal with the demands of İpeklikum.

We were having such a nice time the two of us, we decided to go back to the beach where I'd been previously that day, and watch the sun go down. As much as we loved all of the fantastic characters we'd met so far, we didn't need them right now. This time was just for us. Just two old friends, a beach and a sunset.

We saw that my stone and shell collage was slowly disappearing. The tide was lapping further and further in and each time it lolled forwards, white froth would gently steal some of my design away. I looked around and saw that all the children's sandcastles were ebbing away too. We'd all made our mark that day, but now it was nature's moment to claim it all back.

Other than the sound of the lapping waves, Gillie and I had been sitting very quietly. I could feel the warmth of the wine I'd drunk in my fingers, my toes, spreading right through me and making this moment with my friend even more perfect. The sun was a deep hazy pink and seemed to glow brighter the more it dipped towards the horizon, making its last second in the sky really, truly vivid. Just a second after it vanished Gillie jumped up and crouched down next to where my collage had been. She picked something up.

"Here you go, Jess. You can save these last two as a reminder."

"A reminder of what?"

"I don't know." She shrugged. "A reminder of our afternoon. Or of your collage. Or of this sunset. Whatever you like."

Gillie sat back next to me and dropped two small stones into my open palm. My heart beat strongly for a second when I saw what they were. "Urim and Thummim." I whispered.

"What?"

"Oh, nothing. Just something I read in a book." I clasped my hand around the stones, one white as a winter sky, the other black as midnight.

"Thank you Gillie. I love them."

10

LANGUAGE OF THE HEART

By the looks of things, we were spending yet another night in Beerbelly.

Gillie and I felt great after the full night's sleep we'd had the night before and refreshed by our quality time together that afternoon. And maybe I was imagining it, but that feeling seemed to be flowing throughout the bar too. It was really busy tonight and everybody was smiling, laughing, chatting or dancing. The 'Tokat' dance was still going strong and Kadafi kept stealing away from Demir's office to demonstrate his moves for the English girls, much to mine and Gillie's delight. That young man was certainly a spectacle to behold.

Mesut had created a new cocktail too which perhaps explained the general feeling of joviality. It was inspired by the 'Tokat' dance, remembering that 'tokat' meant 'slap', this cocktail really packed a punch. I couldn't tell exactly what was in it but it was fresh and alive with sharp and tangy flavours. Bad Boy had been given instructions on how to create the cocktail and was trying to cope with the demand behind the bar because Mesut was strangely absent.

When I collected our own cocktails, I asked him if he was

managing okay. "Mesut leave me with all this. He not like the fuss this new cocktail bring but me not like either. Me have better things to do than make stupid cocktail!"

His eyes flicked across the room and I spotted a trio of girls eyeing him from behind their cocktail umbrellas. No prizes for guessing what better things he had to do.

"Well maybe Mesut has better things to do too." I suggested.

Bad Boy just went on scowling and tearing up sprigs of mint. I made my way over to Gillie and Demir who were in deep conversation and set down our cocktails. As I sat and looked around me at all the rosy, smiling faces I couldn't help but feel that something wasn't quite right. Not with everyone else, but with me. I felt good after a lovely day. I felt awake and happy. But there was a pull right in the middle of my chest and I couldn't think of any reason for it. A few months ago, it would have been Jack. It would have been plain and simple sadness. But this pull wasn't sadness, it was quite simply a pull. Like my chest was being stretched with an intense force and it was a uniquely physical sensation. It was weird. But it was probably nothing a cocktail and a flick through my notebook wouldn't sort out.

Although I'd been doing lots of scrawling in my notebook lately, I hadn't really ever read back through the pages. And I remembered something a while ago that Mesut had said about a language of the heart. I felt this book was the language of my heart and probably had lots of clues about where my heart lay. Maybe it was time to translate it.

———

Half an hour later and the pull in my chest was replaced by a pounding. Or rather an alarming combination of the two. I had read through my entire notebook and felt utterly rocked by what

I'd read. Sure, there was all the stuff at the beginning about being free and single and all the wonderful things I'd learned since Jack had left me. But since I'd arrived in Turkey for the second time, there was a definite theme to my writings.

Mesut.

Seriously. He was everywhere. He cropped up at least once on every page and not just his name either. Descriptions of him. The way he looked. The way he moved. The way he sounded, talked, acted. Things he'd said. Definitions of his name. And all of this set against the backdrop of concepts from The Alchemist about omens, destiny, truth, language of the heart.

Fuck.

What was I supposed to make of this? It didn't make any sense. I certainly didn't fancy him. I'd never even had one thought about him in that way. Maybe there'd been a pull towards him of some sort, probably based on the fact that I thought he was interesting and a bit spiritual and perhaps I needed a bit of that spirituality in my life. But that pull couldn't have warranted all these acute observations, these profound thoughts, these compulsive notes?

That pull? Was that what I felt in my chest right now? But Mesut wasn't here right now. He was off god knows where doing god knows what and leaving Bad Boy to do all the work. The more I thought about that fact the more I felt the pull tighten in my chest. It was as if I had an elastic band attached to my chest and somebody was pulling it from the other end at a very, very long distance. Who was pulling it?

"Jess? Are you alright? You suddenly look very pale." Gillie leaned over and placed a hand on my shoulder. "Did you get too much sun today or something?"

"No, I'm fine. Just tired. I think I'll go and chill out in Village Corner. You stay here with Demir." Gillie stood to come with me. "No, really Gillie. Please just stay here. I need a moment."

I gave Gillie a look that I knew she would understand. As soon as I was hidden away behind the curtains of Village Corner, I took a large swig of my cocktail and pulled The Alchemist out of my bag. I needed a diversion. All of this would make sense soon.

For now, I just had to ignore that awful feeling in my chest and get lost in my book.

11

THE COFFEE

I was standing at the top of a sand dune and the wind blew wildly against my cheeks.

My eyes were streaming with tears and although the sun was low in the sky, its golden rays spilled right into my line of vision and I could see nothing. I could hear people far off in the distance, their foreign words carried to me by the wind, and a tone of curiosity in all that they said. I dropped down to the ground and began digging in the sand with my hands. I was looking for something very precious but I couldn't remember what it was. I just kept repeating to myself, "Is it true? Is it true?" But I didn't know the answer. Or what the question was really about.

When I was tired of digging I fell backwards onto the sand and whispered up to the sky, "Is it true?" When the sky didn't answer, the wind whipped harder and raised the sand in great, golden swathes. Suddenly I felt the urge to move my hand to my pocket where I felt two hard, smooth objects nestled closely together. I asked again, "Is it true?" and pulled out one of the objects. It was a black stone. The wind stopped suddenly with my breath.

Yes. It was true.

————

"Jess? Jess? Wake up. You've been asleep for ages."

I opened my eyes. I saw Gillie and Demir peering down at me, Gillie's brow creased with worry. She knelt down and touched the back of her hand to my forehead.

"Are you feeling okay now? I've been here all night next to you. Demir said it was best to let you sleep. I think you were reading your book but fell asleep and dropped it. Here."

I took The Alchemist from Gillie. The cover was all crumpled where I'd dropped it. I flicked to the back page and read the last line. "Yup. I finished it. Must have fallen asleep afterwards, sorry. Hey, where is everyone?"

"Gone hours ago sweetie. Honestly, I don't know how you slept through such a raucous night. Those cocktails really got everyone going. It's almost sunrise now."

"Mesut?" I asked, sitting up. "Where . . ."

"Just over there." Gillie pointed towards the bar. "He's making us some proper Turkish coffee. Says it's sure to wake you up." And there he was, moving smoothly about the bar, dark and silent as a ghost.

I stretched towards the draped ceiling of Village Corner. I couldn't believe I'd slept here all night. And I felt much better too. There was no strange pulling in my chest anymore and that dream I'd been having had left me feeling peaceful for some reason. "But let's go and sit over there. I want to feel the sun on my skin when it comes up."

We settled down at a table near the front of Beerbelly and I sat cross-legged on the cushioned sofa. Demir went into the Mega Tour office for a snooze, but Gillie decided to stay with me. She wanted to try proper Turkish coffee. Gillie chatted away about the events of the evening as Mesut finished preparing our drinks. I half-listened and half-focused on how pleasant it was to sit outdoors like this early in the morning. The rising sun was gradually spreading warmth about us but the slight coolness to the air was enough to refresh and revive me. It made me feel that today might be less full of mystery and more full of possibility.

Moments later Mesut brought over a tray of three tall glasses of water and three coffees in tiny little cups. They looked similar to Italian Espresso cups. I wasn't sure about this. Strong coffee had never been my thing, but I would give it a go anyway. What with the sunrise, the good company, the refreshing morning air, it was an experience I may not be offered again.

Mesut began. "You will like this or not I am not sure. My people love it. We drink it very hot and sometimes, in my city we are putting crushed pistachio into it as well. You can drink the water and it will make your mouth fresh at the same time."

Gillie and I raised the steaming cups to our mouths and took a slow and careful sip. Wow. It was strong. And thick too. I don't know what I'd expected but it hadn't been this. I didn't entirely dislike it, but I didn't love it either. Gillie looked fine with it. That girl's constitution had always been stronger than mine. "Thank you Mesut. It's different to anything I have tasted before." Then I took a swig of water.

He smiled. I would even say that he looked amused. "You know somebody people can tell you things about yourself by looking at your coffee which you don't drink."

"What do you mean?" Gillie asked, slurping away. "Do you mean you can tell our fortunes?"

"I don't know how to say in English. But we are saying 'Kahve Falı'."

"Yeah, we used to have a similar thing in England by reading people's tea leaves. You mean you can tell somebody's future by looking at the patterns left in the cup?" Gillie was beside herself about this.

Mesut let these words settle before replying. I thought he was treading carefully. "Something like that. But is not my thing. Sometimes my mum. But not me."

"Oh no, no Mesut, you have to! Your mum must have taught you a thing or two about it. Come on, read our coffee cups for us. We'd love to have our fortunes told, wouldn't we Jess?"

"Well . . ." I wasn't even sure I could get to the bottom of the cup because the coffee was getting stronger the more of it I drank.

"Come on, Jess. It'll be great. Mesut will be able to tell us if we've made the right decision about closing Firebelly, and what's in store for us next and loads of exciting shit like that, won't you Mesut?" Gillie looked at him, her hands clapped together in delight. He seemed about to protest then let out a long, slow breath and shrugged. Defeat.

Mesut told us to drink a bit more but not right down to the bottom of our cups. That's because there was this thick, sludgy stuff that certainly didn't look fit for human consumption anyway. "Now you are turning the cup, like this." He turned his cup upside down on his saucer so, I guessed, all the thick sludgy stuff would slide downwards. "Then you are waiting. But I am forgetting one thing. You both have jewellery?"

"Erm, yes, but why?" asked Gillie, clutching her new jeweled bangle.

"Don't worry." Said Mesut. "This will be better." He took Gillie's hand and eased off one of her rings and placed it on top of her upturned cup. "This," he said, tapping the ring, "will let your stories, your energy come through. Or is what my mum says, anyway. Jess?"

I took one of my own rings and placed it on top of my coffee cup, just as he asked. My stories. My energy. What on earth would he tell with those? And was I really going to buy into all of this?

Mesut didn't have any rings on, but he was wearing his usual bracelet. The twisted rope of silver with its big glossy spheres. He slipped it off and rested it carefully on top of his coffee cup. I wondered who, exactly, would be telling his fortune. Surely it broke some ethical code of fortune-telling for him to be doing it for himself?

"Come on then," Gillie said, "Let's get going."

Mesut slowly raised a hand in warning. "We are waiting until jewellery is cold. Then we know it has taken all the hot and given all the energy. Only then."

"Okay. You're pretty strict on this for someone who didn't want to do it in the first place." Gillie slumped back in her chair.

Mesut nodded and simply leaned forward to watch his cup. And as he did this I watched him. I couldn't take my eyes off this man. He was alluring in a way I had never encountered before. Alluring in the sense that nothing in the world could feel more right than to be sitting with him right now, waiting for my fortune to be told.

I thought about the excruciating pull I'd felt in my chest the evening before. He hadn't been there. And now he was here, I didn't feel it any more. Had it been the good night's sleep that had sorted me out or was it something to do with him? I didn't know what to think and sat absentmindedly playing with the Urim and Thummim stones Gillie had found for me the day before. Maybe I'd ask them properly later on.

"Come on Mesut, it must be time now." Gillie was getting impatient.

"Okay. I will do." He picked up Gillie's ring and gave it back to her. Then he turned the cup the right way round and peered inside. There was a lot of slick, brown ooze on the saucer but I supposed he didn't need that for now. Gillie shifted forwards in her seat, biting her lip. Mesut looked deeply into the cup for some time before he started to speak.

"I think you are doing two things at same time. They both at same time not good. One is not good because is a secret." He looked at me for a millisecond. "The other is not good because is not good for you. For Gillie." Gillie did not look impressed at that. "But you clever, and you will see. You are choosing something better at the end."

"Oh, erm. Is that it then?" Poor Gillie. Maybe she wanted projections of riches and true love but I had a feeling Mesut was less reading her fortune and more actually reading her.

"No. Is more." He said, and Gillie looked hopeful again. Mesut picked up Gillie's saucer and poured the sludge back into the cup, but there were some markings left over. He began to read these too. "The thing you lost only few months ago was lost years ago really. Now you can be Gillie. Really Gillie. No problem." He replaced the saucer on the table and leaned back in his chair. "And now that's it."

"Right, well, erm, nothing about babies then?"

"No. I am not seeing this."

"Oh." Gillie tried for a smile but it was wobbly. She picked up the ring off the top of my coffee cup and threw it over to me. "Right! Jess's turn!"

"Really, Mesut, if you don't want to, it's fine."

He looked right at me. "Is fine Jess. I do it." He leaned across me to reach my cup and looked into it for what seemed like an age. I couldn't imagine what he was seeing in there. His lashes drooped downwards, thick and streaked with violet-black in the early morning sun, so that it was impossible for me to see what was in his eyes. I was so used to Mesut looking me right in the eye when he spoke and seeing the clarity of his words echoed right there. Now I couldn't see his eyes I felt a strange panic rising. It suddenly seemed absolutely imperative that he look at me right now. What was he seeing? Why wasn't he sharing it? Why wouldn't he bloody well look at me?

He looked up.

"You have two roads in front of you . . ."

And that's when it happened.

With the meeting of our eyes I felt everything fall down around me. All I could see, all I could feel was his eyes on me. In me. Everything around me fell softly and silently away into a writhing counter-current, and I couldn't feel the sun on my skin anymore, I couldn't feel the sofa beneath me, or hear the sea. Gillie wasn't there. Nobody was there. Just me and Mesut and the tunnelled energy between us which seemed to be twisted into one perfect yet utterly terrifying thing.

This man knew me. This man had always known me. He knew all the bad, all the good, all the things from this life and others, it was endless what he knew. He knew things about me I didn't even know myself. He had my soul and I had his and that's all there was to it. I could feel it with every single part of me and every single part of the universe conspired to make it true.

Because here we were. Simply looking at each other.

"Jess, your heart is big and your heart is open . . ." He finished telling my fortune and when he stopped speaking I realised I'd missed every single word. Gillie and the sofas and the sun and the sea all dropped back into reality. Mesut put the cup and saucer back on the table with a clink. I stared at them. It was all I could do.

"Jess?" Gillie said, clicking her fingers, "Earth to Jess, what do you think of your fortune then?"

I tore my eyes away from the cup and saucer to look at Gillie. She looked pretty concerned. She knew something had just gone down but had no way of telling what. "Yeah. Great. Interesting." I babbled then darted away from them, not daring to look at Mesut again. I escaped to the toilets, not knowing where else to run to. It was dark and cold in there which was a welcome balm to my agitated state and shaking limbs, my torrential thoughts and pounding heart. I paced about, took some very deep breaths. I felt possessed with an energy I couldn't identify.

Was it confusion? Was it excitement? What the hell was it?

Once my eyes adjusted to the dark I crossed over to the mirror and looked at myself. Fear. That's where the energy came from. I was really frightened. My face was pale but my eyes were alive. They sparked with something new, as if I'd found a treasure I was terrified of. I looked right into myself in that mirror, in a way I'd never done so before. For perhaps the first time ever I was looking into a mirror for the purpose of looking into me. Not checking my hair or fussing about my mascara. But looking into *me*. The real me.

Was that her staring back? Was that what Mesut had seen just now?

"He's just a man, Jess. He's just a man." I whispered to myself, whilst looking in the mirror. "He's just a man and you are still you." I continued to take deep breaths and kept up the mantra of *he's just a man* over and over in my head until I felt a bit better. I felt the energy inside me shift into something else. There was still some fear but it didn't seem so engulfing. Now there was something else.

"Jess? What's going on? Are you okay?" Gillie popped her head round the door and could see instantly that I was most definitely not okay.

"Can we just go please Gillie? Can we go now?"

"Of course, let's start walking." She marched me out of Beerbelly, Mesut was nowhere to be seen, and with her arm linked through mine we headed off for Shit Class Hotel.

———

We took the shorter route along the beach and all the way, I felt something rising up inside of me.

A heat that had nothing to do with the morning sun rising higher in the sky. As we walked along between the tourists and the locals and the surf and the sand I knew what it was. Anger. Seething anger. I was red with rage at Mesut. With the universe, even. Who was this man? How dare he invade my world like this? I didn't want him. I didn't want it. I just wanted to be Jess and he had no right to do this to me. I didn't think I had ever felt anger like it.

Gillie didn't talk to me the whole time we were walking. She knew me well enough to sense that words were not what I needed and that getting back to the hotel was crucial. She waved off any advances made by vendors on the beach and we just kept on walking like our lives depended on it.

When we got back to our little room, I sat down on the edge of the bed, staring at the cracks on the tiled floor. I knew Gillie was looking down at me, waiting patiently for an explanation of what had gone on but honestly, where would I start?

But Gillie didn't say anything. She sat down next to me and put her arms around me. I hadn't realised I needed to cry until seconds before the tears came. And then they came down furiously as if they'd never stop. Whatever the energy was that had had me in its grip since Mesut told my fortune, it was coming out now with every outraged, bewildered, terrified tear. Gillie rocked me gently and asked quietly "What is it Jess? You can tell me. What is it?"

There was only one, simple answer to that question. "Mesut." I sobbed more loudly. "It's Mesut."

She mustn't have had a clue what I was on about, but she did know that I needed to sob it out. She wasn't going to judge.

She was just going to wait until I was ready to tell her. And once the tears finally subsided, and I'd washed my face and taken a few deep breaths, I did tell her. I told her everything.

———

"Fucking hell. I had a feeling something was going on between you two, but nothing like this."

Gillie had listened to every word I'd said about my fucked-up feelings towards Mesut and what had happened during the fortune-telling. I'd even shown her my notebook with all the feverish references to Mesut. She was flicking through it now, shaking her head in disbelief.

"But nothing's going on between us." I said. "That's exactly it. Absolutely nothing has happened, I just feel like he's impor-tant to me for some reason. Incredibly important. So much so that I'm proper terrified Gillie. This shit is scary."

Gillie nodded and lay the notebook out on a fresh page. "Do you know what I think you should do? Write about it. You don't know the answers, I don't know the answers. But one thing's for sure, you always feel better when you write about things. So why should this be any different? Go on, Jess, take it."

I took the notebook and Gillie scrapped about in her bag for a pen. "Honestly, Jess. You'll feel better. I need to sleep now because I stayed up all night in that bloody bar. But you use the time to write. Breathe. Think of your notebook like you did your dandelion clocks when you were little. And chill out. This might not be as big and scary as you think it is."

So while Gillie snuggled up on her side of the bed, I thought about what I wanted to write. But this was impossible. Nothing came to me.

Then I remembered I didn't have to show this to anybody. It was all mine. Private . . .

The first time I saw him I thought perhaps he wasn't real. He just didn't seem to inhabit this world the way everybody else did. Not real. Not tangible. But apparently his name means 'Happiness' in Turkish. How can he be unreal and happiness at the same time?

To me he represents something dark and wise but I think he probably represents this to everyone. Maybe each person who meets him chooses how much of that they accept, how much of him they allow to occupy their minds and fascinate their hearts. Me? I am fascinated. Not just by his physicality – strong, sleek, lithe like a puma – but by what's behind his eyes, what's behind his heavy brow.

I have my suspicions about him and perhaps they are wrong, but it all seems like a type of omen.

Just when I'm trying to rediscover my destiny, searching back into my uninhibited years as a child to find out what it is I am here for . . . he appears.

Just when I'm finding out about my heart's language, listening for the whispers of the soul of the world . . . he appears.

And his eyes suggest to me he already knows it.

Am I imagining it? Do I just want him to mean something? Sometimes I feel like he is looking right into me. I know he tells more about people from their eyes than their words. Does everyone know this about him?

Is he trying to tell me something I need to hear?

Whatever the answer, I'm going to let his presence trickle over me like a spring, let his strange energy wash over me until I know what I'm dealing with.

If he is an omen, I will figure him out. If he is a sign, I will learn to read him. If he is none of these things, I will remember him as someone who appeared to me and helped me to take notice of my heart's language.

12

TIPPING POINT

The writing had, as Gillie predicted, made me feel better. I still felt like I was experiencing some kind of aftershock though.

I remembered how I'd felt when I'd crashed my car years ago and had been shaky and unsteady for days. This was a bit like that.

Gillie had woken up a couple of hours later and we'd chatted some more. She was remarkably open minded about the things I was revealing. During the whole history of our friendship, we'd never spoken about things as deep as this – there had never been any need for it before. But somehow, right now, we were getting through these strange, unfathomable topics.

When Gillie asked me what I wanted to do next I knew the answer instantly. "I want to go back to Beerbelly. Tonight, after we've had dinner." Gillie raised an eyebrow. "I mean it Gillie. If Mesut means something to me, I have to be around him and then I might find out what it is. If he doesn't . . . well, we can just put this down to experience, can't we?"

"Okay, whatever you say. Let's get our glad rags on then." Gillie disappeared into the bathroom to make herself even more gorgeous than she already was and I thanked the universe she was with me on this extraordinary journey.

What the actual fuck would I have done without her?

———

At Beerbelly, I knew instantly that things were not right.

The joviality from last night was absent and there was a determinably hostile atmosphere. As Gillie and I took our seats we looked around. The Mega Tour office was closed, Kadafi and Demir were nowhere to be seen. Without Kadafi's exuberance there was bound to be an energy drop, but surely not something as drastic as this?

Bad Boy came loping over to us. He looked bleary-eyed but eerily alert, a grim smile poking at the edges of his mouth. "My girls, my girls. You very loyal to us, aren't you my girls?"

"Where's Demir?" asked Gillie, bluntly.

"Don't worry about him. Uh! He is gone. He and Esad take Kadafi to see our uncle in next town. I not want to go so I stay here and I look after the whole bar. The whooooole bar." He shuffled off into the darkness at the back of the bar muttering to himself and vaguely waving at customers he passed by, ignoring their gestures that they would like more drinks. Instead, Mesut was moving swiftly between tables, a white apron tied around his narrow hips, seeing to their demands on his own.

"So Bad Boy's off his face then," remarked Gillie. "I wonder what Esad will think about that."

"Knowing Esad, he probably wouldn't even notice."

"He might notice that business isn't so good though. People are leaving, look." Gillie pointed to where three tables' worth of people had decided to cut their losses and leave. You couldn't blame them. The service was slow, the music was awful, and half of the lights were switched off so the back of the bar looked well dodgy.

"Right, we're practically part of the furniture round here so I'm going to get our drinks myself." I strode off to the bar, knowing full well I was going to have to face Mesut and look into those eyes again. But it was time. I didn't want to run away from this.

At the bar there were two women sitting on bar stools, twirling straws in their drinks and watching Bad Boy over at the DJ booth. They were older than the lasses Bad Boy usually had hanging around him, pushing sixty at least. And they weren't all glammed up either. They both had long hair hanging frizzy down their backs, drab clothes, sour expressions. I couldn't understand the connection. Demir looked up at them and winked crookedly. What the heck was going on?

Then a shadow passed by me and settled behind the bar. Mesut.

"Hello Jess. You okay?"

Slowly, I raised my eyes to meet his. There they were. Dark. Almost black. I felt a ripple of something strong move from the top of my head all the way down to my toes. But no panic. No fear. "Yes, I'm really well thanks Mesut. How about you?"

He moved down to the opposite end of the bar from where the two women were sitting and automatically started making drinks for me and Gillie. "If I honest I tell you I not okay."

"Oh. Anything I can do?"

He lifted his arm and poured a long, slow measure of white wine, set the bottle down and looked at me. "Sometimes I thinking you already do it Jess." I had no idea what he meant. He looked angry again, like the Mesut I'd met right at the beginning of things, and suddenly all I wanted was to see his smile, his warmth coming through.

"Forgive me. Tonight I am not myself."

"Are you upset because Bad Boy is making you do all of the work?" I asked as he pushed my drink towards me.

"No. This I can manage. I am doing all the time anyway." He let out a low, deep sigh, his shoulders almost caving in around him. This was strange. I'd never seen Mesut look anything but strong and sure. I couldn't imagine him having problems that couldn't be solved by gazing up at a starry sky or drinking coffee in the morning sun. "I am confused by myself. I not know which one I really am. Mesut One or Mesut Two."

"I'm sorry, what? Mesut One or Mesut Two? Surely you're just Mesut."

"Yes, but I forget. I am doing a lot of time as Mesut Two, the one who is with the tourists. The one who is making the cocktails and wiping the tables. The one who is being quiet when the rude man speaks or is ignoring when the drunk lady is touching me. Mesut Two is getting the tips and the money and is the only way I am living here. Mesut Two is sending the money to family."

"And Mesut One?"

"He is the one I am when nobody is looking. But he is boring I think."

"No!" I cried, thinking of how fascinated I was by this man. "Mesut One isn't boring. He is just himself. Pretty much everybody has to have a particular persona at work. It's not unusual."

"No, not unusual. But I am thinking is not right either."

He gave me Gillie's drink and moved out from behind the bar. I watched him go and as he was passing the two dour-looking women, one of them reached out, grabbed the edge of his apron and yanked him in to her. She whispered something in his ear and a fleeting look of disgust passed over his face. At least I thought it did. He dipped his head quickly so his hair fell over his face and bowed in her direction before moving off to clear a nearby table. She sneered up at her friend and they exchanged some kind of knowing look. It made me shudder.

When I gave Gillie her drink back at our table, she was chatting away to an old couple we'd met a few nights before. "What kept you?" she asked. "I'm gasping for this."

"Mesut appears to be having some kind of breakdown, that's all."

Her eyes widened over her Pinacolada. "No way! About you?"

"No Gillie, not about me." I remembered Mesut saying *sometimes I thinking you already do it,* but decided to keep that to myself for now. "I think he's freaked out about something. I think it's something to do with those two women." And I pointed them out.

"Ugh. It wouldn't hurt them to crack a smile, would it?" Gillie laughed and fell back into conversation with the old couple.

I tried to follow the conversation, but my eyes kept being drawn to wherever Mesut was or whatever he was doing. If he walked off into the dark depths at the back of the bar, I lost sight of him and could feel that strange pull in my chest again. It reminded me again of an elastic band and I could almost visualise it between us. Becoming tighter and more uncomfortable, the further away he moved. It was ridiculous. We weren't connected. There was no elastic band. Why did I keep feeling like this?

On more than one occasion, Mesut came back to sit with me for a cigarette break. He didn't seem any more relaxed than before. He told me that the two women at the bar were connected to Bad Boy through business. Apparently he'd almost bought a bar with them a few years back but it all fell through because he couldn't get the money together. He owed them thousands but couldn't give it so instead they turned up every season to haunt him. And Bad Boy dealt with it the only way he knew how.

If he 'kept them happy', they would leave him alone until the following year. But this year, one of them had taken a shine to Mesut. Bad Boy had told Mesut explicitly that he would lose his job if he didn't go through with any plans the women might have for him. So far those plans had involved sitting at the bar, making demands about the music, the lighting, even which customers should be served. I had no doubt they were behind whatever drugs Bad Boy was on too. Well at least now I knew why the atmosphere had felt so awful the minute we'd arrived.

During all of these revelations, I started to understand what Mesut meant by having a split personality. He knew that compromising his character was wrong, but if it meant he could keep his job and send money to his family, then maybe he could manage it. This current situation with Bad Boy was taking him to a tipping point.

"Why am I talking to you?" Mesut asked, at one stage, quite directly.

"I don't know. You need a friend, maybe?"

"No. I am never talking to anyone. I am talking to the moon. I am talking to the stars. I am talking to the mirror sometimes. But why, now, am I talking to you?"

I drew in a sharp breath at the mirror comment. Isn't that exactly what I'd been doing earlier today when I'd freaked out over the Turkish coffee? Maybe talking to mirrors wasn't so weird. "I have no idea Mesut. Only you know that."

"But I am not knowing it." He said, holding his hand to his heart. "Really, I am not knowing it." Then he was off. Back to the throng of awful music and the will of those women.

Towards the end of the night, when Mesut was clearing the tables and the last customers were leaving, Demir returned looking for Gillie. I noticed that Bad Boy ushered the two women from the bar and into the darkened depths of Village Corner as soon as Demir appeared. Demir didn't notice them though, he was too enamoured with Gillie and the thought of getting her back to his place for the night. "Do you mind Jess?" she asked. "I haven't seen him all day."

"Of course I don't mind. But just take care, okay?" I was still slightly concerned about Gillie and her intentions with Demir. He obviously thought he had some kind of claim over her yet she insisted it was all just a bit of fun.

Not long after Gillie had gone, first making me promise I would get a taxi back to the hotel sooner rather then later, the atmosphere at Beerbelly changed yet again. Instead of trailing off for the night, the music got louder. And if it was possible, it sounded even uglier than before. Some kind of clanging electro-trance that I simply could not get my head round. I didn't want to hear it so I picked up my drink and went to sit on the cool marble steps leading down to the promenade.

This was better. I took slow, deep breaths and felt my nerves settle slightly as I tuned in to the distant rolling of the waves. Until I came out here, I hadn't realised I'd needed to calm down. I guess that's what Beerbelly was doing to me tonight. Usually such a sanctuary, such a haven, but now those women and Bad Boy had turned it into something toxic. I couldn't understand what Mesut was still doing in there.

I reached into my pocket and pulled out the stones Gillie had given me. Urim and Thummim. Seeing them nestled together in my open palm, one so dark and the other so white made me think of Yin and Yang, the ancient Chinese symbol which represents how opposite forces are interconnected. How one force cannot exist without the other. To me, there was some-thing romantic about this notion, but something formidable too.

"Jess, you are still here?" Mesut had appeared silently and

sat down beside me on the steps. "I am thinking you have enough of my talk and you go home."

"No, I'm still here. But I will go soon."

Mesut nodded and watched me turn my stones over and over in my hand. He didn't ask what they were. He just watched. Then, after some time, he looked back into the bar where Bad Boy was no doubt waiting with the women. "I will go now. I don't want to be this person I am thinking is only way. I might see you tomorrow Jess."

At his words I suddenly felt the same kind of wild anger I'd felt that morning. And not the kind of anger that makes you see red and makes you blind to everything else, but the kind that clarifies absolutely everything.

Here was this man, this incredible, other-worldly man who had changed my entire outlook on life with a single glance over a fucking coffee cup and he was being so weak willed as to let this petty situation overcome the very core of who he was. What was he playing at? A strong, unwavering courage emerged within me, totally accepting that I might lose Mesut with the words I was about to say. But they felt right and real and honest and they just had to come out.

"Mesut, I've heard enough. If you really don't want to be that person then bloody well get back in there and tell them to leave. Own your fucking life Mesut. Own it! Nobody else is going to do it for you."

Then I lowered my voice and looked at him boldly, my eyes blazing into his.

"Life. Is. Yours."

I downed my drink, and walked quickly away in the direction of the beach, eyes of blackened shock staring after me.

———

By the time I got to the shore I was shaking. The beach was deserted. That was one small mercy. So I screamed. Loud and long. I screamed.

When I'd finished I closed my eyes and went back to my breath. It was all I had in this moment. It was my anchor.

Once it was stronger and more even, I opened my eyes. Where had those words come from? I hadn't felt angry with Mesut all the other times he'd spoken to me that night. And since when did I shout at men I hardly knew?

But I knew the answer. I knew it all along. I'd known it since he'd told my fortune that morning. Mesut and I had a connection. Yes, as corny and clichéd as it might sound, we did. Call it past lives, call it soul mates, call it whatever you want. The connection was there. Who knew what we were supposed to do with it, or if we were supposed to do anything at all? But it was there.

And that's why I'd had to speak honestly to him. Lying to him seemed as impossible to me as breathing underwater. All night he'd asked me to listen, to understand, to advise. And on the steps, those final comments he made about going along with something he despised, about being something he really wasn't, were enough to tip me over. I guess lying to a soul mate is like lying to yourself. It just can't be done.

I looked up at the sky. Is it true? I asked silently. Is it true that Mesut could be a soul mate to me? That we do know each other of old? Have I really travelled all these miles to this random, far-away place to stumble across someone who could help me somehow? Then I remembered the stones in my pocket and touched them gently with my finger-tips. Black means yes and white means no. Is it true?

"Jess!"

I turned in the direction of my name. It was him. Walking across the sands towards me. Then I noticed the music pumping out of the bar had stopped and all the lights in Beerbelly were off. And just past Beerbelly, I thought I could see three figures hunched together walking up the hill into town.

"Jess." Mesut stood before me. The wind whipping his hair, his eyes as alive as the stars. "You want to walk?"

13

THE ROCK IN THE SEA

The night was calm and still as it rolled slowly, slowly round to morning.

The sky was turning a deep purple that hinted at magic and the sea stroked our feet in soft, rhythmical kisses as we walked. We'd taken off our shoes and I could feel the sand between my toes. The air was cool and silent. And all the way, I listened to Mesut talk.

Now he was away from Beerbelly, I felt I was dealing with the real him. No more 'Mesut Two' lurking about. Seeing him here, against the powerful, natural setting of the sea, seemed to make more sense. His words flowed more freely and his limbs hung more loosely. Not only did he seem calmer now, but he seemed invigorated too. There was a new energy about him.

"Jess, really you do me big, big favour. When you shouting at me I am seeing everything clearly." He smiled and shrugged at the same time. "First I am upset hearing you. And that is making me feel something too. Normally people not upset me at all. But you did. But then I am listening to your words and when I listen to you I am hearing some truth. A truth nobody else tell me. And maybe because I not normally know people enough to tell me anything true. But you know me. I don't know why."

He went on to tell me more about his life in İpeklikum, the things that pulled him here and the things that kept him here. He told me about the tourists, their expectations, their demands. He said he was lucky to have a boss like Esad because he just let him run Beerbelly however he wanted, that Bad Boy had no real impact on the place. He was glad he wasn't part of the family network because it meant he could leave if he ever wanted to. But Esad was like an older brother and he would not let him down if he could help it.

He knew Demir didn't like him and that had been apparent for a long time now. Mesut didn't think much of him either, thought he was manipulative and not to be trusted. He said I should watch Gillie's back for her, just in case.

He said that, just before I had arrived in İpeklikum for the second time, he'd been having some worries about what on earth he was doing here. He felt there was something else waiting for him. "And then you and Gillie come here. And I am feeling shocked because I talk to you. Normally I am not talking to English girls. They not interesting for me. But you . . ."

"What? I'm fabulous? Wonderful? Amazing?" I teased.

He laughed. "I don't know what you are Jess but you are here and that is that." Then he stopped walking. "Look, we are here."

I hadn't realised we were walking with a particular destination in mind but Mesut had stopped next to a trail of rocks leading off into the sea. He pointed right out to the end of them. "You see the big one at end? We are going there."

"What do you mean we are going there? How?"

But he'd already put his shoes back on and was half walking, half crawling across the rocks. Was he mental? We were going to get soaked. But, I supposed, there was no going back now. So I slipped on my shoes and followed him.

When I got to the very end, Mesut was already sitting on the last large rock before the ocean took over. He patted the space next to him. "Come. This is your place."

"Excellent." I said and plonked myself down. "I like it. Er, what is it for?"

"It is for sitting, of course. And for the watching of the sun." He pointed out towards the westward hills and I saw that we were perfectly situated to watch the sunrise.

"It's so beautiful. Is this your favourite spot then?"

"Yes. I am coming here a lot after working. Is much better place than pier or balcony or somewhere. Is natural. And . . ." he looked all around him at the deserted beach, "is private."

"Yes, it certainly is." I agreed. I couldn't think of anywhere I would rather be right now than on this rock with Mesut about to watch a sunrise. I wasn't scared anymore. Of his eyes and how they might affect me. Of his heart and how it might pull me in. And it didn't feel romantic either, although in any other situation with any other man I'd certainly have my suspicions. This just was what it was. The two of us. On a rock. Waiting for the sun to rise.

We fell into a peaceful silence. Mesut was all talked out. And I was ready for the quiet appearance of the sun.

It came up slowly, teasingly from behind the mountains. At first a fiery tinge touched the wide, white clouds, clearing the purple haze of the night and then a smooth, orange circle sliding into the morning. From this spot we could see how the sun cast new, glittering light over everything in İpeklikum. It gave the buildings, the paths, the beach a momentary glow so beautiful it was hard to believe this happened every single morning whilst people slept in their beds. A transient magic. A gift from the universe.

"Wow." I said, humbly.

"Of course." Mesut smiled and I thought his dark skin had never looked more beautiful as it did just then, touched by the sun. "Wow of course."

"Mesut, can I tell you something?" I asked, taken by a strange courage.

"Yes, if you want it."

"I do. I want to tell you about a thought I've had. Actually, no, it's more of a feeling. I didn't think it could be true just a few days ago but now I'm certain of it. I'm certain it's true."

"Feelings are always true Jess."

"Well, it's just that I feel I have met you for a reason. I feel you are important to me for some reason." He kept watching me, still and waiting. "I think that maybe I did not meet you by accident but that something else has happened. You have 'appeared' to me. Do you understand? You have 'appeared' because you can help me in some way."

"And what you feel I can helping you with?"

"I don't know." I said, hiding my head in my hands. "I just don't know."

"Jess," he said, touching my hands and gently pulling them away so that my eyes were there for the taking. "I am thinking you do know. What is it?"

Now it was all or nothing. "My destiny Mesut. I have been wondering what it is since I got here. I feel maybe you can help me rediscover my destiny."

"Rediscover?" He hadn't even blinked at the responsibility I had just laid on his shoulders.

"Yes. I think I probably knew it when I was a kid. When nothing was impossible. But now, although I have lost it, I think I am very close to rediscovering it. I can't remember my destiny but I feel you can help me figure it out all over again."

He turned away from me and looked out to sea. I couldn't

make out his expression, just his long, violet-black lashes dipped towards his cheeks, his hair picked up playfully by the breeze, and the curve of his cheek tinted by the sunlight.

Then he stood up and held out his hands to help me up so that we were both standing on the rock in the middle of the sea together. He gave me a long, kind look, bowed slightly and said "I hope I can help you." That was it. No, 'Are you crazy'? Or 'Get away from me you insane woman', or 'Sort your life out Jess.' Just, 'I hope I can help you.'

We clambered back over the rocks and headed on up the beach back to Beerbelly. We weren't holding hands. We hadn't kissed. Not even a cuddle. But I felt closer to this man than I potentially had to any other before him. Inexplicable as it was, our hearts were touching and that was all that mattered.

Back at the bar it was peaceful and still. Gillie and Demir were enjoying a pot of Turkish tea and a bowl of olives, so we joined them. Gillie's face was twitching with curiosity so I just winked and gave her a grin. That would keep her guessing.

"So Mesut," She just couldn't help herself. "Where did you whisk my friend off to for all this time."

"Nowhere really." He said, and leaned back in his chair, looking at me intently. "We just walking and talking."

"Have you been up all night Jess? Again? But you don't look tired. To be honest sweetie, you look amazing. Have you got fresh make-up on?" She came to sit right next to me, looking into my face and inspecting it for glittery eye shadow and blusher.

"No, of course not. It's seven in the morning. It's just what's left from last night."

"Then by rights you should look a hot mess. But you don't. You look beautiful. I'm not joking. Whatever, you've done Mesut, you've done something right. The girl looks fantastic."

Mesut nodded. "Definitely she has beauty." He said. "Is in

here too." And he pressed his hand to his heart, giving me a look that made me feel anchored to the core of the earth.

And then I knew that the way I looked had nothing to do with the precise application of last night's make-up, and everything to do with the way that I felt.

14

THE PURE PATH

I'd like to say the following few days were full of magical, intense, out-of-this-world experiences. But actually, they were more kind of comfortable.

And beautifully so.

Now that Mesut and I had established we obviously meant something to each other, no matter how weird, we relaxed into each other's company. While Gillie was fussing around Demir, or answering one of her bizarre, secret phone calls (which were becoming more and more frequent), Mesut and I found ourselves together. Sometimes alone, sometimes not. Sometimes chatting, sometimes not. But together. And all the better for it.

Mesut was definitely smiling more. And it suited him well. He got Bad Boy to take on more work at the bar. He took regular breaks just so he could stroll along the beach with me. Mornings became our real magic time though. We would sit on our rock in the sea, or perhaps sit on a swing-seat in the Çay Bahçesi (Tea Garden) sipping coffee and looking through trails of climbing roses to watch the sun's first rays reach out and caress the water. It made me wonder how I'd ever managed a morning without a sweet, milky coffee, a beach and a sunrise.

Mesut and I talked about all sorts. Our ideas about life, philosophy, dreams, desires. We talked about the language of the world and the soul that we thought whispered through every living thing, the energy that bound everything together. I felt years of physical insecurities – even those planted there by Sandra's horrible boyfriend – slowly start to slip away as we discussed how important gratitude was to his faith. Gratitude for health, gratitude for nourishment, gratitude for a body that god designed for you – a body that gives us the chance to experience all the wonders of the world every single day that we're alive.

Even though I hadn't thought or talked about it in years before this holiday, I told Mesut about the constant criticism I'd endured as a little girl, under the devious, yellow-grinned tyranny of Sandra's bloke. I guess I'd shoved it so far back into the depths of my consciousness I'd never given him credit for the ways in which I felt my body failed me even to this day.

"I know it's shallow, Mesut, and I know there are a million more important things than how my body looks to me or anybody else. But what he said cut deep – maybe deeper than I know."

"What was this person's name Jess? This man who said such things to you?"

"That's the weird thing – I really can't remember. I just remember his horrible, devious smile and his sallow skin and his prodding, pointing fingers and his laugh and, of course, the words he used against me."

"And I'm guessing he not exactly beautiful himself?"

"Ugh! Not at all. He oozed cruelty and ugliness." I shuddered at the memory.

"Oozed?" Mesut tried the words out in his mouth.

"Yeah. Oozed. Like the ugliness just flowed very slowly out of him. From the inside."

"I think I know your mean. And anyway by the way, I have a name for him."

"Oh yeah? I hope it's suitably horrible."

"From now on he is called, 'Man-I-Kill'. In my head anyways. You not need talking about him again if you not want it."

"Man-I-Kill?" I laughed. "It almost sounds Celtic. And excuse me but that doesn't sound very in-keeping with the Islamic faith. You can't just go around thirsting for the blood of people who do things you don't like."

Mesut leaned back in our swing seat, causing us both to rock ever so slightly. He sipped his black coffee and his eyes dipped darkly down into his cup. Then he looked up at me and stopped the swing abruptly with his foot. "We talking about you being child, Jess. Is not right. I am thinking Man-I-Kill will find this out. One day."

Fuck, he was so intense sometimes. I can't say I didn't love it.

"Well, I'd prefer to forget about him for now, so hold off one your killing spree. I know what he said and did was wrong, and I need some time for that to filter through to the deeper layers of my mind so that I can adjust my actions and maybe, you know, one day feel okay in my body. It's not a bad body really. It's done me proud so far."

"Yes. You can be proud. Is *really* not bad body." I might have been imagining it but I thought I saw his lashes flick up and down over my torso – the very bit I'd always had issue with. And what was that behind them? Hunger?

Maybe he just needed breakfast.

"Anyway," I said, trying to edge the topic of conversation away from my body before any devouring was done, "I've been reading this amazing book. Here, have a look. Do they have this in Turkish? Have you read it?"

And it just so happened that The Alchemist was one of Mesut's favourites. "Ah, I reading this when I college student long time before now. Is very famous book in Turkey. When I see you reading it Jess, I nearly say something but I not want take your experience. Is important, I think, you make own discoveries. So I say nothing." But now, as I told him I'd finished it, we got really stuck into the book's themes and ideas and the adventures that Santiago went on. I began to think that this little book really had life-changing magic woven through its pages.

"Honestly, Mesut, if somebody had told me at the start of this holiday that you and I would find common ground in a book we've both read, I never would have believed them."

"I know Jess. But books have more magic than we understand. You not think?"

"Yes. I do think." I said smiling at his seemingly innate ability to zone right in on my thoughts as they occurred.

Of course, we disagreed sometimes too. Over things like past lives, karma and religion. And this made me feel even more certain that he had appeared to help me find my path. Mesut challenged my views in a way that helped me evolve, rather than feel shunned. And I think I did the same for him too.

One morning, as we shared a basket of bread and olives together, sat on brightly-coloured beanbags we'd pinched from the Çay Bahçesi and relocated to slump happily against the harbor wall, we realised our conversation was sadly lacking some basics. Whilst we'd pretty much bared our souls to each other, we hadn't even touched on the simple stuff like how old we were, our families, education, home towns etc. It was like we'd started on the very inside and worked our way outwards. And here we were now, ready to give it a go.

"Okay, here's my profile Mesut. Age: twenty-eight. Family: one brother, three cousins. Home town: Ashton in the North

East of England. Education: Creative Arts Degree. Erm, anything else?"

"Yes. What about your birthday. You know it?"

"Of course I know it, you loon. It's the seventh of April. Now. Your turn."

"Okay." He said, "I am twenty-six years in age."

"What? I can't believe you're younger than me!"

"Why not? I am looking younger than you Jess," He looked positively victorious.

"Shut up! You've got to be at least two hundred years old. Maybe more." And I wasn't really kidding. I still had that feeling, and god knows where it came from, that he had walked this earth before now. Possibly with me.

"Alright then. I am two hundred years in age. And family: well, I am one in nine children and really, too many cousins for me to be counting."

"Woah."

"Is normal in my part of Turkey to have big family. Home town: Manevitaş in South East of Turkey. Very mystical and historical place. Is really where life started, did you know?"

"What?" I asked, chomping so enthusiastically on this beautiful fresh bread, I wondered if I'd heard him right. "Life started there?"

"Tabi. Of course. Some people is thinking Garden of Eden is there. One day I take you Jess. You see for yourself."

"It's a deal." I said, knowing that we could be treading on the playful edges of prophecy here.

Mesut continued. "Okay. What is next? Education? Not really. I am not liking school and I am not behaving so my mother is cry and send me Muslim school."

"Muslim school?"

"Yes. Is good for children who are not being good. But not for me. I not behaving there either."

"So basically, your poor mother cried through your whole education. You horrible child."

"Yes, I really was. And my birthday? Well not many people are knowing their birthday in Turkey. Is not so important for us and we are not being obsessed by it like you English. But I know mine because my uncle always is reminding me is same day he start new job as teacher."

"Which was?"

"Twenty-fifth September."

Well that date rang a bell. Not only was it in under a week's time but wasn't it the same as Ekrem's? All this did was remind me what a genius decision I had made by ending things with him. Otherwise right now I'd be gearing up for an unbearable night in a god-awful night club followed by some equally unbearable shenanigans under a single red light bulb. This listening to your heart stuff was really serving me quite well.

"Jess, I realise I am not knowing your whole name. I just knowing Jess."

"It's Jessica Emily Parker. And you?"

"Is simple. Mesut Akyol. That is all."

"I know Mesut means 'happiness' . . ."

"Yes, is meaning very deep happiness." He puffed his chest out at this. "I am thinking you are lucky to sit here with me Jess."

I loved how Mesut's sense of humour was coming through more with every day I spent with him. He had a beautiful, child-like sense of play.

"Ha ha. What about your surname, how did you say it? Ak-yoll? Does that have a meaning?"

"Yes. Is simple again. Is mean 'pure and honest path'."

"Pure and honest path?"

"A path that you take that is honest and true. A path that is meant for you."

I felt that shiver that was slowly becoming familiar whenever I was around Mesut. Could it be something to do with this 'language of the world' that Paulo Coelho talked about in The Alchemist?

Another omen then. Mesut was a path personified, just as I'd suspected. My heart had known it first and now here it was laid out for me plain to see, in his very name.

A path that you take that is honest and true. What more could I want from the universe? All I needed now was the courage to take the next step.

———

That evening, Gillie and I decided to have a night in at Shit Class Hotel with a bottle of wine and a tray of baklava. I'd told Gillie about the whole birthday thing and she was quite taken with the concept that we should give Mesut something really special for his birthday. We'd had a look around the shops but honestly, what do you buy for the person you suspect you may have known in a past life? Nothing seemed to cut it.

Then I remembered the palette of paints I'd bought a few days before and resolved to make Mesut a painting. I didn't have a canvas or anything, but was pretty certain Gillie and I could fashion something suitable from what we had available back at the hotel room. We hadn't come this far as community artists to not know how to work within our means.

And I wanted to include some words somewhere on the painting. Knowing Mesut loved the book, Gillie and I had spent the best part of the afternoon flicking through The Alchemist to find a suitable quote. There were so many beautiful concepts to choose from but I wanted to hit the nail right on the head. I'd almost given up when Gillie said "Right, that's it, I'm going to open this bloody book on a random page and you are going to choose the first thing you see. Agreed?"

"Agreed."

And there it was. Clear as day and absolutely perfect.

'To realise one's destiny is a person's only real obligation'.

Demir had reluctantly agreed to translate the quote into Turkish for us, but not before he made it clear he wasn't happy about our idea. "I not know why you want to do this for him. He is not child."

But now dusk was falling outside our hotel room window and we were starting our work in the settling evening light, Gillie and I didn't give Demir a second thought. We ripped the back page off an old jotter Gillie had brought with her and were now wrapping a scrap of fabric round it to give the painting some background texture. Then we got out the paints, agreed on a colour theme of midnight blues and deep, cranberry reds and each started painting at opposite ends of our homemade canvas.

Gillie and I hadn't worked together like this for so long. No words were needed as we worked round each other's brushes. We silently added small swishes of silver and white, responded to each other's mark-making with balancing strokes and harmonizing colours. And when we were happy with the small abstract piece, Gillie stood at our balcony door and rolled a cigarette while I started writing the words of the quote on paper ready to be added to the painting.

"Jess?"

"Uh huh?"

"Do you fancy a change of scenery?"

"What do you mean?"

"I mean, don't you fancy seeing some more of Turkey? We haven't seen much outside of İpeklikum really."

"You're right, we haven't. Do you fancy going on a day-tour again?"

"Well, no. I was thinking of going a bit further away sweetie. Maybe, İstanbul?"

I looked up from my work. Gillie was biting her nails. "İstanbul? How long would it take us to get there?"

"Eleven hours. I asked Demir and he said eleven hours by coach."

"You asked Demir? Would he come with us?"

"No. He has to stay here and work. And he doesn't like the idea either. But I think it would be good for us, don't you? It would be good to see more of Turkey and İstanbul is supposed to be amazing. And then I was thinking we could go somewhere else too. Maybe Cappadocia where they have all those weird little fairy chimney thingies and the hot air balloon rides. That would only be another twelve hours or so by coach. And the coaches are supposed to be fab. Air conditioned, reclining seats, free tea and coffee, the works." She'd spluttered all of this out in a rush and now seemed to be holding her breath, in anticipation of my answer.

"It sounds like you've given this a lot of thought."

"Well, erm, a bit." Then her phone rang. She picked it up and clasped it to her chest. "I'll be back in a minute, just got to take this." And with that she was gone, out of the room, down to reception and no doubt off into the street below to talk to her mystery caller again.

I looked down at Mesut's artwork drying on a page from a magazine on the bed. And the words, carefully written and torn, ready to be stuck to the surface of the painting. But we'd miss Mesut's birthday if we went away. I wasn't sure how I felt about that. Yes, I liked the idea of discovering more of Turkey, but why now? Why hadn't we discussed this before?

I wandered over to the balcony and looked out at the street below. And there was Gillie, sitting on the edge of a wall, chatting away to whoever it was on the other end of that phone. Did the mystery caller have something to do with this? Why wouldn't she just tell me what was going on?

I thought back over the last few days and how Gillie had been supporting me through such a tumultuous time. She'd just accepted everything, no matter how freaky it might have sounded, and gone with it as if it was the most normal thing in the world. Maybe I shouldn't be questioning her here. Maybe it was my turn to go along with what she needed.

And maybe she needed time away from Demir. He was pretty intense and Mesut had told me he wasn't to be trusted. Perhaps new landscapes were something that would benefit Gillie right now. And although time away from Mesut would be strange for me, it would give me time to see how I related to the outside world now that he was in my life. And, more importantly perhaps, how our friendship would stand up to time apart.

When Gillie reappeared I'd already stuck the words on Mesut's painting and held it out for her to see. "Yes, Gillie, let's go to İstanbul. And Cappadocia too if you like. I think it's a good idea."

Gillie smiled. "Great," she said. "We leave tomorrow."

15

SURPRISE

These long-distance Turkish coaches were a bit of alright.

Air conditioning, tea and coffee on demand and a cheeky little cake too if you asked nicely. Clean loos, comfy seats; aside from an HD Ready TV and a king-size bed, there wasn't much else you could have asked for.

Gillie had arranged for us to leave İpeklikum at ten o'clock that night, and Demir had sorted the tickets with a sour look on his face. He clearly wasn't happy about Gillie leaving and when I'd asked her why, she'd whispered something about a woman's place, so I decided to keep my mouth shut for fear of getting on a very large soapbox and never getting off it.

Mesut, however, took news of our leaving all in his stride. He said we'd enjoy İstanbul "a very lot" and gave us a few ideas for things to see and do. We'd given him his painting all wrapped up in a scarf (it seemed there was a shortage of gift-wrapping paper in İpeklikum) with strict instructions not to open it until his birthday. He'd nodded silently and tucked it away under the bar.

When we said goodbye at the coach park, he covered my hands with his and pulled them to his chest. We both opened our mouths to speak but nothing came out. The whole eye contact thing was more than enough, and the fact that I could feel his heart beating steadily underneath my fingers. We would see each other again soon, even if I did have that strange elastic-band-pulling going on in the general area of my heart.

Despite the comfort of the coach journey, it was all pretty exhausting. Gillie and I chatted a while, pinched as many cakes as we could from the refreshments man, and took naps when the need overwhelmed us. Gillie was definitely not herself though. I wondered if Demir had finally pissed her off with the whole 'woman's place' comment. And she suddenly seemed very keen on the subject of me.

"So Jess, what's going on with you? I've been spending so much time with Demir I've hardly got round to find out how things are going. You and Mesut are so sweet together. Have you snogged him yet? Please tell me you've snogged him?"

"Urm. Nope. Not even close."

"Why on earth not? How could you not be tempted sitting on rocks and watching sunrises and stuff? I wouldn't be able to stop myself if it was me. He's gorgeous, in a native American kind of way. There must have been an opportunity."

"Well, yes, I suppose there have been lots. But to be honest, it hasn't really crossed my mind." And I meant it. The sunrises and the rocks certainly hadn't been wasted on me. I was well aware of how they would have been ridiculously romantic in any other situation. But it seemed that Mesut and I were sharing something that could be irreversibly cheapened by a snog. I was scared of cheapening the whole thing. Of turning it into the worst kind of holiday cliché, on a par with Ekrem / Eric and his throng of Cockney lasses. I just loved what we had right now.

"Come on, you must fancy him, Jess. You do, don't you?"

This was a weird one. I was definitely attracted to him, his presence and his energy. But did I fancy him? He wasn't anything like my usual type. Far too skinny and scruffy and long-haired. But he certainly made my heart beat faster. He certainly made me want more of him. Like, all the time. "Oh bloody hell, Gillie, I don't know! Can I get back to you on that one?"

She looked at me with that *I-know-something-you-don't-know* kind of look and sat back in her seat. "Okay sweetheart. I'm ready when you are."

"Anyway, never mind me. What about Demir? You can't tell me you've spent all those nights at his place and nothing's happened."

"Okay, stuff has happened." Her mouth was set in a grim line.

"Stuff ?"

"Well, half of the time Kadafi is around and it feels weird knowing he's in the next room and I haven't gone as far as Demir would like. I really like him, Jess. He's so sexy. And he seems to really want me and that feels amazing. I deserve it, after Marcus, you know? Somebody who wants me that much."

"But?"

"But . . . well, I just haven't gone that far yet."

"Is it because you're enjoying being adored so much? He still has that puppy-dog look whenever you're around. That's something you don't get off the average English bloke."

"Totally. He's so soppy and I'm not used to it. It's nice. I deserve it. I do. I deserve it." And she did. Of course she did. The girl was amazing. I had a feeling though, that Gillie needed to walk down the path of Gillie for a little longer before she could really, wholeheartedly accept adoration from anybody else.

"So why hasn't it been right yet then?"

She frowned for a moment. "I'll see if it feels right when I get back." And that was it. I knew it was conversation over from her tone. She didn't want to be pushed any further on this one. Plus she was suddenly distracted by her beeping phone which went off for the umpteenth time during the journey. And then she did her off-into-the- distance type of stare, which happened every time she checked that damn phone. Maybe whoever was on the other end of it would give me some clues as to what was going on with my friend.

———

When we finally arrived in İstanbul, it was nine in the morning. Rush hour. Now I've witnessed rush hour in a lot of cities but in İstanbul it is quite something. Getting off the coach we were not only blasted by the petrol-laced heat but by an overwhelming soundscape of engines, horns, voices, yells, screeches, growls and rumbles. And the colours. The bus station was a vast cement creation, a smooth, shining, off-white slab which reflected the bright orange early-morning sun in sharp fragments across bright yellow taxis, grey and black luggage mountains, and the odd flash of pink, blue, orange or green as brightly-dressed children darted confidently in between growling vehicles with shuddering engines. Trails of smoke rose from cigarettes in just about every direction you turned, women chatted behind patterned headscarves held over their mouths, clutching babies that wailed from rough bundles of fabric. Coach drivers ate rounds of bread, sitting on the hot concrete floor whilst endless crowds of people waited in the shadowy depths of the bus stands.

We looked into the shadowy depths ourselves, hoping we'd find a way to get out of this place. And as luck would have it, after just fifteen minutes of panic-stricken wandering, and pretty much vowing we'd never come here again, we found the main taxi rank just outside the bus station.

We agreed a fare in advance with the taxi driver (as previously insisted upon by Demir) and wound our way through the city. This place was beautiful and bewildering. One minute a domineering silver-grey high rise, the next minute a golden-topped mosque with pearly minarets powering upwards to the sky. The whole city seemed to be a contradiction in terms, but a fascinating contradiction at that.

Apparently Gillie had already sorted our hotel, which was in the 'old' district called Sultanahmet. I couldn't get over how organised she was with all of this. How did she know which part of İstanbul would be good to stay in? I did a silent prayer that she'd not booked us into some dodgy back-street establishment that would have us running for the next Bosphorous ferry. Surely she would have done her research?

As we drove up to the hotel I looked out the window and thought Gillie may well have just landed on her feet this time. The 'Yaşmak Sultan' looked pretty impressive from the outside. Okay, so I'd grown fond of Shit Class, but that didn't mean I couldn't play the field a bit. And if playing the field meant a room bigger than a broom cupboard then I was totally up for it.

We stumbled, with our backpacks, through the grand doorway of the Yaşmak Sultan and found ourselves in a reception area that was big on mood lighting, marble and curves. I felt a slight sense of panic that my modest bank balance would not be able to fund even an hour in here never mind a few nights, and was just about to find a discreet way to lean over and whisper this into Gillie's ear, when she let out a little yelp and skidded deliberately across the shiny marble floor.

Strangely, she'd flung herself towards a random man and was now engulfed in a vigorous hug with him whilst leaving me there, in the middle of the hotel's opulence, feeling more than a little baffled.

So I stood there, in my baffled state, rolling my eyes in what

I hoped was a jolly way at the receptionist, whilst Gillie and random man finished their hugathon. And it wasn't until they finally let each other go and Gillie stepped back that I realised that I knew the man too.

It was Oliver.

16

GAME PLAN

"Hello matey. Fancy meeting you here." Oliver smiled that lovely friendly smile that I hadn't seen in so long and hugged me close.

I looked at him. Then at Gillie. I opened, then closed, my mouth.

"Jess! Oliver's always wanted to visit Turkey. So I thought, why not meet up with him? You know, while we're here! And İstanbul was the first place he could get a flight to. Isn't that great? Isn't that an awesome surprise?"

"Surprise!" Oliver said, looking awkward for the first time ever in the history of Oliver.

Why couldn't I speak?

Oliver joked, "It's okay, she's just in shock." Then he grabbed Gillie's hand and said, "Let me show you the rooms. They're amazing. I knew this hotel would be great. I'd heard good things about it."

They trotted off down the corridor, Oliver having managed to make a porter magically appear and take our bags. I trailed after them, past swirly golden walls and smooth marble pillars and honestly felt I might have stepped into some sort of parallel world because surely, surely, Gillie couldn't be serious? Oliver? Whilst deciding whether or not to sleep with Demir? What was going through that girl's head?

After trailing down many a surreal corridor I finally stopped / stumbled into a doorway of a room. Gillie was inside gasping, her hands clapped to her mouth and turning her head this way and that as she took it all in. There was a whole lot of burgundy going on. Not to mention gold-encrusted everything and a sleigh-style bed fit for four or five people at least. I suddenly yearned for a bit of Shit Class.

Then Oliver was in front of me, a hand on each shoulder. "Jess. Matey. You're through here." And he ushered me across the corridor into a slightly smaller, more modest arrangement of burgundy-festooned and gold-encrusted stuff. I sat on the bed and worked my gaze up to meet his. "I hope you like it. I promised Gillie I'd find somewhere nice and this place was recommended to me. We're perfectly situated in the old district. Not far from the Blue Mosque, or Hagia Sophia and the Grand Bazaar is walking distance too." His tall, angular frame burst into a bold silhouette at the window, his long arms demonstrating just how delighted he was with the location. And it was all I could do to just sit there, watching him, as if he was an apparition that was going to dissolve at any moment.

"Alright, that's enough. I have to ask Jess, because you seem kind of stunned. And like, not able to speak. It is okay, me being here, isn't it?"

Bless him. In any other situation I would be over the flipping moon to see Oliver and right now I needed to put him at ease. "Oliver, of course it's okay. I'm really pleased to see you. It's just . . ."

"I know, I know. You and Gillie are having crucial time to yourselves and I know how important this trip is to you. But don't worry Jess, we'll all have a great time together. And I'm paying for the hotel . . ."

"What? No Oliver, I can't . . ."

"I'm not taking no for an answer. I got lucky with a photography contract and I can't think of anything better to spend my money on. It's a done deal."

As I had earlier this year, I wondered again what cloud this bloke had floated down from.

"And may I say you look bloody gorgeous. Something about being out here is obviously agreeing with you. But I'm sure you'll tell me all about it later." And with that he winked and dashed back across the corridor to find Gillie.

I watched the door close gently, then lay back on the bed, allowing myself to be slowly, slowly enveloped in velvety-soft bedding. I stared up at the ceiling looking for answers but really just noticing how the lampshade hung at a strange angle, casting thin streams of ruby light in all directions. How could I find answers if I wasn't even sure of the questions?

I didn't know what Gillie was up to. And I doubted if she did either. I knew she and Oliver had been getting cosy back at home, which was why I'd been more than a little surprised at how she'd been going on with Demir. Especially as, to me and the rest of the world, Oliver seemed like the infinitely better choice. And all those secret phone calls and texts must have been from Oliver. That was weird. Why hadn't she just told me it was him?

Some part of Gillie obviously thought it was okay to string both of these men along. And that was a part of her I wasn't entirely familiar with. How strange, after so many years of friendship, to unearth this aspect of Gillie's character. Not that I was perfect or anything. But how on earth was I supposed to play this one?

The air con suddenly made me shiver so I dug under the

layers of soft bedding and climbed in. Surely this was nothing a good nap wouldn't sort out. So I closed my eyes, lay still, and let my attention wander to my breath.

The easy, steady rhythm rocked me slowly, gently and I knew, as I drifted off to sleep, that in its own seriously messed-up way, everything was as it should be.

———

I woke up later to find Gillie beating on my door and insisting I must get up right that instant.

"We're going to see the Whirling Dervishes. Oliver sorted tickets. Come on!" And the irony was not lost on me that I resembled some kind of whirling dervish myself as I dashed about getting freshened up in the thirty seconds Gillie had allotted for me.

The Whirling Dervishes were performing their 'Sema' (meaning 'Sky') ritual at Sirkeci train station just ten minutes walk from our hotel. Apparently the best place to see them was Konya, where the ritual was founded in the thirteenth century. But, here we were among the throng of İstanbul's tourists hoping to get some sense of this mystical ritual. We'd managed to bag seats near the front and Oliver was giving us little insights from a guide book about what we could expect from the performance.

"It all comes from a branch of Islam called Sufism which focuses on love, tolerance, worship of God, community and personal development through self-discipline and responsibility. Apparently the spinning ritual is based on the idea that the fundamental condition of our existence is to revolve. All beings are comprised of revolving electrons, protons, and neutrons in atoms. Everything revolves, and the human being lives by means of the revolution of these particles, by the revolution of the blood in his body, and by the revolution of the stages of his life, by his coming from the earth and his returning to it."

"I still don't understand the dodgy hats though." Gillie said as we watched the men dressed in black cloaks, white robes and tall brown hats come and set up their musical instruments.

"Hang on a minute, it says something here about that." Oliver smiled. "Here we go. 'In the symbolism of the Sema ritual, the semazen's camel's hair hat represents the tombstone of the ego; his wide, white skirt represents the ego's shroud. When he removes his black cloak, he is spiritually reborn to the truth.'"

And with that, the lights dimmed, the echoing train station stilled and the semazens drifted out across the floor and took their places. They started with their arms crossed over their chests, heads held straight and still, as they sang a calm, measured stream of what I assumed to be Arabic words. There was a drum beat, then more chanting and a thin, eerie sound of a flute stretched out across the room. I found myself holding my breath.

The whirling started slowly and steadily, with the semazens' arms gradually stretching outwards as if they were waking from a long, deep sleep. I noticed each man held his right hand turned up towards the sky and his left down towards the earth, his eyes fastened down there. They revolved from right to left and it occurred to me that they didn't appear to be in any kind of trance, as I'd expected. More like completely awake, channeling something powerful. I wanted to clap but remembered something Oliver had said about this not being appropriate. This was, after all, a ritual, not a performance. It was about connecting with God, about being spiritually reborn to some kind of truth.

The ending was strange. You could sense the urge to applaud from the multi-cultural audience, jarring with that knowledge that applause wasn't valid here. Instead there were some whispered gasps and some silent smiles from members of the audience, as the semazens crossed their arms over their chests again and walked quietly out of the hall.

"Is that it?" Gillie whispered. "I mean, I'm starving, can we go?"

"Of course." Oliver smiled at her and took her hand. "Let's go and see what we can find."

I followed them through the crowds of people all pushing to buy souvenirs of the Sema ritual. Postcards, CDs, key rings, figurines and posters, were all on offer on a table at the back of the hall. I just didn't get it. It seemed a bit empty to be taking home something so cheap and tatty when it was supposed to represent something deep and mystical. I'd stick with the memory thank you very much.

A few moments later and we were sitting under a huge white awning in a side-street cafe, swept away from the main thrash and crash of the city. It hadn't taken us long to find a place that was filled with Turkish people, which we banked on being a good sign that the food would be halfway decent. We were right. Gillie and Oliver had ordered the biggest, most crammed-full lamb kebabs wrapped in floury flatbread, and I, being a vegetarian had chosen the only option available: half an aubergine stuffed with tomatoes, garlic and herbs. This was simple, honest food but it was fresh and flavoursome and just tasted totally different to anything we'd had in İpeklikum. I can still remember how that aubergine tasted to this day.

I can also remember how bizarrely stunted the conversation became. The three of us had a good chat about the Sema ritual and what we thought of it, but after that things dried up. We oohed and aahed about the food for a while of course. I commented on the blackness of the sky, the whiteness of the stars, the engaging soundscape of the city whilst we were sitting in this little cocoon around our table, somehow removed from it all. But after that I don't know what went wrong. Gillie and Oliver continued to smile. They seemed jovial enough, but their answers became mono-syllabic. Maybe they were tired.

We agreed on a walk round the Sultanahmet district. The night had got a little nippy, not something we were used to down south in İpeklikum. The chill was refreshing though, and kept us moving quickly throughout the district's winding streets and little avenues. We learned to keep our wits about us when we walked along the main streets as trams had a tendency to appear out of nowhere. On more than one occasion, I had to yank Gillie off a tramline seconds before she would have met her maker.

We stopped for Turkish tea in a tiny little ethnic souvenir shop. We sat on beautifully embroidered cushions, looked at glittering tapestries on the walls, admired hanging mosaic lamps in deep, lustrous colours. Then we paid the price for it when we realised the tea cost four times what we would have paid in İpeklikum. This was the city, after all.

Oliver was all excited about going on a Bosphorous cruise, so he dragged us up and down streets that were lined with various tour companies, looking for the best deal. He tried his best to get us an 'indirim' (meaning 'discount') which Gillie would have usually been impressed by as she loved a bargain. But tonight she seemed distant and when Oliver asked her what she thought, she just replied "Anything Oliver. Whatever you want." I nodded in agreement and Oliver dashed off to book the tickets at the first place we'd been to, whilst we waited at the bottom of the street.

"Right Gillie, what the hell is up? Spill it."

"Just tired Jess, I wasn't sleeping like you this afternoon."

"Oh really? What on earth were you up to?" I asked in my best nudge-nudge, wink-wink kind of tone.

"No Jess. God, is that all you think about? Oliver and I had a lot to catch up on."

"Well, of course, but haven't you been speaking on the phone these last couple of weeks? Isn't that who has been calling and texting you all this time?"

"Yes."

That was it. That was all I got. A yes.

"So how are things between you two? And while we're on the topic, what's going on with Demir? God Gillie, talk about having your cake and eating it. Does Oliver even know about Demir?"

"No, he bloody doesn't! Just leave it please."

"Hang on a minute, I can't just leave it. You're my friend and you're doing weird shit. This isn't like you. What's your game plan here?"

"Jess." Gillie sighed, looked down at her feet and looked utterly exhausted in that moment. "I'm on it, okay? Just leave me to it."

Under the cold, harsh glow of the tall street lamp, I noticed drooping lines around Gillie's mouth and creases in the centre of her brow. And being typical Gillie, just as she had done through her entire relationship with Marcus, she didn't want to let me in on a thing. "Fine Gillie. If that's what you want. But you know you can talk to me about this stuff don't you?" I took her hand and gave it a squeeze. She squeezed back.

"Yes, yes. But I'm fine. Honestly."

And sweeping off in her trademark way, she went to join Oliver in getting his indirim.

"Of course you are," I whispered to the wind. "Of course you are."

17

COLD SHOULDER

There were no two ways about it. This hotel had the best restaurant. Ever.

Oliver and I were sitting at a table for two in the Olive Restaurant which was on the rooftop, no less, of the Yaşmak Sultan. There we were, supping sweet milky coffee, eating bread, olives and fruit for breakfast and looking out over the amazing panoramic view before us. Within that view there was an incredible fusion of past and present, of heritage and optimism. We could see Hagia Sophia, Topkapı Palace, The Blue Mosque, all swathed in the shimmering drama of the Bosphorous. The Golden Horn curved protectively to separate the sacred history of the city from the rest of its pulsing, contemporary ambition. The contradictory nature of İstanbul was alive here. What a metaphor for the constantly tipping balance of life. I liked it.

Oliver, on the other hand, was having a hard time. Bless him. This was the first time I'd seen him appearing to be at all human. Until now, he had been this weird, angel-like entity to me, offering me grounding, confidence, hope and aspiration. Now I guessed it was my turn.

"I really think something's up with Gillie," he said. "I just don't get it matey. Before you both went away, I really thought things were going well. We get on. We like each other, I'm sure of it. And when she asked me to come out and meet you two over here, I jumped at the chance. But I can't figure out why she didn't tell you I was coming. And I can't figure out why I'm getting the cold shoulder now."

"The cold shoulder?" I asked, chowing down on some deliciously warm bread, and popping an olive in my mouth.

"Well, you know the kind of thing. Not engaging in conversation any deeper than chit chat. And . . . God, I feel like a lovesick kid saying this out loud . . . she doesn't want to hold my hand or touch me at all. I thought after the reception I got when she first saw me, things would be great. I guess I was wrong matey. Wrong, wrong, wrong."

"I'm sure she's pleased to see you Oliver. We've just had a lot going on during this trip, there's been some serious soul-searching. She's probably just readjusting to, you know, the city, seeing someone from home and all that." I hated this. Why should I skirt around the truth? Oliver deserved more than that. But Gillie said she was on it and I felt my loyalty was ultimately to her.

"Readjusting. Yeah. You're probably right."

"Where is she now, anyway?"

"She said she wanted longer to sleep. But I was bristling to get up."

"Me too. Good timing on both our parts." I smiled and managed to crack one out of Oliver too. He downed his last gulp of coffee, leaned back in his chair and seemed to take in the view for the first time since coming up here.

"Anyway, wow." He said. "Maybe it was worth coming just for this."

I nodded in agreement and we spent a good few moments

just looking and appreciating. I could feel the breeze on my cheek, the morning sun starting to tickle my neck. My breathing was soft and slow as if being up here and having this perspective on the city, gave me a certainty that everything was coming to me at exactly the right time. Even Oliver and his saddened confusion over Gillie.

He poured us both some more coffee and leaned forward, seemingly back to his old, twinkly self. "Right you. I want to know what's going on with you. Come on, let's be at it."

Resistance was futile with this man. I knew that by now. "Oh bloody hell. I haven't got a clue where to start Oliver."

"Trust yourself Jess. You'll start where you're meant to start." He leaned back in his seat, hugged his cup of coffee and waited. I wasn't going to get out of this one.

"Alright," I laughed, "you asked for it."

———

I'd given it my best shot. Gillie, Oliver and I were on our Bosphorous boat cruise and I felt like I'd spent the entire day jollying them along.

The weather had seemingly decided to go along with the mood evoked by the two of them by throwing cold winds and slick drizzle at us from all angles. And there wasn't a joke I had not cracked or a funny story I'd left untold. I'd used my entire bag of tricks when it came to the cheering up of grumpy people and there was nothing left inside it. Nothing.

Perhaps, I thought, as I shivered with the cold afternoon whipping across the deck of the tour boat, perhaps I just needed to leave them to it.

After breakfast, and after telling Oliver a condensed version what had been going down for me over the past couple of weeks, we'd both been positively peppy. Oliver had decided to give

Gillie a bit of space and time, and I'd relaxed into the weirdness of things. But then Gillie had hit the scene and things had turned around. She was behaving a like a strange, robot-like version of herself at first. All forced smiles and platitudes. But she wasn't able to keep that up for long and she slowly slid into a more real representation of herself. Avoiding any eye contact. Slinking away from Oliver's touch. Feigning sickness and tiredness.

Well, I was sick and tired now. Hadn't she asked me to come away with her so we could spend some time together? Why would she pull me into this bizarre scenario when I could be back in İpeklikum watching endless sunrises with Mesut? Fuck it. I never thought I'd choose a cheap holiday resort over one of the most culturally rich cities in the world.

I looked several seats behind me to where Gillie and Oliver were sitting. We'd all been given transparent rain ponchos to protect against the drizzle from our tour guide. Only there hadn't quite been enough so the tour guide had thought fit to give Gillie and Oliver just one to share between them. And so they sat hunched together, enveloped in their plastic tent-like poncho, with their shoulders, legs and arms pressed together, but their heads looking out in different directions.

I noticed Gillie's eyes were welling up and wanted to rush over there and hug her, wet poncho and all, but there was something about her stare that spoke of isolation. I searched in the direction she was staring and saw a massive industrial dock, with cabins and cranes and stacks and stacks of what appeared to be blocks of metal. Why would that upset her? Okay, maybe that's not what we'd hope to see on a historic cruise, but a city had to have its industries.

Then I saw it. Emblazoned across one of the huge dockside cabins was a load of bright white chunky lettering, utterly unfathomable to me apart from one word: 'Demir'.

Oh Gillie. Please don't see this as a sign. Please don't think that Demir is the one for you. Oliver or not, Demir is a dodgy option.

And, would you believe it? As the boat channeled relentlessly through the grey waters, the word 'Demir' was there time and time again. Sometimes in bold, fat letters, stretching across cabins and massive, moored cargo ships and other times in rusted, peeling signs at the edges of the dock. That word was bloody everywhere. Now that I thought about it, I seemed to remember Demir saying something about his name meaning steel or iron or something, as he did a flexy-muscle thing in Gillie's general direction back at Beerbelly.

I looked at her now. She'd closed her eyes but I could see the tiny stream of a tear slipping down her cheek. Lucky that Oliver was in his own huff in the opposite direction and totally unaware of where Gillie's head was.

We were passing directly under the Bosphorous suspension bridge now. It stretched majestically across the Bosphorous Strait, all one thousand, five hundred and sixty metres of it, linking Europe and Asia in a single graceful curve. I could appreciate the beauty of it, and I could see it was a feat of engineering, but in all honesty, on that day, I just felt its weight. Its heavy presence. Its shadow and its dramatic, ominous grace.

———

The whole day had been a bit of a write-off really.

By early evening we'd arrived back at the hotel and shuffled off to our rooms to get hot showers and put on dry clothes. Minimum words had been spoken. The whole dynamic between the three of us was utterly weird and I wasn't sure how much more of it I could take. For the first time I wondered if me slinking off to İpeklikum on my own would be against the rules of whatever game we were playing.

After a hot shower and wrapping myself in the fluffiest dressing gown known to man, I decided to nip down to the hotel spa. I wanted a brochure. If this trip was going to continue to be unbearable then the least I could do would be to indulge in a little pampering.

I was crossing the insanely polished marble floor of the reception area when I spotted Gillie. She sat on a sofa in a shadowed corner, dressed in a fluffy bath robe identical to mine. She had a piece of paper rolled up between her fingers and was looking at it longingly. She was tapping her foot. And biting her lip.

"Jesus Gillie," I said, as I parked myself next to her, "Just go out and buy some fags, will you?"

She looked up. Briefly. "Oh. I'm okay. I don't want to smoke. Oliver doesn't like it."

I took a deep breath. To speak truth, or not to speak truth? That was the question. "Right. So you'll go round with a face like a slapped arse all day, not respond to anything Oliver says, not engage in any conversation with the man who has travelled over two thousand miles to see you, but you'll refrain from smoking one little fag? Really Gillie, I just don't get it."

"What's there to get, Jess? I'm just so bloody confused. Can't you get that?"

"Of course I can. But honestly sweetheart? You've done this to yourself. You've invited confusion right in the front door!"

Gillie drew her breath in sharply, then it shot out like gunfire. "Okay, okay, so maybe I'm not bloody perfect! So maybe I'm not on some fucking soulful journey and making all the right moves and turning all the right sodding corners. But I deserve some happiness too, Jess. And I deserve for a man to treat me with respect and love and tenderness and passion and all the things I never even got close to with Marcus. And surely you, in your fucking heightened state of euphoria with your sunsets and your mystical man and your starry nights can see that you're not the only one in the world who deserves that!"

"Of . . . of course Gillie. Of course I can see . . ."

"Really? Because sometimes I think all I ever do is follow you around on your fucking stupid hippy trip. But where's mine? What's happening to mine while yours is going through its fucking oscar-worthy moments? It's fucking lost Jess. It's lost." She scrunched up the roll of paper in her hand and threw it across the floor before pulling her knees up to her chest and tucking her head right in. Still. Silent. Closed.

I stared at the floor. I counted five breaths. This was new to us. What now?

Should I put my arms around her? Comfort her? Walk away? Shout back? Get Oliver? Buy fags? Whisk her off to the spa? Nothing seemed quite right. In the end, I just waited. As she had done for me for the last eight or nine months since Jack left. I just waited.

Finally, Gillie uncurled her head and looked tentatively at me. There was a torrent of anguish beneath that steady gaze. "I'm sorry." She whispered. "I just don't know what to do."

Remembering Oliver's way with words I whispered back, "But if you did know what to do, what would you do then?"

The answer was there in a flash. "I'd tell him to go home."

"Okay then," I said, "so there's your answer." She took a huge, shaky breath, that I'm pretty sure took a vast energy reserve, and reached out for my hand. We stood up together, a vision of sisterly courage, holding hands in our fluffy white robes and quietly walked back along the corridor.

It was time to speak to Oliver.

18

TEN YEARS' TIME

I hadn't seen Gillie since the hotel lobby last night. We'd got to her door and I'd kissed her on the cheek before she disappeared into her room to speak to Oliver. And now here I was, having a glorious, sunny breakfast up on the roof-top restaurant again, feeling not-so-glorious about what my friends must be going through.

Last night I'd messed about with my notebook, writing up abstract reflections and even having another go at the 'three positive things' exercise that had helped haul me out of heartbreak earlier this year. I just wanted to see what I could rescue out of this tight tangle of strangeness.

And, as always, they were there, waiting patiently for me to tease them out . . .

1. *Discovered the Yaşmak Sultan's amazing rooftop restaurant and had lovely catch-up with Oliver about the happenings since I arrived here in Turkey*
2. *Finally got some truth out of Gillie, even if she did feel the need to shout it in my face*

3. *Was reminded in one single bloody gorgeous text
   message that Mesut is still in this world, still
   thinking of me*

And oh my word what a moment that had been. There I was, absentmindedly doodling in my notebook and half-watching bright, twinkling Turkish pop videos on the little telly in my room, when the text message came through.

Hello Jess. I hope u having good time in İstanbul. U should know if you want to come back early there is a heart here beating for u.

Oh. My. Lord.

There is a heart here beating for u. What did that mean? And he was inviting me to come back early! Did that mean he was missing me? Did that mean he was shunning all advances from all other similarly fascinated girls with his fascinating self and waiting for me?

Me? Mesut was waiting for me?

And then all of a sudden I hated that message. I hated that it was making me feel like this. Confused. Silly. Emotional. I hated that it was pulling me into a sequence of excruciating doubts and the absolute certainty that I was now ripping apart the value of all the honest, soul-enriching times we'd had together. I might as well write into 'Take A Break' magazine and have them slap a dodgy picture of us on the front cover and invent a trashy headline like 'Turkish Text Scandal Sends Brit into Deathly Despair'.

And then I read the text again and loved its every word. And then I hated it again. And then adored it. And then cursed the tele-communicative technology on which it was created. And the entire evening pretty much went like that.

And all the while Gillie and Oliver were across the corridor having their own emotional battle.

———

I was about halfway through my breakfast when somebody plonked themselves down in the chair opposite me.

Oliver. Right. What delicious breakfast goods could I tempt him with to comfort him over his split with Gillie?

"A very good morning to you Jess. And isn't it a bloody gorgeous one?" I looked up. There was a smile. A smile that did not suggest he'd just been dumped. At all. "Pour me a coffee will you matey? Caffeine is my friend today."

"Erm, of course. Here you go." I passed him his coffee and he started assembling his breakfast plate with mountains of everything. "So, erm, how are things? How was your night?"

He leaned in towards the centre of the table as if he was going to let me in on a secret but then, at the last minute, thought better of it. "Marvelous." He said. "Just marvelous. Today is going to be a good day."

"Really?" I smiled, pretty much getting the picture about why he looked like the cat who got all the cream. Gillie had chickened out then. "Right, well. I'm glad things are looking up for you."

"They certainly are matey. What about you? How was your night? Did you go to the spa after all? Gillie said she saw you loitering around the entrance."

"No, I thought better of it. Just had an early night really. It's so good to have a room where I can stretch out on the bed without hitting my toes off a wall or a piece of furniture."

"Yeah. Gillie told me about your hotel in İpeklikum. What have you been calling it? Shit Class?"

"Yup. Well, it lives up to its name."

"God. I can't imagine. Still, it's done the job though, hasn't it? You don't want too much luxury whilst you're busy searching your soul. It would be distracting."

"Indeed it would." And I had a little pang. Or maybe it was a big pang. For Shit Class? For İpeklikum? For Mesut? "Oh, and I got a text. From Mesut."

"Nice one. What did it say? That's if you don't mind me asking."

"Of course I don't. Here, have a look." Oliver looked at my phone and nodded, a twitch of a smile telling me he was clearly amused.

"And? What did you say in return?"

"Nothing."

"Nothing? Come on Jess, you can't leave a man hanging like that."

"Honestly Oliver, I don't think Mesut will be *hanging*. It's not his style."

"He's only human Jess. And he's kind of put himself out there with that text. He's obviously going to be waiting for you to text back."

"I really don't think he will. I can imagine him sending it and then just trusting it to the world, you know? He doesn't need me to justify his words or his feelings. He just does what feels right to him."

"You can imagine that, can you? Well, the imagination can be a powerful thing." He sighed and put his coffee down, leaned back in his chair and let his arms dangle down by his sides. He looked around him at the people in the restaurant, the tops of ancient buildings, birds circling the tips of distant minarets. His features were soft and unguarded. Even his normally spiky hair had fallen down, over his brow. He was the vision of a man slowly falling in love. "What do you think, Jess? What do you think we'll be doing in ten years' time?"

"Oliver, I don't even know what I'll be doing in the next ten minutes, never mind the next ten years." I said.

"It's interesting though, isn't it? Imagining what we might be up to? I mean, we didn't even know each other a few months ago and now here we are, on this glorious rooftop in an amazing city, thousands of miles from home. Who'd've thought it?"

He had a point. "Not me. I thought my life was all planned out. Me, Jack and the dog . . . and maybe a few babies one day. I thought I'd be running Firebelly till I was old and grey."

He laughed. "And now look at you – gallivanting around watching sunrises with people who potentially featured in past lives you didn't even know you'd had; completing bizarre challenges for no good reason other than to see what happens. A slight departure from what you had planned, don't you think?"

"Slight." I smiled, remembering why I loved this man.

"So who knows where either of us will be in ten years . . ." He pondered this over a massive slice of watermelon, chewing thoughtfully. I could almost hear the cogs whirring in his mind from where I was sitting. Then he dropped the watermelon and sat up straight. "I know! I've got the ultimate idea. Let's meet back here in ten years' time. You and me!"

"What, here?"

"Yeah. No matter what we're doing or where we are in the world, let's meet back here, at the Yaşmak Sultan in İstanbul, in this very restaurant." He grinned. "We can bring the kids."

"Kids . . ." Who the heck was I going to have kids with? This was weird. "Okay, so we meet back here, on this rooftop in exactly ten years' time?"

"Exactly." He looked at his phone which was lying on the table next to him. "On September twenty-first, ten years from now at ten seventeen in the morning."

"Sounds good to me. In this part of the restaurant? Do you think we can remember this spot?"

"Of course we can. Look. A few yards left of the buffet table. In the top right hand corner with a view of the . . ." We looked all around us. "Hell, with a view of everything worth looking at in İstanbul!"

"Agreed!" I clapped my hands together. "Oooh, I like this idea! It's like something from a film."

"Jess matey, it's better than a film." He lifted his coffee cup up and motioned for me to do the same. We clinked them gently together. "This, my friend, is real."

Once we'd eaten enough to feed an entire village, we started thinking about the plan for the day. I had just one request. "Please Oliver, no more boats."

Oliver chuckled. "Okay. Now here's a thought. Look around you. Why don't we just go and see everything we can see from here? It's not like we need to travel very far. Let's do the Blue Mosque first."

"Okay. Agreed. What about Gillie? Do you think she'll be alright with that?"

"She will. She'll be fine. And there's something I want to tell you. It's pretty exciting."

"Okay." Please, please don't let him be in love with Gillie. Or be about to propose to her or something mad like that.

"Tomorrow, all three of us are going on an adventure. To Cappadocia."

"What?"

"You know, it's the place Gillie's been wanting to visit since she got to Turkey. Rough, alien landscape with little fairy chimneys sticking up out of the ground everywhere you look. It's been featured on loads of sci-fi films. I've been out this morning and bought us all coach tickets. And I've found a little hotel set in the mountains."

"Woah, woah, Oliver. You have to stop buying stuff. I have to pay my own way. And tomorrow? Are you sure?"

"Tomorrow's as good a time as any. In fact," he drained his coffee cup, wiped his mouth with a napkin and stood up to leave, "I'm going to tell Gillie now. She'll be well chuffed. See you in thirty minutes in the lobby?"

I nodded and off he dashed. Cappadocia? Tomorrow? That would mean another ridiculously long coach trip. And I wasn't sure Gillie had wanted to go to Cappadocia with Oliver tagging along. But let's face it, I didn't have a bloody clue what Gillie wanted or what she was doing from one minute to the next. It was all too much for me to keep up with and, if I was going to survive this trip, I had to learn to keep my emotions separated from everybody else's. Not my circus, not my monkeys.

So the choice was before me. Go with Gillie and Oliver or don't go with Gillie and Oliver? I could stay in İstanbul and do a bit more sight-seeing. I could go back to İpeklikum and see if Mesut was really waiting there for me, his beating heart and everything. I could go wild and back-pack around Turkey on my own, seeing if my destiny decided to show up in some other fancy place. Oh, what was a girl to do?

Well, right now, this girl was going to tackle one thing at a time.

First item on agenda: Blue Mosque.

19

A WISH

It was prayer time.

Most of the other tourists had left the mosque now. But we decided to stay, just the three of us. We knelt down at the back of the vast space and watched quietly. Gillie and I wore headscarves we'd borrowed at the entrance, with our bare feet tucked under in the expected manner. We waited.

It truly was a magnificent space. One high, central dome was surrounded by several smaller ones, all adorned in thousands of hand-painted ceramic tiles, mostly blue, gold and red. Sunlight streamed in through hundreds of tiny windows, settling on huge, wide pillars and stroking the soft red carpet on the ground. Enormous metal rings hung on chains a long distance from the curved ceiling, each one dotted with many golden light bulbs making the whole place feel magical and even holy. Which, of course, it was.

As the prayer began, and the hundreds of men gathered closely together knelt forward on their prayer mats, making all the moves and whispered words their God was waiting for, I looked down at the ground. It didn't feel right to watch them. This wasn't a show. It was their life.

I wondered how many thousands of men and women had had conversations with God here. How many wishes, yearnings, dreams and fears did these ornate, curved walls know about? If the soul of a place like this could speak, what would it say? To me, coming from my own place in my own time, space and culture, I didn't feel a magic here brought by a God, I felt a magic brought by people.

And in that stillness, in that quiet awareness of where I was sitting, how I was feeling, I could sense that magic right now. A beautiful, concentrated magic. Far bigger, far brighter than anything one person could conjure on their own, but every soul on earth equally integral to it. And I became intensely grateful for Gillie, sitting at my side. For Oliver, sitting next to her. For everybody back at home and for everybody whose path I had ever crossed, even those I disliked or who had challenged me. And I became deeply grateful for the man with the long, black hair waiting for me somewhere in the world.

If I listened hard enough, beneath the chanted whisper of the prayer, I could hear that heart beating for me.

————

It's true that some traditions work no matter where you are in the world.

With Gillie and I it had always been ice cream. There was no problem that could not be solved without a few huge dollops of chunky double chocolate. Sadly, that particular ice cream choice was not on offer at the kiosk Oliver had left us at whilst he'd gone off to collect brochures about Cappadocia. In fact, by the way the ice cream man with the fancy waistcoat and fez was pulling and yanking it about in and out of its container, I'm not entirely sure it was ice cream at all.

Nevertheless, we sat there on a bench on a busy street,

eating it anyway. Me with my vanilla cone, Gillie with her lemon. It was our first moment alone together all day and I had absolutely no idea what to say.

"Right, before you say anything," Gillie turned to look at me, "I know I have some explaining to do."

"And some." I said, happy to be let off the hook.

"I just . . . well . . . look, I went into the room last night, all ready to tell Oliver that this whole thing had been a bad idea, and I just wasn't ready for . . . well, you know . . . him. The buggar had gone and made everything all romantic. Candles, music, he'd ordered some mega-expensive stuff off the room service menu. He had wine ready to be poured and just the sweetest little look of hope on his face that I just couldn't Jess, I just couldn't."

"Okay, that must have been tricky. But yesterday you . . ."

"I know, I know, I was feeling all confused and I'm so sorry I shouted at you. I didn't mean to. I just had Demir on my mind and Oliver was here demanding my attention and I know I made this all happen, I know I did. I asked Oliver to come here. How could I send him home again? He's such a nice bloke. He doesn't deserve it."

"He is a nice bloke." I said, suddenly feeling very defensive of him.

"Exactly. So, I decided to just go with it and see how I felt. I let him do the whole romantic thing. I ate the food and drank the wine and one thing led to another and well, I just thought, why not? Why the hell not? It's not often I'm in a swanky hotel with a lovely man and having all that fancy stuff thrown at me. Why shouldn't I enjoy it?"

"Well, Gillie, because he has feelings for you. Real ones."

She sighed. "I know. And I like him too. But I needed to have last night to see how deep those feelings really go. I needed to give him a chance."

"Give him a chance? Gillie, it's not a fucking audition. Sorry if I sound like your mother, but shouldn't you have waited before going that far? Those feelings can develop without sex you know."

"Can they? Jess, you have no idea how amazing it is for me to feel wanted in that way. You're lucky. You had that stuff with Jack all the way through to the end. He adored you until he walked away from it all. But my relationship with Marcus didn't work like that. Well I want it now. I want it. Why shouldn't I have it?"

"There is absolutely no reason why you shouldn't have it Gillie, just not with a man who is quite clearly falling for you. Especially if you're going to go off and shag some random Turkish bloke straight afterwards! And for your information, it wasn't always like that between me and Jack. We were together for seven years for God's sake. We weren't always ripping each other's clothes off."

"Okay, fine. But you know what I mean. Good lord I'm enjoying the feeling Oliver gives me though. I need it right now."

"Well please, please be careful Gillie. He is a man with a big heart. Just be gentle with him."

"Gentle?" She laughed. "What if he doesn't like it like that?"

"Ugh! God, Gillie! I don't want to know!" I cried, pushing her away, giggling in spite of myself. How did she always get round me like this?

"Don't want to know what?" Oliver asked, standing before us, his arms full of travel books and brochures. "What are you two giggling about?"

"Oh, nothing, nothing." Gillie smiled and jumped up to help him with the books. "We're just wondering what's in this bloody ice cream. It's not exactly Ben and Jerry's now, is it?"

"Hang on a minute, I'm sure I've read something about that." Oliver snapped open one of his books and started reading something about tree sap and flour made from orchids. Bless him. He was completely in his element here in İstanbul, completely in his zone. And somehow that made him seem vulnerable to me. But Gillie was vulnerable in her own way too, I had to remember that. They were just two confused human beings walking down rocky paths that led to who-knows-where. There was no crime in that. And I should, perhaps, concentrate on my own path. After all, I didn't particularly want to veer off it now that I'd unearthed it. It was crucial to keep going.

The rest of the day was a manic rush of sightseeing.

We drove through thick, pulsing crowds to get to the Grand Bazaar – a curious land strewn with avenues of fabrics, foods, spices and trinkets. We breathed in its rich scents, tasted its floral sweetness and bought from its endless variety. Gillie seemed to forget the careful budgeting plans we'd discussed on the coach to İstanbul and bought her own body weight in beautiful, sparkling scarves. At least she had all the fashion seasons sorted for the rest of eternity.

We walked round the grounds of Hagia Sophia and Topkapı Palace, being happily tugged along by the pull of the tourist swarm. Polished pavements, blue skies and clusters of buildings all attached to their central, ancient domes gave us plenty to absorb on this crisp, sunny afternoon. Gillie and Oliver sauntered along ahead of me, hand in hand, chatting about the things they were passing, the things that synthesised Ottoman and Byzantine empirical history. They seemed happy enough for now.

Luckily, on the way back to the hotel, we came across an

unexpected gem. The moment Oliver stepped onto that particular street he recognised it. "Wait a minute. I've seen this street
before, in one of the books. It's where we'll find an underground
reservoir, apparently. The Basilica Cistern. Built in five
hundred and thirty something. They used to dump dead bodies
down there."

"Ugh!" Gillie cried. "I'm not going down there."

"Oh, come on Gillie. That was many moons ago. It's clean
as a whistle now and supposed to be beautiful in an eerie kind
of way. Let's go."

About fifty downward steps later we were draped in a cool
darkness and standing on damp, wooden platforms, wondering
which way to turn. The water beneath the platforms was black
and silky, rolling gently with the sleek disturbance of shivering,
ghostly carp. Water dripped from the vaulted ceilings all around
and there were hundreds of carved columns before us, eerily lit
up in greens, reds and golds by strategically placed spotlights.
This place certainly knew how to do atmosphere.

For some inexplicable reason, Gillie, Oliver and I silently
went our separate ways to explore this watery cavern. There
was soft, classical music playing over some hidden speakers
somewhere and it just felt like this needed to be a quiet, lonesome experience. When I looked around me properly, I could
see that most other tourists were going it alone too.

I didn't know where to look first. The vaulted ceiling with
its millions of bulging dewdrops waiting to meet the water
below; the ornate, carved columns with their fine, intricate
features that looked as though they'd been ripped from ancient
temples; the sleek, shadowed walls bathed in hundreds of years
of crushing humidity; the endless sheet of black water that ever-
so-slightly rolled and rippled below; or the other-worldly reflec-
tion that shimmered with the dark promise of solitude.

The symmetry and sheer majesty of the place was breathtaking. I didn't like to think how many hundreds of slaves might have lived, worked and died here all those years ago to make this concept real. It invoked a deep sense of respect and reverence in me – as well as a distant sadness – that clung to me as I walked around this incredible place.

In a far corner of the cistern I found the renowned and sinister head of Medusa carved into a huge marble block at the base of a column. The odd thing was that it was placed sideways. And just a few steps away there was another Medusa head, this time upside down at the base of a column. Both were lit the same intense green I would imagine the snakes on her head to be and despite the intense inertia of the marble, I could almost see them squirming. Why weren't the heads the right way up? What was that all about? As I knelt down to inspect that legendary face, I wondered if by placing them this way, the strength of her deadly stare was somehow diminished. Who knows what mysterious powers the builders of this place had believed in back then. Maybe the construction of the cistern had been so fraught with danger that the last thing they needed was Medusa throwing out her petrifying glare as well. An ancient version of a risk assessment, perhaps.

After about half an hour of wandering, I came to a stop at a shallow pool which was bathed in a silvery-white light. It seemed a little more friendly, a little more welcoming than any other part of the cistern. All over the base of the pool were thousands of glimmering coins which, I guessed, represented the wishes of as many tourists over the years. *Just imagine how much energy must be vibrating from the bottom of that pool*, I thought. *All the love and desire that went into each and every flick of a coin, all the visions and imaginings pulsing from down there.*

It was, I realised, a little like my own childhood ritual of wishing with dandelion clocks. I got a rush of powerful nostalgia and stuck my hand into a pocket, finding, along with my Urim and Thummim stones, some loose change. Now, what would I wish for? World peace? An end to hunger? Health and happiness for everyone?

I thought about the poor souls who had been responsible for building this cavernous wonder and felt compelled to offer them a wish. After all, it was because of them I was standing here now, on my own path of self-discovery, making this ancient place an imprint on the map of my life. I threw a coin in, watched it plummet and wished for their peace and rest in whatever reality they may be inhabiting now. Who was I to rule out that their energy, their souls were out there somewhere?

Now it was my turn. One of these coins had to be for me. As I smoothed my thumb over the embossed surface of the coin, turned it over time upon time in my hand, I tried to feel my wish rise up in me. This wasn't going to come from the head. It was all heart. I felt random moments over the past few months fight for my attention, visions of people, places and things squabbling into a cluster of frustration. What was it that Jack had said all those months ago on that grey, murky hillside?

Figure out what it is you want. What do you want?

I just want to know what I'm here for, a voice spoke up from somewhere. *Destiny. I want to know what my destiny is.*

And as that coin spun up into the air and then gracefully, elegantly turned downwards into the pool to join all the others, I did actually feel that I might just be a tiny bit closer to finding that out.

20

CAPPADOCIA

It was as if we'd stepped onto a distant planet, rather than off a coach onto a different part of Turkey.

We'd spent the whole evening travelling and were absolutely exhausted, but every single one of us, as soon as we touched the edges of the Cappadocia region, found a new energy strong enough to awaken slightly wider eyes and a new curiosity.

Having just woken from a long, juddering sleep, when I awoke and saw what was outside my window, I felt as if I'd been picked up and dropped into a fairytale. The hills all around looked as if they'd been grabbed by a giant's hands and clawed upwards into hundreds of mounds and crevices formed into the fiery rock. Towering grey boulders rose up out of the earth of swirling orange and white for no other reason than it seemed their regal right to do so. The stone seemed as if it would be soft if you were to reach out and touch it, a parade of whipped marshmallow straight from the surreality of a children's story. Never mind Lucy in the Sky with Diamonds. The Beatles would have had a field day with this place.

We got off the coach in a town called Ürgüp, greeted by the

cold, crisp air of a cloudless early morning. I shivered, and pulled my cardigan round my shoulders. "There shouldn't be too long to wait," Oliver said, checking his phone for the time. "The bloke from the hotel should be here to pick us up soon. I think it's about another twenty minutes to get to where we're staying."

I plonked myself down on my rucksack and had a glance round. In some ways Ürgüp seemed like a typical Turkish town. Uninspiring bus station, lines of shops and restaurants, dusty streets and uneven pavements. But looking up and beyond that, there was the dramatic backdrop of a rock face, which would have been enough on its own to inject some intense theatre. But this was no ordinary rock face. This one was clawed into with hundreds and hundreds of caverns, all with house-fronts strangely fused into the rock, paths hewn in and around them, deep-set windows and wooden doors marking them as genuine homes of genuine people.

It wasn't long before the hotel man came to pick us up. Announcing himself quietly as Levent, the man who was "helping you be here in my best home town", he packed us into his vintage VW Golf and we trundled out of the main road of Ürgüp. Once out on the open road, we were treated to even more of this remarkable landscape. I was tired and rubbing my eyes anyway, but I have to admit I was kind of reluctant to believe this was actually reality.

Levent said one thing to us on the whole journey to our hotel, he was obviously well used to allowing tourists some time to collect their thoughts about this strange place. He said, "You are coming from İstanbul, yes? Well then. This is being different for you. You like." And that was it. No background information about how any of these strange, twisted rock formations came about in the first place. No hard selling of discounted cave tours or balloon rides (they were pretty big out here). Instead, Gillie,

Oliver and I sat looking out of the car windows, occasionally exchanging confused, weary glances.

We were staying in a village called Akköy, which Oliver had sought out because of its quiet, traditional nature. Apparently village life consisted of cooking, baking, preparing foods for storage, and gathering wild mushrooms so we weren't exactly here for the all-night parties. We were staying at the only hotel in the village, called 'Akköy Evleri'. And when we arrived there, after driving ever-upwards into the mountains, it more or less looked as if we were staying at somebody's house.

At the top of a steep, narrow, winding road, it was a sweet little place, not cavernous exactly, but a creamy-white building sticking out of the rock face, and adorned in climbing pink roses. There were steps leading up to a vast, wide balcony in front of it, that hung over the road below and looked out onto a breathtaking mountain scene. Gillie gave a low, quiet whistle. "Woah."

"Woah exactly." I whispered, as we all followed Levent into our rooms.

"There is two rooms," He gestured, "This one is through balcony and other one is this way." He led us through the first room and into a second one, which was a tad more interesting, as the wall which the bed was against was a shimmering rock face, jutting out majestically. "This is double and other one is single so . . . ." He looked at us, searching for the relationship dynamic here. I was far too tired to be cajoled into giving him any clues, but I noticed Oliver slink an arm round Gillie's waist, just to give the poor man a break. "Okay." He said. "You is tired from your long journey with bus. I leave you now. When you is feeling hungry you coming find me and food for you is making."

And he left us to it. I knew this place had magic. I knew it was out of the ordinary and that there would be plenty for me to discover here. But I was tired. To the point where any discovery on any level was going to have to wait. I shuffled past Gillie and

Oliver back into the first room, dumped my bags and collapsed onto the single bed.

Perhaps some ghost of a thought drifted through my mind about whether or not Gillie and Oliver actually wanted the double room (were they a couple or weren't they a couple?), but sleep washed over me and that was that.

21

THE BALLOON RIDE

It was early the next morning and as I waited, yawning against the biting cold, I wondered if I'd ever be awake enough to consider Cappadocia anything other than a dreamy vision.

I looked at Gillie standing next to me and could see from her rubbed-red eyes and bed-head that she wasn't far behind me in the sleepy stakes. It seemed Oliver was tanked-up on an energy we weren't able to tap into. Or maybe that's what falling in love does to a man.

When our host, Levent had left us the previous day we'd managed about two hours of sleep, tops, before Oliver urged us to get up and sample the food that had been promised to us. Which would have been great, had Levent and his ageing father (who also seemed to be head chef) ever heard of a vegetarian. I tried to explain that chicken does actually count as meat, it having once been living, breathing, walking and clucking etc but was simply met with cynical stares. I guessed bread and cucumber would have to do for now.

Oliver had managed to become best buddies with Levent over lunch and talked him into driving us back into town – something neither Gillie nor I had felt particularly up for but were too tired to argue. It emerged that Oliver's main mission was to secure tickets for a hot air balloon ride, and that is why we were standing there the next morning at an insanely early hour.

We'd been picked up by a minibus at five o'clock, to be driven to the spot where the balloon would be launched. The bus was crammed full with pale-faced, droopy-eyed tourists who all looked like they'd been plucked from their beds without warning, and there was scarcely a whisper amongst them. There was only Oliver who seemed to have the strength of spirit for a jaunty expedition such as this. "We might not even get to go up in a balloon," he explained to us, "it all depends on the weather forecast, you see."

"Great." Gillie remarked. "This could all be for nothing then."

"Not for nothing, Gillie." He said, wrapping an arm around her. "They'd pick us up again tomorrow to have another go." Gillie stared at me and mouthed the word *Again?* And I had to fight back a giggle.

Looking around, it didn't seem as if we were in a particularly inspiring place to start our balloon ride. The grey, rocky landscape was rough and fierce but seemed drab in comparison to some of the fiery, whipped-up rock we'd seen on the way here in the minibus. And it had been raining. Hence the delay and the doling out of hot coffee and little chocolate cakes to the tired, tutting tourists.

There were huge, deflated balloons laid out on the ground as far as I could see: flat stripes of red, white, green and blue, expanses of orange, slack swirls of yellow and purple. Upturned baskets attached with drooping ropes paused obediently as if waiting for the sudden command to rise. Middle-aged Turkish men clustering together, shaking their heads and licking their fingers, raising them up into the air, only to then look at each other quizically and descend into rapid chatter about the misbe-having weather.

My gaze shifted to the jutting sheets of rock which surrounded us and I noticed they were starting to glow with a feint pink tinge and a slither of silver glitter was crawling up and over the rough ground beneath our feet. Sunrise. If we weren't quick getting up into the air we would miss it. And that, according to Oliver's brochures, was the whole point.

There was a sudden cry from one big, bearded man who was standing on a basket so everybody could see him. He gave the universal thumbs-up sign and there closely followed a cheer and then a loud grinding whir giving all of us inexperienced balloon riders a bit of a start. Huge, industrial fans were in action, blasting air into each balloon's trembling depths. The immense, circular stitching on the inside of our balloon started to swell and spread into perfect symmetry, held tight by the now straight, taut lines attached to the basket.

Once our balloon was bobbing about eagerly, a flame was lit near its base, which sprang upwards, licking dangerously close to the sides. Almost instantly the balloon wanted to drag up and away but I noted with relief that the basket was attached to our minibus and was held down by our launch crew too. I looked over at Oliver who was beaming from ear to ear and snapping photos of this spectacle with his fancy camera. The man was in his element. Gillie, on the other hand, looked rather white.

"Jess," she whispered, "Remind me again why I agreed to this?"

"Because we're international explorers. We're fearless adventurers. Intrepid globetrotters."

"Yep. Great. Absolutely." She nodded. "But you'll hold my hand, yeah?"

I hugged her in. "Of course I will. Oh, look. I think it's time to get in."

The droopy-eyed tourists from our minibus now seemed altogether wired as they clambered into the high-sided basket with broad grins and wide eyes. There was no door and the only way to get in was to kiss goodbye to your dignity and climb over. So we did that as gracefully as we could (i.e. not very) and found ourselves in a little quartered section inside the basket. We hadn't known it would be split into sections and Oliver had clambered into a different section to us. The basket was jam-packed now, with maybe twenty five people so there was no way he could have changed his position. I gave him a little wave and a shrug and he just smiled back, camera at the ready.

"Don't worry about him." Gillie said. "He's a big boy. I'd rather hold your hand for this anyway." So we joined hands, held tight, and nestled snugly up against the side of the basket, waiting for lift-off.

We didn't have to wait for long. The ropes tethering us to the minibus were freed and the men who had been pressing the basket to the ground, against the fierce drag of the balloon, deftly whipped their arms away in one smooth, synchronised movement. That was it. We were going up.

Even though I'd been expecting it, even though I'd been waiting in the freezing cold for half an hour, anticipating it, the ascent into the sky came as a surprise. My heart lurched initially, and I could feel that familiar, heavy thud of anxiety in the first moment I saw the ground race away. How could we be moving so fast? How could there be nothing but basket between me and thin air? I held Gillie's hand tight.

Maybe I was surprised by the smoothness of it, the ease and the grace with which we rose. I could feel the cool air sliding over my cheeks alternated with the rushes of hot air our pilot was blasting into the balloon to make it go higher. Once my initial flash of fear had subsided, I started to feel the pleasant buoyancy of it all, the effortless draw up towards the clouds.

As I looked round at everybody else in the basket, I noticed the whispered hush as well as the silent adrenalin that gripped people in different ways. Over zealous smiles, flushed cheeks, white knuckles gripping the edge of the basket. The promise of the rising sun settled broad rose-pink streamers of light across all of us and seemed to very gradually diffuse the tension. I could feel the breath in my body start to calm and I felt in that instant that there was nowhere else I would rather be in the world.

Gillie nudged me. "Jess, look at that!" She was pointing straight out in front of us. It was difficult to say for sure but perhaps a hundred and fifty other hot air balloons were rising slowly, steadily into the sky, all with their own set of awe-struck people crammed into their own baskets. It really was an incredible sight to see. The colours and the patterns that adorned the sky right now were as bright and beautiful as you could imagine – like an endless cluster of floating lanterns, glowing with the sun emerging among them, the deep turquoise of the sky and the white of the wispy clouds as their eternal backdrop.

We could hear the occasional roar of distant flames as the various balloons were powered ever upwards above the rocky plain. It felt like an altogether harmonious, shared experience if you looked across at the myriad of colourful balloons, and at the same time a humbling, private experience if you looked into yourself.

Gillie squeezed my hand and we talked quietly about the things we could see. The previously uninspiring launch area was, I now discovered, at the centre of a mass of undulating rock and stirred-up earth, and so had been the perfect place to start our ride. What we saw below us now didn't seem to belong to the planet we knew. Savage, fiery mounds breathed up towards us, thousands of years in the making and quivering with pent-up energy. It was a relief to float up and away from them, closer towards the clouds and into a dreamier place.

The fiery colours below calmed and so did the roaring fire of our balloon as the pilot said we were high enough now and could use the wind to navigate our way. Gillie saw in the mountainous folds below a depiction of ice cream. "Caramel and vanilla," she said, "that lovely soft, whippy kind I used to get when I was little." I nodded and took my phone out of my pocket so I could take some photos. They might not turn out as well as Oliver's, but they'd be good enough to inspire some paintings when I got home.

The rest of the balloon ride was just breathtaking. The pilot had us one moment high among the clouds and gazing down at Cappadocia in its awesome glory, the next moment he'd swoop us down low enough so we could almost touch the branches of trees sticking out horizontally from bronzed cliff edges. People laughed. People gasped. People were struck silent at times and incensed to talk with immense animation at times. It was a ride of a lifetime in more ways than one.

Throughout it all Gillie and I held on tight to each other. Oliver was in his own little world of photography, but Gillie and I were doing this one together.

At some point, maybe after about an hour or so, we started to descend. To all intents and purposes it seemed as if we were making a bee-line for a large truck parked below. As I looked around at the many other landing balloons, I could see that they had all managed to land right on the back of a truck and that people were now clambering out all over the place. How on earth was the pilot going to manage that? It seemed like it was going to be a tight fit even if he did get the positioning right.

As if reading my mind, he laughed, "Sometimes I am doing the landing on the vehicle very well. Sometimes I am missing it completely." Suddenly lots of panicked faces gawped at him. "Is okay," he continued, "I am in good feeling about today's landing."

And just as we were all mentally calculating how we would stunt-roll out of the basket without getting concussion, we felt the gentle collision of the bottom of the basket with the flat truck-bed. And we cheered. Relieved and grateful.

Ten minutes later I was reminded yet again why Turkey has its well-earned reputation for hospitality, when bottles of champagne were popped open, fizzing glasses were poured and given out and dishes of fresh strawberries were handed round for us to share. And if that wasn't enough of a lovely surprise, our pilot then called each of us, by name and handed us a personalised certificate to prove we'd really ridden in a hot air balloon. Now that was something for my notebook.

After this, Gillie, Oliver and I sat on a nearby rock, sipping our drinks, inspecting our certificates and basking in the ever-rising early morning sun. "Well girls, what did you think?" Oliver asked, enthusiastically. "Did it live up to expectation?"

"Oh good lord." Gillie said. "It was just beautiful."

"Yes." I agreed. "Once in a lifetime, awe-inspiring, soul-searching, life-affirming . . ."

"Cool." Oliver grinned and checked his watch. "And it's only eight o'clock."

———

We were still reeling from our experience in Cappadocia's skies when the minibus stopped without warning outside a grey building on the edge of the wide, quiet road.

Being the obedient tourists that we were, we allowed ourselves to be herded into the building, not knowing at all what to expect. The room we found ourselves in was small – too small for a load of hot and bothered people – and seemed to be some type of workshop. Having failed woodwork twice in my life with over-whelming adeptness, I was unable to identify any of the tools or equipment scattered about the place. "I think it's metalwork of some kind." Oliver contributed. "Or maybe a jewellery workshop."

And minutes later we found out Oliver was right. We'd been offered the chance to see some master jewellers at work with an apparent 'no obligation' approach. Yet another masterful trick of the trade showed by our tour guide who just happened to be the brother of the man who owned the jewellery workshop. Family ties. Now that's a language that speaks volumes all over the world, not just in Turkey, as was now demonstrated by the beeps and swishes of credit card machines at several different till points around the sales section of the building.

I looked through the glass counter-tops at the finished jewellery on show. Ruby earrings that reminded me of a vivacious primary school teacher of mine, an opal and turquoise choker that Ella would have died for and just there, a chunky silver band that reminded me eerily of Jack's engagement ring. I shivered. And I wondered if he still had it.

I trailed my gaze away from that ring and marveled at how the thought of Jack did not bring about instant tears anymore. It didn't even make my heart hurt. If anything, I felt a fondness, a warmth towards him. How weird was that?

"Can I help you with anything Madam?" A fresh faced, pretty young woman asked me from the other side of the counter. "It looks like you are having your eye on something, yes?"

I was about to say no, I wasn't interested in anything but then I realised she was right. I had my eye on a necklace directly below me. I must have been gazing at it lost in thought and as it came into focus now, I realised I really liked it. I nodded at the lady and she dipped her hands down to bring it out so I could see it better.

It was made of silver. Not quite a choker, but a shorter style of necklace in a thick, twisted rope. When I looked really closely at it nestling in my hands I could see impossibly fine strands of silver which had been meshed together to form this rope effect. At the front of the necklace were about twenty silver spheres all slightly mis-shapen and glossy, each one winking pearlescent light back at me. "You want to try Madam?" The lady asked me and tilted a counter-top mirror in my direction.

I shivered at her question. The last piece of jewellery I'd bought had also been a necklace, earlier that year. And it hadn't been the most genius purchase I'd ever made. I'd bought a matching one for Jack as a last-ditch attempt to make him realise we were meant to be together and, well, let's just say things had kind of gone tits up. Or had they? Because in the end I'd managed to palm those necklaces off on some poor soul on eBay and they'd more or less funded my ticket to Turkey. So here I was now, standing in this jewellery shop, looking at an entirely different necklace only because of that first, apparently costly mistake. Maybe it hadn't been so costly after all.

"Oh, okay." I smiled. "Why not?" Once I'd got it on, I flicked back my hair so I could get a better view. I'd thought that such a chunky piece of jewellery might have been too heavy for me. It was, I suppose, what you'd call a 'statement piece'. And I wasn't used to making statements with jewellery because I usually went for delicate pieces that promised to draw no attention whatsoever.

But this necklace was different. Unlike the one I'd bought for both me and Jack, this one seemed to be saying, *I am here, I am me, I am Jess*.

Later on, when we were trundling home in the minibus and my credit card was safely tucked away, still smarting from what I'd just done to it, Gillie asked what was in the little parcel I held in my lap. "I treated myself," I grinned. "I don't know what made me do it."

"Don't be an arse. You're allowed to treat yourself." She said. "Come on then, let's have a look at what you bought."

The necklace tumbled out into Gillie's waiting hands and she gasped. "Oh Jess, it's gorgeous. I didn't spot anything else as unusual as that."

"That's Jess for you," chimed in Oliver. "An eye for the unusual, haven't you matey?"

"Maybe." I smiled. "I bloody love it though. It sounds corny but it just spoke to me."

Gillie had the necklace held really close to her eyes and was squinting at it. "It just spoke to you, did it? Well, does it remind you of anything sweetheart?"

"Not really. Why, should it?"

"It should." She said, matter of factly and dug her phone out of her handbag. She flicked the screen to her photo album and started looking through her holiday snaps.

"Aha. There it is. Let me just zoom in . . . there. Look." She handed the phone to me and it was a photo of Mesut, casually leaning against Beerbelly bar, polishing a glass as he often did. The bit Gillie was pointing to though, was his left wrist or, more accurately, what was on it. His bracelet. "See? It's almost like a matching set." She smiled that smile that told me she knew me better than I thought she did. "Just like the two of you."

22

SEE WHAT HAPPENS

The shouting had stopped at last.

There followed an inevitable hush and I could sense that crackling of silent emotion, splintering the air. Rapid, angry breaths. I could hear them even from here. They were probably staring at each other. A quiet challenge to go even further but both knowing, really, that enough was enough. Sitting out here on the balcony, watching the sun set over the surrounding mountains, I had been forced to give up the peace I'd been looking for. Even in a wild, remote place such as this there was no escape.

I'd been sat there for hours – along with my notebook, pens, a sketchbook and paints – working frantically, to find some sense of what was going on with me. What did I really want? What was my destiny? With sketches, musings, poems and doodles, I'd been trying to get that elusive grasp on the carefree, fearless attitude of a child. What had the little girl in me always wanted? What did I just know I could do to bring light into the world? Right now I could really do with one of those Moments of God Marcus raved on about. However, it was possible I'd disappeared so far up my own arse God would never be able to find me.

Shit, I needed to get a grip.

And that's when it all started. Gillie shouting at Oliver. Oliver shouting at Gillie. They were in the back bedroom at the time so I didn't hear everything that was said but there was a lot of "Why the hell didn't you . . . ?" and "Why can't you just . . . ?" I suspected it was all started by a certain expensive looking package Oliver had carried home with him from the jewellery workshop. He'd kept it in his white-knuckled fist until he and Gillie had gone into the bedroom for an 'afternoon nap' and now I was guessing he hadn't quite got the response he'd been looking for when he'd bestowed it upon her. Poor bloke.

Just then the silence was broken by some quick, light foot-steps and somebody rummaging in a bag. Then a deep, resounding sigh that I thought probably came from Oliver. In the next split second Gillie was outside, her hair blazing out behind her, her cheeks flushed and zipping past me towards the main house where Levent and his father lived.

"I don't want to hear it Jess. I'm going out. Don't wait up."

"Right. Hang on, are you okay?" I asked, standing up.

"Fine!" She looked over her shoulder just before she disap-peared into the house and threw a twisted smile at me. "I'm going out with Levent."

Levent? That was odd. Why would she go out with Levent? I hardly had time to contemplate the notion when the two of them were suddenly rushing down the steps, ripping past the roses and climbing into Levent's car. Levent looked like he'd just stepped into some kind of dream if the dopey smile on his face was anything to go by. Was there any circumstance in which that girl could not work her magic?

I sank back down to the ground, watching the car wind its way round the twists and turns of the village road and it wasn't long before it was out of sight. There was quiet again. And just me and the fragments of my broken afternoon out here on the balcony.

I started to pick up my stuff when a couple of envelopes fell out of my notebook. Marcus's challenges. Could I really be bothered with another one? Could I?

Oh, what the hell. I tore the envelope open.

Challenge 5 — The Great Giveaway

Giving can be great. Give away something
that's valuable to you and see what happens.

Really, Marcus? Really?

I wasn't an idiot. I obviously knew that giving was good for the soul. I had about six different direct debits set up back at home for various charities that I'd been guilted into donating to once a month, even though I could barely afford my own bills. And that felt good. Well, kind of.

And of all the places I could open this particular challenge, why, oh why had I opened it here? There was nobody for miles around. It was possibly one of the most remote places I had ever been to in my life. Who was I meant to bloody well give something to? Gillie had done a runner with Levent, Levent's Dad was probably cooking up new ways to get me to eat steak and Oliver, well Oliver was going through his own stuff. This challenge was really not doing it for me right now.

I knew what I'd do. I would go to bed and get an early night. Maybe the challenge would make more sense in the morning. If

I was going to give anybody anything right now it was going to be me and it was going to be sleep.

I'd had the blankets pulled up around my ears for a good few minutes and was finally feeling my body let go of tension and give itself up to the grasping tendrils of sleep, when a sound stirred me. It was a kind of a shuffle, a hushed tread. I looked up and saw the hunched figure of Oliver making his way out towards the balcony, having had to use this room as a thoroughfare. Bless him. He usually stood so tall and straight. This was not his night.

I settled back down and pulled those blankets tighter around me. He'd probably need some time alone after today. What could I say, anyway that would make him feel any better? It was a wise choice to just leave him to his thoughts and let him work it out for himself. Besides, I needed sleep more than ever right now. I could feel the edges of my dreams pulling me seductively in, the fuzzy promise of peaceful abandon was mine, if only I allowed it. I took a deep breath in and then out and waited for it to come.

It didn't come.

I couldn't get Marcus's bloody challenge out of my head. The Great Giveaway. Why wouldn't the idea of it leave me alone? I had nothing to give right now. Nobody to give to. Why couldn't I just indulge in the sleep I so needed?

Then the shadow of Oliver's pacing frame crossed the room and I knew exactly why I couldn't go to sleep. I had to give Oliver something now. My time.

That's what I had to give away.

———

"Bloody women." Oliver sniffed at the night air.

"Oi." I nudged him. "We're not all bad you know."

"I know that really. Just let me have my huff with the fairer sex for one night, will you?"

"If you must."

"I must." He replied, and stretched his legs out along the floor of the balcony, his weight on his elbows and his head turned up towards the stark, white moon. At least I'd managed to get him to sit down. When I'd joined him he'd been full of a fretful energy that was bordering on destructive. I'd paced with him, up and down and up and down, perpetually chasing the lengthening shadows until they merged into a darkness that wrapped us tight in the velvet-black of the night. That was when he'd sat: when the words started to slow and the breath started to deepen and the darkness gave him some slither of comfort.

He'd told me all about the ring he'd bought for Gillie. A cluster of deep-red garnets encased in white gold, he'd felt certain she would accept it in the spirit it was given – with deep fondness and with the possibility of love. But apparently she'd freaked. "She got all defensive and weird. She said I was moving too fast and what the hell did I think I was doing coming out here and demanding all these things of her. I didn't know what she meant by 'all these things' and told her so but apparently that was the green light for her to really rip into me. And Jess, I don't appreciate being yelled at. Even if it is by Gillie."

Now the moon looked down on us and shed occasional beams of silver-white revealing solitary glimmers of hope in all that was being said. "I knew it was a risk coming out here. None of this is Gillie's fault, really. It's mine. I remember having a tiny feeling of doubt before I bought that plane ticket, but I pushed it away. Locked it up and pretended it wasn't there. If I'd just listened to it then I wouldn't be in this shit-fit of a mess."

"Oliver, you've taken a massive knock. You're bound to be feeling crap. But this mess hasn't been so bad, has it? Just look . .

." I reached out to touch his chin and gently tilted his head so instead of looking at the balcony floor, he was looking up and out over the starlit mountains. "Look at where we are."

"True," he sighed. "If I could just put the whole Gillie thing to one side for a moment, I could, maybe, feel like a lucky man right now." We sat in silence for a while. Lucky. Yep. It was hard to sit here and not feel lucky to be alive. Heartache or no heartache. We'd been out here so long our eyes were accustomed to the darkness so we could make out the dark mass of mountains before us, the harsh, jagged lines that they cut into the black sky, and the stream of stars that blessed all they touched with specks of glistening white. Although we were sitting on a blanket on the smooth, marble floor of the balcony, we were so enveloped in the landscape that it felt we were part of it. Or somehow floating within it, with our own words to keep us afloat.

"I remember going climbing in the hills with my dad when I was little," said Oliver with a smile. "He was a good climber. It was his thing, you see. And, of course, I wanted to do it too because then I'd be like him. My Mum used to worry herself sick because we'd go out first thing in the morning and not come back until after dark . . . but I loved the part where it got dark the most. That's when my Dad said there was magic in the hills. He used to say there'd be trolls following us, wanting to steal our climbing gear so they could build dens with it. Then he said there'd be pixies following the trolls, looking for food that dropped out of the trolls' knapsacks. And then fairies following the pixies looking for magic thorns in their hair." Oliver laughed. "We both knew it was utter rubbish, but, even as I got older, I never asked him to stop saying it. I loved the idea of a trail of creatures following us in the darkness as it closed in. I think, the more I listened, the longer the tale became and it meant more time with my Dad."

"Were you close to your Dad, then?"

"Sometimes yes. Sometimes no. Isn't that the same for most people?"

"I guess so." I said. Oliver continued to tell me about his dad. And then his mum. And then his only brother and what it had been like growing up in a house on a hill that all his school friends thought was posh but was actually falling to pieces and not even owned by his parents. He spoke of draughts and leaks and a mean landlord who used to put the rent up on an almost monthly basis. He talked about the first camera he was ever given. A second-hand classic that had a button that used to stick and take multiple shots and waste a whole film.

"I loved that piece of rubbish," he said. "It helped me see the world in a whole new way. What was possible if you just found a different viewpoint."

"Have you always known you wanted to take photos, then? I mean, ever since you were given that first camera?"

"I can tell you exactly when it happened, Jess. I was twelve and I'd already had the camera for a few months, and I'd just been messing around with it, not really knowing what I was doing. I was getting on my Mum's nerves, like really getting on her nerves because I was clicking away at her all the time. So she told my Dad enough was enough and he should take me out for the day. A long day, preferably. Going up in the hills or whatever it was that we did, to *'show that boy there are other things in life worth picturing.'* I remember Dad wasn't keen because the footy was on or something but he knew better than to mess with Mum when she was in that kind of mood. So, we trudged out the house with no particular plan.

"We didn't go up into the hills like I thought we would though. Basically, my Dad just started walking into town and I followed him, not saying anything, just hoping he had something amazing up his sleeve. When we got into the centre of town, he sat us both down on a bench and pointed across the square at another bench. 'See that bench, son? That's what you're going to take photos of. All day. Until I come back to get you.' Well of course I was confused. And massively disappointed. Why would I want to take photos of a bench all day? I remember he said, 'Don't argue. I've given you the best position you could hope for. There are a million different stories on that bench. Pick out the best ones, okay?' I knew that tone of voice and that there was no use arguing so I nodded and off he went."

"And?" I asked, wondering what twelve-year-old Oliver had done next.

"I took photos of the bench. All day. Like he said." A wide smile spread over his face and his eyes flicked upwards, glazed with the tenderness of a cherished memory. "I was freezing cold, I was desperate for the loo, I could have eaten a horse but I stayed there, rooted to the spot, hardly taking my eyes off that bench. And if I closed my eyes now, I think I could remember every single picture that I took."

"Tell me some."

Oliver closed his eyes. "A great big blackbird, pecking crumbs from the splintered arm rest, orange, beady eyes looking right at me. A tired young mum, her brow creased with worry, her baby nestled in the crook of her arm and letting out an almighty wail. A gang of teenaged girls, clicking through a plastic bag full of eye shadows, and one of them holding up a bright turquoise one against the intense purple of her jacket. The afternoon sun, splashing the seat of the bench with golden light interrupted only by the shadow of a swooping hawk. A market trader, chomping into a bright orange, flaky pasty, the shadow from the peak of his cap hiding the ecstasy of his shut-tight eyes. An elderly couple sitting close together, hands clasped, backs straight, both looking down at an unwrapped sticky bun with crooked smiles. The tears of a red-faced toddler splashing to the ground as he climbs onto the bench to look for an absent parent. And finally, at the end of the day when I was tired and exhilarated, starving and confused but sitting in total clarity, there was my Dad, sitting on the bench opposite me, leant forward, elbows on knees, eyebrows raised and a smile I'd never seen before."

"And is that when you knew? When you wanted to be a photographer?"

"Not exactly. I knew something big had happened. I walked back home with my Dad, holding his hand and wondering what on earth had just gone on. But knowing that the tingles down my spine and the loud thumping in my chest were important to me somehow. It wasn't until I got the photos back, about a week later, that I knew photography was for me. Every picture seemed so loaded with meaning, so embroiled in narrative, even the ones that were accidents, that I couldn't ignore how they made me feel."

"And that was it for you then? Photography has been your thing ever since you were twelve? God, I'm so jealous."

"Come on Jess, I'm only human. I've been sidetracked. I've had doubts. Who doesn't? For a while I was going to be a journalist. And then a teacher. I even dabbled in accountancy for a bit. But about fifteen years ago, when I was going through a bit of a hard time, my Mum sent me a parcel of my old stuff because she was having a clear-out. You know, as mums do. And in the parcel were all those photos, bound together in an elastic band. And that was a turning point for me. I got that rush of feeling back, that excitement of what it is to picture a story in just one click. It was as if my twelve-year-old self was sending me a message. This is it. This is what you do. Bloody well get on with it."

"Bloody well get on with it." I echoed softly. "And it was as easy as that?"

Oliver looked at me like I was mad. "Of course not. The universe has a way of testing your resolve. I was up against all kinds of obstacles."

"Such as?"

"Money. Time. Confidence. A relationship that wasn't working. But once I'd had my resolve tested again and again and again, things started to flow better. And now, well, now I know this is what I do. No matter what. Anybody who comes into my world has to accept that in me. Not just accept it, but embrace it I guess. I'm living my destiny, matey. That's what it's all about."

I lay back on the blanket and heaved a huge sigh. "Yeah. That's what it's all about." I closed my eyes and enjoyed the feeling of the chilled air as it tickled my cheeks, my forehead, my eyelids. "Get me another blanket will you, Oliver? And a cushion?"

"Yes m'Lady." He quipped and I heard him shuffle off into the rooms. Seconds later there was a brief gust of air whipped across my body, followed by the settling, comforting warmth of a fleece blanket. Oliver knelt down beside me, lifted my heavy head and propped a cushion underneath it. He kept my chin in his hands and I opened my eyes to find him smiling right at me.

"You, Jess Parker, are a great friend." And he kissed me lightly on the forehead before moving off into his room, his heartache still clinging, but no longer clawing, at his soul.

23

THE RETURN

I can't say what woke me.

It could have been the warm promise of the rising sun that was beginning to spill indulgently over the mountain tops. It could have been the intense silence that had settled, like a vast silken sheet all around. Or it could have been the beating of my heart, quickened by the clamouring strands of my dreams.

I sat up, stretched out and then crossed my legs. I pulled the blanket Oliver had brought me last night around my shoulders and up over my ears. Gillie. Was she home? I twisted round to look into the rooms, where the glass door hung wide open and saw that she lay sprawled on my bed, fully clothed and snoring. She was out for the count.

I shifted myself forwards right to the edge of the balcony and planted my feet on the rough rock jutting out at the end of it, so that I could feel as much a part of the landscape as possible. For some sleepy reason it seemed important to be close to nature right now. I wanted to really feel the closeness of the mountain this hotel was carved into. I wanted to be on it, in it, part of it. Suddenly, I remembered a quote I'd heard long ago that had stuck with me: *The only zen you can find on the tops of mountains is the zen you bring up there.*

I closed my eyes and let the morning drift towards me. I found my breath. I found memories from the night before. Giving Oliver my time, my ears, my understanding. Watching his heartache come to him, grip him, smother him and finally leave him to his own means. Listening to his stories. Seeing the tender edges of healing drawing in around him as he came into alignment with himself.

Then a night teeming with dreams. Had they been dreams? Or had they been memories? Or maybe even messages? My mind was too foggy to make distinctions but my heart was telling me, with its quickened pace and incessant pounding, that whatever they were, they had been of some importance. I closed my eyes and breathed in and out slowly, hoping to bring some of them back.

I'm just a girl running on the beach, amazed at the heaviness of my legs and the lightness of my laughter. I'm drawing and writing in a giant-sized scrapbook, recreating a movie I've just seen about two cartoon dogs falling in love. I'm dunking a huge, heavy paintbrush into a bucket of water and slinging it at the sandstone walls of my old house, making patterns that resemble my dreams before the sun dries them out. I'm making my best friend laugh with the doodles I'm drawing on her hand, her tears from falling over almost forgotten. I'm lying at the bottom of the field, laughing helplessly at the sky and the incredible pictures I can see rolling out of the clouds. I'm dipping my fingers in paint and swirling them round and round onto a huge sheet of paper, to evoke the memory of a merry-go-round. I'm writing a story about a boy who got lost, alive with the possibility of a happy ending. I'm decorating a book with lace and gold sequins, a book full of stories and pictures, ideas and conversations that were worth capturing at the time. I'm typing at my Mam's old-fashioned typewriter with more joy than I ever thought possible, crafting a story from something or anything that makes me smile or quickens my pulse. I'm standing at the bottom of my village at the very edge of where I'm allowed to go, blowing the heads of dandelion clocks so that their wispy seeds float out with the intentions of love as far as the wind will carry them. My heart is calming and my breath is settling and I can see stars, sunbeams, pens, pencils, paints, words, pictures, sea, trees, hands, footsteps, smiles, sand, soil, flowers, clouds . . . and I'm moving with them . . . they're moving with me . . . and we are going amazing places together.

I opened my eyes and intuitively looked down at my side where a pile of my stuff lay. My notebook. My pens. My little palette of paints. 'The Great Giveaway' challenge from Marcus. I'd spent hours alone with them yesterday, unable to hear what they were trying to tell me.

But now, on this softly stirring mountainside, my psyche still strolling through the avenue of my dreams, the realisation swooped down on me like a rogue angel yanking hard at my heart.

Stories. People. Words.

That was where my destiny lay.

It lay right in the core of all the things I had ever loved. The stories of all the people who had ever confided in me. The way my own stories echoed back with my dreams, fears, vulnerabilities and truths. The way I could tease and feel my way round a story, the way I could unearth strings of words to create understanding, clarity and comfort, and the way I could summon a creative energy to cultivate strength in myself and others.

It was so clear now. I needed to gather. I needed to pay attention. And above all, I needed to write.

Fuck! This was amazing! Who'd've bloody well thought it? I'd only gone and had an actual epiphany on an actual mountainside. This was the stuff of dreams! No, fuck that, this was the stuff of movies. This didn't happen in real life. Not to me, anyway. Wasn't I the girl who kept my overdraft meticulously in check? Wasn't I the girl who folded my knickers into little colour-coded triangles? I didn't rough it on mountainsides and wrap myself in a blanket and watch a sunrise against a rugged landscape and listen to the language of my heart. I didn't do this kind of thing.

Evidently, now I did.

I sat there in what really was some kind of euphoria for I don't know how long. My heart, having been yanked by that rogue angel, now felt as light as a feather and a blissful feeling of certainty and calm swelled through my whole body. This, I thought ironically, was my payback for having refused every kind of drug offered to me during the university years. This was a high you could not buy off one of the grungey kids round the back of the canteen.

And the best thing about this wonderful, life-affirming realisation I had just gone through, was that I was already living it. My destiny was already here. Hell, I was already writing stories, poems and ideas down. I'd been doing it for months now. I was already creating paintings with abstract words that spoke of truth and beauty. There was a beautiful man in Southern Turkey about to unwrap one of them in just a couple of days from now. And I was listening more carefully than I ever had done to the breath of the world, the beauty of its people and the pulse of its soul.

I realised I'd been doing a compromised version of this for years. Firebelly had been my way of working with people, listening and responding to them with the language of creativity. Through Firebelly's work, I'd been able to put the focus on them – the kids, the adults, the communities, the schools, the villages. But now it was my time. *My* time to use *my* creative powers. No more compromises.

I grabbed my phone from the folds of my blanket and found Marcus's number. It somehow seemed right to be messaging him, even though this moment was mine and mine alone. If it wasn't for his challenges and his daft sense of humour, I may not be in this place right now. So I tapped in the first words that sprang to mind.

Marcus, I've done it. I know what my destiny is. I'll tell all when I return.

When I return.

It felt like I'd already done that.

24

A THOUSAND TIMES BEFORE

"Aw, Gillie, his eyes look so big and sad."

"Please don't Jess, I feel bad enough as it is. Just pull the curtain across or something." Gillie had her head down, pretending to look for something in her bag.

I gave Oliver a last wave from my side of the coach window and he smiled at me before I awkwardly drew the curtain across. It seemed wrong just leaving him standing there alone in the bus station. He'd done his best to help us with our bags and wish us well on our journey, but I knew he was still smarting from how things had turned out. Nevertheless, he'd decided to do a bit of travelling round Turkey on his own. Just him, his camera and a lot of soul searching. I hadn't been sure about leaving him but he'd been adamant it was what he needed and reminded me I had good reasons to return to İpeklikum so I should really make a move. He'd given me the warmest hug ever, nearly lifting me off the ground and whispering into my hair, "Thank you Jess. I really mean it." I felt his gratitude settle over me and gently fuse with my own.

When it came to him and Gillie saying goodbye, it had been the briskest of embraces but with a long, lingering look from

Oliver. Gillie was on the bus like a flash. Things weren't going to be right between them for a very long time.

This final bus ride felt different to the others. Yes, I was going to İpeklikum and yes, I'd been there before, but this time I had fresh eyes, a fresh heart, fresh everything. I was still on a high from the whole epiphany on a mountainside thing and couldn't get over the buzzy feeling I had all over my body. Even Gillie's revelations about how she just couldn't get it on with Oliver any more, and how she thought maybe Demir was the one for her, weren't enough to put me off. I felt all at once a thousand feet high and more grounded than ever. I was away with the fairies but firmly at home. Buzzing like a raver but settled like a hermit.

Everything that occurred in the story of The Alchemist made a new kind of sense to me now and I knew, without a doubt, that what had happened to the shepherd boy Santiago was happening to me too. Minus bejewelled swords and mysterious men who turn things into gold, but still . . . .

————

I was sitting on the steps of Beerbelly in the blinding white mid-afternoon sun.

Gillie and I had checked back in at Shit Class, got ourselves washed, refreshed and filled up with some classic holiday cuisine (egg and chips) and then made our way to Beerbelly. Gillie had held my hand tight all the way there. Partly, I think, because she was nervous about seeing Demir and knowing without even saying it, that she was planning to take things to the next level now that Oliver was out of the picture. But also, I think, because she saw through my calm veneer. I was doing my best to just be the usual Jess, but who was I kidding? My heart was hammering and my mouth was dry at the prospect of seeing Mesut again.

Now Gillie was tucked away in the Mega Tour office with Demir and I was sitting here, alone, intent on soaking up some rays but actually feeling like I'd been stood up for a date or something. Mesut was nowhere to be seen.

All of a sudden I heard a loud whoop, a bright flash of colour swished past me and somebody smelling absolutely delicious sat almost entirely on my lap. Kadafi.

"Hah! My lovely Mrs Jess! You came back to us!" He had his beautiful, bronzed arms clasped tight around me so that I could barely breathe. "I am very so very pleased to be seeing you!"

I practically ripped myself free from his embrace. "Yes, Kadafi. We came back. And it's just fab to see you too. Gillie's here too, did you know?"

"Yes, yes. I see her come into office to see Demir. I am giving them . . ." He stretched his fingers into the air to make quote marks, "quality time." Then he slapped his own thigh so hard it made my eyes water and he laughed like a hyena. On acid.

I nodded and looked out at the street and the beach beyond it. No Mesut out there either. "Erm, Kadafi?"

He fixed a serious chocolate brown stare my way, looking the most stern I'd ever seen him. "Mrs Jess, is okay, I know what you are going to ask me."

"Do you?"

"Yes. You are looking for Mesut. I am right, yes?" I nodded. So it was obvious then. Kadafi continued soberly. "Well, he is asking me to tell you, to make sure you know, that he has gone back to his hometown to live with his family again. He has been gone for few days now."

"Oh . . ."

Fuck. Gone? I swear I felt the whole world slip away in that moment. The warmth of the sun, the sounds of the street, the presence of Kadafi next to me, everything started to disappear and swirl irretrievably away . . .

Then I felt a stinging slap right on the centre of my back, "Oh Mrs Jess, Mrs Jess, I am feeling so sorry! Your face is looking so sad! I didn't mean it . . . it was me joking. He is here! He is here!"

I turned to look at Kadafi. He didn't look so serious now. He was half laughing and half embarassed. "What?"

"He is here. Honestly." He had his hand on his heart now. "Come with me. I show you."

He grabbed me by the hand and pulled me up to my feet. I was tempted to viciously slay him then and there for the emotional burn-out he'd just put me through but that would potentially ruin my chances of finding Mesut.

Kadafi guided me past the bar toilets and down a little corridor I'd never been down before. At the end of it was an opening with a shabby orange curtain drawn across. He grabbed me by the shoulders and twisted me round so that I faced him. He'd gone all serious again. And he was whispering. "Now, lovely Mrs Jess, your Mesut is here. You lucky because he is alone. The other boys will not return for a while so you go see him now." And with that bizarre piece of information, he winked, held back the curtain and pushed me gently into the room. Then he scarpered.

The place was a mess. I counted three sets of bunk-beds, none of them made up. Blankets, sheets and clothes were strewn everywhere and the floor was covered in crumpled newspapers, empty glass teacups, backgammon pieces, and dirty plates, high-lighted by a single stream of light cast from a small, glassless window high up on a wall. The smell wasn't anywhere near as unpleasant as it might have been but strong nonetheless. I could detect aftershave, sweat, spices and the sleepy, heavy scent of men resting. I stood in the middle of the room, not even knowing where to place my feet.

The room was empty. All of the beds were dishevelled and vacant, the dark, shadowed corners stayed still and silent. I felt out of place in this heavily masculine, dormant space and if this was Kadafi's warped sense of humour again then that vicious slaying was most definitely back on the cards. I sighed heavily from my spot on the floor and knelt down to collect my thoughts. What was I doing here? Where was Mesut?

Just then, from the corner of my eye, I saw a movement in one of the bottom bunks. A pile of blue patterned blankets had just shifted. I'd been sure there was nobody here but now I could feel my heart pummeling my chest. And I could feel something else. A kind of lightness that clashed delightfully with the thudding.

Hope, maybe?

The blue blankets slowly rose upwards, gave a little quiver, then slipped back to reveal a tangled mass of black hair at one end and toned, cocoa limbs stretching out of the other. A hand appeared and long, tanned fingers dragged the strands of hair apart until I found that unmistakable stare. It was him.

Most of his face was covered in hair that stubbornly clung to clammy skin but I could tell he was smiling. Broadly. His eyes said it all. And before I knew it I was smiling back the kind of smile that spreads a glow through your entire body and stays a good long while. Those moments of just looking at each other and smiling did a better job of speaking than either of us could have done. The universe may have been whispering and murmuring and scheming away, but we were lingering in the bliss of silent smiles.

Mesut held out his arm and gestured for me to move towards him. "Come." He said. "Come here." There was a little voice in my head exclaiming, *What, under the blanket? In bed with him?* But before I knew it I was there, my head on his chest, our bodies pressed close and his arms wrapped tight around me. It was perhaps forty degrees outside but he covered us both with the blanket so that the heat closed in heavily, fusing any gaps left between us.

"Jess, Jess." He spoke in a whisper and I felt his breath stirring strands of my hair against my forehead. "Jess, Jess, Jess." My name sounded like an incantation when he spoke it. It sounded like a spell that would evoke the truth of this strange longing. Distinct from the heat of the day, and the heat of the blanket settled over us, I felt a different kind of heat spreading now. It had been nestled in my chest since he'd put his arms around me: a tingling, scalding sensation which was now spilling out slowly across my stomach and spreading down, down into a part of me that knew there was no going back. This feeling was real. This feeling was true. And I knew, with the quickness of his breath and the pressing warmth of his body that this was stirring in him too.

It would be so easy to just tilt my head and find his lips. Kiss him with all the heat and desire that was coursing through me right now. But what would happen to my world? What would happen to his? All of the moments we had spent together and apart had led to this moment in this bed. Our skin sticking, our breath merging, the roots of our spirits clawing for each other. If we came together just that little bit closer, would we be able to take it? I feared whatever lightning bolt was waiting for us would strike with such fierceness we might be blasted apart and then how would I find him again?

He said my name once more, so that this time it sounded like a pledge. "Jess". He moved his hand to tilt my chin upwards but I was already there. We kissed hard. We kissed so that we could stream all of our fears into each other in one go. I felt the reassuring, wild touch of his teeth on my bottom lip and the ferocity of that tore through me, something that echoed back in his pressing body. There were excruciating thrills as his tongue found mine and we locked together in a delicious, unbearable heat.

His hands, which had felt heavy and urgent on the small of my back, now moved up to my face and rested firmly on my cheeks. He drew an inch backwards so that our lips were no longer touching and although he was short of breath, he fixed that steady, unsettling gaze he had right on me. We looked at each other for some time. That stare that would have scared me half to death at the start of this trip, now with our breath steadying and our pulses slowing, was so beautifully familiar I felt like it had been designed for me.

We kissed again. And now that I'd poured my heart into him with all the wild abandon of the first kiss, this time was slower and calmer. Softer and fuller. And the weird thing was that I felt like I'd kissed him a thousand times before. The lightning strike I'd expected never appeared, but instead there was an intimacy that seemed to be age old. The familiarity of it was unsettling. In terms of our lips and our mouths, the kiss felt new and brimming with the promise of magic, but inside, in my heart, I knew I'd kissed this man before.

In the same way I'd 'returned' to my destiny just two days before on that breathtaking mountainside, I was now returning to this man, to this soul.

25

SOMEONE RANDOM

Mesut and I spent the majority of the afternoon in that scruffy bottom bunk bed, for all the world acting like we were in the lap of luxury.

And we did have luxury. We had the luxury of each other's kisses, flowing with an urgent depth that was beyond sexy. And we had the luxury of each other's company. Breath, conversation, touch. That was all we needed.

It turned out, however, that we also needed privacy. But when the boys got back from the market it transpired that we were never going to get it in the barmen's digs. In fact, Bad Boy, on crashing into the room and seeing me on his territory spat out a stream of angry words at Mesut. This was obviously a no-female zone. Mesut simply took my hand and led me, dishevelled and smiling, out into the bar area. It occurred to me that the Mesut from a few weeks ago would have practically melted Bad Boy with his death-stare had he been spoken to like that. But this Mesut was all smiles.

Gillie pounced on me when I arrived at the bar. "Jess! Where have you been all afternoon? Kadafi kept tapping his nose and saying it was a secret. I could have strangled him! What's going on?"

I took a huge breath and smiled broadly. "I've just been in the digs where the boys sleep. With Mesut."

Gillie looked over at the bar where Mesut was preparing coffee for us. He looked relaxed. Calm. He was smiling to himself which, pretty much everybody knew, was not normal. Gillie's eyes widened as she did some mental calculations. "Oh Jess, my God! Have you two been . . ? Have you really? Bloody hell!"

"No, no, no. Chill the fuck out." I ushered her over to a chair, sat her down and lowered my voice, hoping she'd do the same. "No. Of course we haven't. But, well, I have had a pretty amazing afternoon."

"Aw, sweetheart. I'm so happy for you. This is great!" She flung her arms around me Kadafi-style and pulled me close. "But just tell me, pleeease tell me. What was the kissing like? Everything you imagined it would be?"

"Well, yeah, but I think you imagined it more than I did. No, seriously, I guess it was good."

Gillie looked confused. "You guess it was good? That doesn't sound encouraging."

"No, I mean. Well, it's weird, right? But at first, when we kissed it was like we couldn't get enough of each other. It was pretty wild and . . ." I shivered. ". . . in a good way. And then, well, it just felt so natural. Like we'd been doing it for years. Do you think that's weird?"

"Yes, but so what?" Gillie leaned back and clasped her hands behind her head. "Right now, everything's weird. I'm going to Demir's apartment tonight. He's cooking me dinner."

"Really?"

"Yes. Really. With candles and Cappadocian wine and he's

getting rid of Kadafi for the night *and* apparently he's got something to give me."

"Oh-oh. Sounds suspiciously like a repeat of the Oliver episode."

"Yes, but this is different because it's what I *want*. I want Demir to treat me like this."

"Are you sure honey?" I still wasn't convinced by Demir, despite the imminent promise of romance.

"Yes. I'm sure." She nodded. "Now, where's your hubby with those coffees?"

———

The afternoon fused slowly into the evening and Gillie and I were still lounging in the comfort of Beerbelly's familiarity, along with long, cool drinks and good conversation. Although Cappadocia and İstanbul seemed like an age ago, I felt I carried some of the wild terrain and the pulsing history of them with me. They were woven into the fabric of me now, in the same way that İpeklikum was – ever present and momentous.

We were visited by members of the Beerbelly clan sporadically over those few hours. Kadafi had literally bounced in and out of our little zone, listening for the threads of the stories of our travels. Esad had spent an hour or so half-dozing, half-listening to the conversation from the deep cocoon of a wicker chair, inexplicably clad in a bright red beanie hat and dark woollen suit.

Demir kept joining us to paw over Gillie and massage her feet, all the while his shifty little brown eyes darting about (*looking for what?* I wondered).

And Bad Boy shuffled to and fro, muttering incessantly under his breath and glaring at Mesut who sat, loose-limbed and smiling right next to me.

Now I didn't speak Turkish, but it was pretty obvious that Mesut had given the bar over to Bad Boy tonight, because he'd hardly moved from my side since we'd sat down. It didn't seem unreasonable, considering that the running of Beerbelly was usually taken on entirely by Mesut. But Bad Boy was obviously not amused and the gaggle of young girls drooling over him from the pool table didn't exactly improve his motivation.

"Don't you think you should be helping Bad Boy out a bit?" I whispered to Mesut.

"Why?" He asked, smiling.

"Well, he's obviously not used to actually working. And it's getting busy now, isn't it?" I gestured to the gaggle of girls playing pool and then, unbelievably, another gang of sixteen year-olds who had just walked through the door and made a beeline for Bad Boy.

"Yes. Is busy." Mesut nodded. "But I give him warning that when you come back I will not be working."

"Really?"

"Yes. And still he is asking the girls to come. He is learning lesson tonight I think. I am not messing with lesson." And he sat back with a wry smile, stretching his legs right out under the table and his arms out across the back of the sofa. I'd never seen him looking so loose and limber. It seemed a far cry from the tense, mysterious man I'd met originally, but it suited him, there was no doubt about it.

As his arm stretched out behind me, he brought his hand up to gently rub my neck when his fingers came across the necklace I'd bought in Cappadocia. He played with the rope chain for a few moments before leaning in closely to have a good look. I tipped my chin back so he could see properly and he was so close I could feel his breath on my neck, sparking an exquisite heat down my spine. Gillie looked across at me and winked. She'd clocked Mesut's discovery of the necklace and I thought back to her little prediction back on the tour bus about us being a matching pair.

And just as I had this thought, without even a single word, Mesut looked me square in the eyes and slipped something cold and smooth into my hand. I looked down. It was his bracelet. The very one that he had used to stream energy into his coffee cup when telling our fortunes on that morning when I'd felt my world spinning out of control. The morning when I knew he meant something to me. Something crucial. Something inevitable.

"Is yours now." He said, simply, and helped me fasten it onto my wrist. "I am thinking it was always yours." I didn't know what to say. My stubborn Englishness made me want to protest wildly and give it straight back to him. But what good was my Englishness here? Cultures, languages and weird, insanely over-emphasised manners were blown out of the water here. So I took it. Now I was at the receiving end of one of Marcus's 'Great Giveaways' and do you know what? It felt bloody good.

"Oh my God, Jess!" Gillie said suddenly, snapping me out of my blissful exchange with Mesut. "Demir's just asked if you're still doing the challenges. We totally forgot. Have you got any left?"

"Actually, yes." I said, and started flipping through my note-book to find the last envelope. Gillie still didn't know about the Great Giveaway challenge as it was all tangled up in her experi-ence of Oliver, and I wasn't going to bring that up now, whilst she had her feet in another man's lap. So I dragged out the chal-lenge envelope and covered the number six as I opened it. Everybody leaned in to listen as I read it out.

Challenge 6 — Textnology

Losing touch with ourselves can be caused by
losing touch with people who were once
special. So . . . text someone random today.

"Oooh! That's brilliant! I know I've got loads of numbers on my phone for people I haven't spoken to in ages. What about you Jess? Who are you gonna text?" Gillie asked, eagerly.

"I don't know. There's bound to be someone on here I haven't been in touch with for a while." I dug out my phone and handed it to Mesut. "Here. You'll do a better job of random than me." He shrugged and flicked through the contacts on my phone, none of the names on there meaning a thing to him. His finger came to rest on the screen with a little tap and he handed it back to me.

"Gillie, it's Jason Reeves."

Gillie's eyes widened. "Shit Jess. How have you still got his number?"

"I've no idea. But apparently, he's the one."

"Do it! Jack is a thing of the past now." She darted a look at Mesut. "Just do it."

"Okay. But this might not even be his number anymore." I bent my head to tap out a text. Jason Reeves was a guy Gillie and I both knew from our university days. He'd been a technician in the Creative Arts department and a firm favourite with all the students. Not limited by the same red tape wound around lecturers, Jason was a regular at student house parties and long, lazy nights at the pub. He had always seemed to be around and was one of the friendliest men I'd ever known. He was a great big hunk of a man, an avid rugby player and, if my memory served me right, he did an amazing Robert De Niro impression. Jason was one of the good ones.

If only Jack had thought the same thing.

Looking back now, I could see that it had never taken much to make Jack jealous. In fact, Jason might have been the first man we ever argued over. I remembered the night clearly. It was cold and damp and the drizzle soaked me to the skin as Jack and I stood outside the pub, screaming at each other through the mist, about the apparent way Jason had looked at me. I remembered feeling astounded at Jack's reaction and devastated that the man I was falling in love with could possibly speak to me with such venom.

That night had turned into one of the longest of my life as I battled it out with him and his demons. Somehow I'd been able to convince him that Jason was just a friend and I guess I'd taken pity on the way his vicious insecurities ripped through him. Me being me, I thought I could fix him, that my love would conquer all. Seven years later and I found out that had never been possible.

I'd kept Jason as a friend but it must have been obvious to him that whenever Jack was around I'd been slightly cooler. This is not something I could imagine myself doing now. This new Jess would not treat people like that. So as a confirmation of this new promise to myself, I texted:

Jason. Hello stranger. How the heck are you? Just reaching out to an old friend to see if you're still around. Love Jess (from the uni days).

That would do it. I put my phone down on the table.

"Now," Gillie said, smiling. "We wait".

26

LUCKY

Later that night and I was walking on the beach with Mesut, the steady beat of the nightclubs long since faded and the night taking on that kind of heavy blackness that settles in before morning.

Gillie had been whisked away by Demir, leaving Kadafi to sleep in the bar and deter any late-night stragglers looking for a drink. My world now consisted of barefooted steps in the cool, sinking sand, the warmth of a fleece blanket thrown over my shoulders, and walking in-step with a man who was listening to my every whispered word.

It had been difficult to know where to start, telling Mesut about my time away from him. But, in the same way that Oliver always told me that wherever I started would be right, Mesut's eyes urged me on, with kindness and curiosity. So, inevitably, everything about our time with Oliver came flooding out, as well as the raw magic of the two places we had visited.

Mesut didn't say much during my tales. He didn't nod and agree and ooh and aah the way most people would when listening to somebody recount their experiences. Nevertheless, I had a feeling he was deeply present. And I realised this was how

I always felt with him. We were holding hands now and he gently increased the pressure when I told of how difficult the whole Oliver thing had been. And just like that, I knew he understood.

But how to tell him about my moment on the mountainside? I'd even glossed over this with Gillie because it had felt so weird saying the words out loud. Somehow it was perfectly fine to have an internal monologue going on about rediscovering my destiny and being on an authentic path and living every moment with perfect love and self-compassion. Saying it out loud to an actual person in real time? Now that was another matter.

But, I reminded myself, being authentic was about taking those kinds of risks. Why not speak the language of my heart more often? Look where it had brought me so far. There was no telling where I could go with this.

So, I took a deep breath and off I went . . .

————

"So, you are thinking your destiny is to use your stories? To write? That is what the mountain is telling you?" Mesut and I were sitting down now, on a blanket, under a tree, the rippling waves of the shoreline not more than thirty feet away. He was trying to make sense of what I'd told him during our walk.

"Well, the mountain didn't tell me, exactly. I think the answer was in me. I think the mountain helped me to remember it. As if it had been deeply buried inside for a really long time."

"Yes. I think so. And how you feeling? When you remembering this?" He asked this and I instinctively drew his palm to my heart.

"Oh Mesut, it felt incredible. It's really hard to describe. I had this tremendous feeling of weightlessness at first, then a crashing sense of victory that made every one of my senses kind of sing loudly. And then this rush of warmth, like arriving home after a long time away. I still feel it now. It's blissful."

"Blissful. Is good?"

"Blissful is very good." I said, and curled myself into him, my nose in the crook of his neck, as he draped his arm down my back. Despite being very much at one in a soulful way, we were still getting used to how our bodies fit together. I wouldn't call it awkward, exactly, but there was definitely something slightly strange. I mean, how do you find a physical language that matches a language of the heart? I'd never been with anyone so slim before and wasn't used to the smooth, hard touch of him, the closeness of his bones to the surface of his skin and all the angles of his body. Similarly, I'm sure I wasn't usual for him either. Although he clearly wasn't in the league of Bad Boy, I knew Mesut would have had more than his fair share of women. Was I his 'type'? Did this feel weird to him too?

"Jess, Jess, Jess." He stroked my hair and chanted my name softly just as he had done earlier that afternoon. My heart began to beat just that little bit faster. "You are so different for me."

I gasped. "Really? I was just wondering about that."

"Yes, really you are different." He pulled gently on a strand of my hair. "I am never thinking I am going for a yellow woman."

"Hey!" I exclaimed, sitting up and turning round to face him. "For starters, you mean blonde, not yellow. And just what, may I ask, is wrong with blonde women?"

He laughed and tucked his own hair behind his ears so it was out of his eyes and he could look at me properly. "Nothing is wrong. Just is not my type."

"So what made you break the rules this time?"

"I am not thinking about rules with you Jess. In fact . . . with you I am not thinking at all."

"So what's going on here then?" Oh God, Oh God, did I really want that question answered?

"Is just feeling, isn't it? Is feeling from here." He pressed his hand to his chest, then to mine. His touch made me catch my breath and I just nodded. "All I know is, that before you, I am mainly talking to the stars. Yes, over years there have been women – all of them dark, by the way." He grinned wickedly at me. "And even my mum is arranging marriage for me once. But is never right for me. I know myself. I know I not want any of it."

"So what did you want?"

"I am not knowing then. Before you, I am not knowing. I just accept it and get on with life in Beerbelly, in İpeklikum. I have friends, yes, and I have happy times, yes, but is not really good enough."

"And then?"

"And then, let me tell you . . ." he pulled on my shoulders with a sharp jerk so that I gave a surprised cry, and before I knew it I was lying down, wrapped tight in his arms. "And then . . . just when I never expect it, a woman come along. A yellow – sorry – a *blonde* one. And first I am thinking she just a tourist and she will come and she will go like everybody people. But no. This one is staying. And this one is talking. All the time talking."

"Hey! I do not talk all the time!" He kissed me softly so that I couldn't protest any further.

"And then, one day, this woman, who is usually talking all the time, she is now shouting at me. Shouting at me on the steps of place where I work, with fires in her eyes and I know she means it. She is meaning it with all her heart. And after that, is my turn to talk. And her turn in listening." He pointed up to the stars, which we could see glinting fiercely under the crooked branches of the tree we were lying under. "Before you, I am always talking to the stars, whenever I am feeling bad. I leave Beerbelly, I come out here where nobody people is finding me and I am looking up, asking the stars what to do, telling them everything that is inside me. I am thinking because they are part of the soul of the world that they can listen well and tell me what to do. But now, now I am finding somebody who can do that better. I don't talk to the stars now Jess. I talk to you. And the stars are jealous."

We fell into a deep kiss that I felt over every inch of my body and deeper still. The simplicity of Mesut's words clung to me like a dewdrop to a leaf and saturated me with what I could only imagine was love. Love for this moment, love for this world, love for myself and yes, love for him.

Let the stars be jealous.

I don't know how long we kissed for or how many times we went over and over the artful workings of the universe that had brought us together, but we were finally interrupted by the fated sounds of the creeping morning. The distant clink of breakfast cutlery being laid out on tables, the dragging sound of the combing machine that cleaned the beach daily and the buoyant sound of birdsong, directly above us in the overhanging tree. Mesut sat up and stretched out indulgently. "The birds is waking up." He said.

"Yes, noisy buggars." I looked up at them and couldn't believe how many I saw. They must have been roosting the whole night in that tree, just above our heads. Now they were flapping and tweeting and practically having a rave. Then I saw something drop to the ground and I shouted, "Oh shit, Mesut! Watch out!"

The birds weren't just having a party, they were doing their morning ablutions – all over us! We sprang out from under the branches as soon as we realised what was happening but it was too late. We were covered in bird shit.

I looked at Mesut standing there with slimy, grey filth dripping through that beautiful black hair of his and realised I must have looked just as ridiculous with the same gunk blotting my own hair and clothes too. Mesut's face was like a storm until he looked at me and his features smoothed into a smile. He laughed, and so did I. Heartily. I gathered up the now decorated blanket and rolled it under my arm. Mesut slung an arm round my waist and we wandered off away from the tree.

"Is our bad luck, eh Jess?"

"Bad luck?" I said. "No, anything but Mesut. In my culture, getting shit on by a bird is very good luck."

"Really? No. I am not seeing how."

"Absolutely, it is. In fact, if getting shit on by one bird is good luck, then we've just had a whole lifetime's worth of good luck splattered all over us. Can't complain about that."

He stopped walking and pulled me against him by my waist, then slid his hands up to hold my face tenderly. He kissed me once. "That," he said, then smiled widely so I could see deep crinkles beside his eyes, "is not surprising me."

27

MESUT'S BIRTHDAY

"A flight ticket?" I nearly choked on my bread and olives.

"Yes. A bloody flight ticket. All the way back to Newcastle. Leaving today." Gillie said, her eyes blazing over her coffee. "Can you believe the cheek of the man?"

Well, yes, I could really. "Hmmm," I chewed thoughtfully. "And he thought you would see this as a present? A kind gesture?"

"Seemingly so." Gillie said, crossing her arms and snapping down her sunglasses to ward off the glare of the early afternoon sun. I'd been in bed all morning after my night on the beach with Mesut, and Gillie had been at Demir's apartment all night. We'd met here at The Four Seasons for a bit of brunch and a catch-up. She was filling me in on the events of the night which had, in the most part, seemed fine, but this last bit was messing with my head.

"So, let me get this right. He cooks you dinner, gives you wine, sleeps with you, then kicks you out of the country? Nice. The bloke's got style."

"Hang on a minute though. It was all going really well up until that point. I mean, he was charming, and romantic and in bed he was . . . well . . . let's just say he left no stone unturned . . . and then, when I woke up this morning he'd left the flight ticket on my pillow and he was gone."

"Gone? Gone where?"

"To work. Well, I assumed that's where he was. So I went straight there and had to wait half an hour whilst Kadafi went and got him out of some meeting or something, and that's when I had it out with him."

"What did he have to say for himself?"

"Oh, something about his uncle's cousin's girlfriend not needing the ticket anymore and they thought I might want it for free. I told him, 'I've got my own bloody flights booked, thank you, I don't need you to usher me out early.' And then he was all kind and sweet and said he didn't mean it that way and if he had his way he'd have me stay forever blah blah blah . . .'"

I reached over the table and grabbed Gillie's hand. It was still warm from gripping her coffee cup so tightly. "Gillie, come on. What do you think this is all about?"

She gave a long, drawn-out sigh and tipped her head back, talking to the sky. "Honestly? I think it's probably just a misunderstanding. A cultural thing. I think because he comes from an insanely poor family, he thinks anything free is worth having. I think I've made him see that giving me a flight ticket home was not exactly the best thing to give a girl you've just slept with. You should have seen the look of realisation on his face when it finally clicked."

"Really? You think it was just an honest mistake?"

"Of course. He's been a player in the past Jess, I know that. But for now he's with me and that's that."

"Okay hun. As long as you know what you're doing." I wasn't convinced. By Demir or Gillie. Her body language was not matching her words. Her mouth was set in a grim line, there was still a fire behind her eyes and her shoulders were

scrunched rigid and tight. She was utterly impenetrable sometimes, which made me sad when we'd known each other so
many years, and after a holiday so jam-packed with soulful revelations too.

"Anyway," Gillie sighed, "what about your man? Isn't it his
birthday today?"

Your man. That sounded weird. "As it happens, it is. Fancy
a slow saunter over there to give him his present?"

"Didn't we already give it to him before we left for
İstanbul?"

"We did. But he told me he'd wait until we were there to
open it."

"That's sweet. But, Jess, don't you think it should just come
from you? I mean, you're the one he wants to spend time with
on his birthday."

"Don't be silly." I said, standing up and throwing some
money on the table to cover our bill. "We made that painting
together, so we should give it to him together. Come on."

————

Mesut's long fingers, rested on top of the little fabric-wrapped
parcel that was balanced on his knee.

He looked at Gillie and I, peering past the hanging strands
of black hair that fell in front of his face. He looked so serious.
But I knew him well enough now to know that he was
teasing us.

"Oh for God's sake Mesut, just open it will you?" Gillie
shifted on her patchwork cushion in Village Corner and glanced
through the sheer curtains into the depths of Beerbelly. I think
she was as nervous as me. From the reactions of everybody else
when we'd strode into the bar, cheerfully wishing Mesut a
happy birthday, it was fairly obvious the Turkish culture didn't

really 'do' birthdays. Now, perhaps, I could understand Demir's reluctance to translate those special words for Mesut's painting. I couldn't, however, understand the major huff he'd gone into when Gillie had disappeared into Village Corner with me to give Mesut his present. I swear that man was part toddler.

"Okay, okay," Mesut smiled. "I open it."

He unwound the strip of fabric that bound the whole thing together and let the wrapping fall away. The painting lay on his lap, face up, the deep tones of the paint showing a subtle sheen across the contours of the texture we'd created and the little words stuck hard and proud to the surface.

Kaderini yaşamak bir insanın tek gerçek yükümlülügüdür
   (*To realise one's destiny is a person's only real obligation*)

I think I actually heard Mesut gasp. "Really, really, I not expecting something like this." He said, choosing his words slowly, carefully. He brought the painting up close to his face, looking at all the details as if he'd never seen anything like it before. Then he turned it over in his hands and read the English translation we'd included on the back and the little message: *For Mesut from the Beerbelly lasses, Gillie and Jess.*

"Do you like it then?" Gillie asked

Again he turned the painting over and brushed his hands across the top of the canvas, feeling the bumps and ridges of the fabric we'd painted onto. "Really, I am liking it." He murmured. "I am keeping it now, very close to me and then one day I am giving it to my first son."

Suddenly something like an electric current rippled through me making its final thumping exit through my chest. It left my whole body jarred with a faint pulsing sensation reminiscent of déjà vu. Something like the mountainside thing. What was that all about?

"Really?" I blurted out, feeling the need to fill the crackling silence, "Why your first son?"

"In my culture, the first son very important." Mesut chuckled and held the painting in towards his chest. "He needing this."

Gillie darted a look between us and knew something weird was going on with me. I didn't realise I was holding my breath until she brought a hand down firmly between my shoulder blades and then rubbed my back affectionately. "Well, we're so glad you like it, aren't we Jess? We just wanted to make something special for you."

"Really, is special. Thank you." Mesut said and bowed towards us. Then he stood and held out his hand to me. "Let's we find somewhere safe to put it Jess." And just like that I was brought back to reality with the warmth of his touch. As we stood, Gillie slipped through the curtains and shot off in the direction of the Mega Tour office.

"I'm just off to find his Majesty!" She chirped, leaving us staring after her.

"I have no idea why she chases him, Mesut." I said, honestly. "I think he's getting more and more dodgy as the days go by."

He guided me by the hand over to the empty bar. "Really you right." He said, and placed his painting on the top shelf behind the bar, straightened it, then stood back to admire it. Then he turned and leaned his elbows on the bar reaching his hands out to find mine. I grasped them and leaned in to him, our noses almost touching, now needing no more than a whisper between us. "Let me I tell you story. Do you have some time?"

"For you?" I breathed softly, "All the time in the world."

———

I'd never seen a grown man drink from a baby's bottle before. And he didn't look particularly pleased about it either.

Earlier that evening, Bad Boy and Kadafi had thought it a fitting joke to present Mesut with the plastic bottle with a neon pink teat. And when I'd asked what the heck was going on, Mesut had shown me that the drink they planned to ply him with all evening was Raki, the aniseed-tasting alcoholic beverage Turkish holiday resorts were famous for. I'd learned that it was traditionally enjoyed with water mixed into it, turning it the colour and consistency of milk. Hence, the baby's bottle.

"They is thinking is hilarious. Look at them," he said, tipping his chin over to where his friends sat, their shoulders shaking with the sheer force of their merriment. He shrugged and tipped the bottle towards his lips.

Oh well, I thought. *When in Rome.*

Right now I was sitting having a few peaceful moments to myself as Mesut was being tormented by all manner of people over at the bar. Courtesy of a load of regular tourists he knew of old, he had also been presented with an England football shirt (classy), an over-sized leprechaun's felt hat with a light-up shamrock buckle (classier still) and a blow-up doll complete with accompanying blow-up sheep (there are no words).

I didn't have time to wallow in cynicism about the traditions of British benevolence because I was still processing the story Mesut had told me in the tea garden that afternoon.

The situation itself didn't seem to be too out of the ordinary. Mesut had a few mates who'd had past drug problems and apparently Demir had never liked them anywhere near Beer-belly. Not that it was Demir's call, of course, but Esad, being Demir's cousin, had relented and asked Mesut, respectfully, to keep them away.

Whilst Gillie and I had been on our travels, one of them,

called Ömer, had been hanging around more than he should have been and things had kicked off.

"What happened?" I'd asked Mesut.

"Is not that bad. Ömer is wanting talk to me so he wait at bar all night until I finish. Esad say okay. But then Demir is coming back from tour and is seeing him there. He is making big noise and is shouting and all customer is getting little bit scared."

"What did Esad do?"

"Nothing. He is already going home and leaving bar to me. So I in charge and I tell Demir to be quiet and Ömer is staying." Apparently after that Demir had took a swing at Mesut, which Ömer blocked and simultaneously managed to knock Demir off his feet. That's when all hell broke loose and there was a full-on fight between Demir and Ömer, which Mesut had to break up, getting a few punches himself in the process. The police turned up and sent everybody home, meaning nobody paid their drinks bills and Mesut did not get paid that night. Or the next night as the police closed Beerbelly for a day as was the minimum penalty if any of the bars in İpeklikum had trouble with violence. Knowing what I did of Demir's little world, I could see how this would just exacerbate the whole situation. Demir deemed Mesut to blame for all that happened that evening, which resulted in the temporary closure of his elder cousin's business, meaning profits were interrupted which was serious stuff. Money, family, business, loyalty – a strong, complex web woven by Demir that would give Al Pacino a run for his money.

"I wonder if Demir told Gillie about all of this? She hasn't mentioned it."

"He is not mentioning this type of thing."

There was something in Mesut's tone of voice that just didn't seem right. "What do you mean, 'this type of thing'?"

"I am meaning Demir is not telling Gillie everything."

Mesut went on to tell me that Demir only tolerated him working at the bar because Esad valued him so much. Mesut stayed put because he really didn't care what Demir thought of him and could handle his tantrums. Clearly, Demir was of the opinion that blood flowed thicker than water and couldn't handle the fact that Mesut was firmly rooted in the family business. "But is not matter what he do, Jess," he'd said, "Demir's hate not touching me."

I couldn't help thinking what would happen now, though, that Gillie and I were in the picture. How would Demir feel about me snuggling up to Mesut and then making sure Gillie knew what I knew? If he gave two hoots about Gillie then this was going to get interesting.

Just then I felt the tickle of hot, rapid, aniseed breath on my shoulder. "What you think Jess? We get out of here?"

I turned to find that dark stare ready and waiting for me. I looked behind him and could see virtually everybody in the bar waving at Mesut, shouting for him to stay, clinking bottles and clashing glasses.

I found his eyes again, and matched his broad, steady smile. "Absolutely".

––––––––

We'd been walking for a good half an hour when he said we were nearly there.

And now, instead of negotiating crumbling, rocky paths under foot, it was some sort of overgrown, weed-ridden field that the moonlight was barely touching. I could just see the glinting ends of stiff, papery stems topped with clusters of dried flower-buds and I could feel them dragging on my skirt and scratching at my legs. But Mesut's grip on my hand was firm and I could make out the broad shape of his shoulders ahead of me so I knew where to walk, where to place my feet in rhythm with his slow, careful pace. "Really, I am doing this walk so many times, Jess. But not with other person. I hope is okay for you."

"Well, it's different anyway." I said, feeling slightly out of breath. "Not how I thought you'd want to spend your birthday."

"I am not caring about birthdays," he said, "only that I am with you. The rest not important."

It was always weird when Mesut said something like that to me. Although it was a fairly new experience for me to hear it coming out of his mouth, he always said these things with such matter-of-factness, that it didn't occur to me to feel embarrassed or flattered. There was no room for that here. Each time he did it I just kind of shrugged inside and thought, *yeah, you're right.* It was weird it was so normal.

"So remind me again, where exactly are we going?"

"Remember I am telling you about Esad's fiancé?"

"Yes, erm . . . Beryl? Your Geordie mate?" Mesut had told me a while back about a woman called Beryl, who Esad had been engaged to since forever and who was, strangely enough, from a little village only about half an hour from where I lived back in the north east of England. Apparently she was pretty much Mesut's best friend in the whole of İpeklikum but I hadn't met her yet because she was back in the UK for the summer. She didn't particularly like the heat, he'd told me, or the fact that she never saw Esad during the summer months. She was due back tomorrow though so I'd be meeting her soon.

"Yes. Beryl is buying this house before she is meeting Esad. When she is starting live with him, she not wanting sell this house, so she let me I use it. That is where we going."

"So why aren't you there every night?"

He turned and smiled and I could see the white of his teeth, the dark mass of his hair framing his face. "Is because of this walk. Mostly I am lazy, Jess. The bar is easier."

"Fair enough," I said. Then something occurred to me. "Shouldn't Esad have offered this house to his family? Demir and Kadafi? Or Bad Boy? How come you get it?"

"Is not Esad's house." Mesut shrugged. "Is not his choice. Beryl is trusting it with me."

"Yet another reason for Demir not to like you then?"

"Yes." He said. "Another reason."

A few paces later we emerged from the tall, scratchy plants and were back on a solid path. In front of us was a block of at least ten semi-detached houses, looming grey with white sparks of moonlight jumping off the solar panels on the rooves. Mesut's pace quickened and I shivered. The cloudless night was getting cold.

We walked to the far end of the cluster of houses and stopped at the last one. This one stood alone on a high concrete plinth and had an authoritarian air that beamed out over the other houses. Mesut let go of my hand, found a key in the back pocket of his jeans and clicked the heavy, metal door open. We ducked inside and let the echo of the slamming door vibrate out into the night.

When Mesut flicked on the lights throughout the house I could see it was stark and bare. Nobody had lived here properly in a long time, although there were a few tell-tale signs that a woman had, at one point, laced it with her character. Among other things, there was a deep red, star-shaped ashtray on the windowsill, a dramatic, framed photo of fork lightning hitting the ocean on the wall, and a wild, multi-coloured hand-hooked rag rug sprawled on the tiled floor. I would guess that the lady of the house was strong-willed and vivacious. I liked her already.

"Coffee?" Mesut said, flicking the kettle on in the tiny little kitchen. I nodded and said I was going for a wander. I went up the freezing cold marble staircase that led from the living room to the landing, and found four doors. One of them led into a modest little bathroom, not unlike the arrangement Gillie and I had at Shit Class. The soap on the sink was dry and cracked and there were white water marks around the base of the shower. Nobody had washed here in a while. The cynical part of my brain that thought I was utterly mad to be even entertaining the thought of a relationship with a Turkish barman breathed a sigh of relief. No women had been in here of late.

I tried another door but it was locked. It had a window at the top of it and I could see that it led up onto the roof. I briefly remembered something Mesut had said about how, in the part of Turkey he came from, whole families would sleep on the roof during the summer because it was too hot to be indoors. It was chilly tonight though, and I was fairly certain he wouldn't be suggesting that. It struck me then that I would most likely be spending the night in this house. With Mesut. Not that I hadn't spent entire nights with him before. But tonight there was no beach, no bar, no rocks in the sea.

Tonight it was just me, him and four walls.

I wondered which four walls it would be and tried another door. This room was small and square and had absolutely no furniture in it at all. All it contained was a little plaque hanging from the handle of the window reading, 'Life is yours.' My breath stopped for an instant as the meaning of that dusty plaque realigned itself with where I was right now. It was that little mantra again, that I'd pinched off an inebriated Esad on my first holiday to Turkey earlier this year.

And just look where it had brought me.

Knowing we couldn't sleep in a room with no furniture, I tried that last door on the corner of the landing. This was it. This was the room Mesut used when he came here. It smelled of him. That deep, musky smell of tobacco and the sea-salt surface of his skin.

It was so dark in there. No street lights working outside, just the bare, waning light of the moon coming through one slim rectangular window. I sat down on the single bed and switched on a lamp, which sat on a little upturned wooden box. Once the room was bathed in the soft, yellow light I noticed signs of the man who was slowly stealing my heart.

A black dream-catcher hung above the bed, its speckled feathers and tangled web of tiny wooden beads casting shadows that breathed mystery onto the wall behind it. There was a clay dish laying next to the lamp, with small objects nestling inside: a set of amber prayer beads; a carved wooden head of a Native American Apache; glass pebbles of white, blue and green all smoothly polished by the sea; several items of jewellery in chunky silver, black leather and woven with coloured threads. There was a large purple cushion pushed up against a wall, with a stack of books beside it. There were no pictures on the wall, but there was a small bundle of photos leaned up against the skirting board, next to the clay dish, tied in a piece of string.

"You are liking my room?" Mesut whispered at the door. Standing there, holding two steaming mugs of black coffee, and smiling altogether with gentility and strength, I thought I had perhaps loved this man forever.

"Yes," I smiled. "Yes, I really do."

"Is good." He said, setting the coffees down on the upturned box, next to the lamp. "I am not bringing anyone here before now. Is mine. I not share it."

I didn't want to have this conversation right now. I didn't ever want to have it, but the words came out against my better judgement. "Haven't you brought other women here before?"

"No," he said, with such simplicity, it made my heart sing. "No, I am not sharing it. Really Jess, I am not knowing what you are doing to me."

"I'm not doing anything. You just brought me here, I

thought you'd want to stay with all your friends at the bar. It's your birthday remember."

He covered my hands with his and held my gaze in that way that only he knew how. "I am telling you already, yes? Birthday is not important. The rest is not important. I am wanting you. I am bringing you here because I am wanting you." His voice was cracking slightly. From fear or desire, I couldn't tell but I didn't care, I just had to kiss him.

I kissed him so deeply and with such feeling that I thought he must surely feel the quickened pound of my heart steal up from my chest, surge through my lips and into his mouth. How could he not feel it? It consumed me so completely in that moment that I couldn't imagine he might be hesitant. But he broke away.

"Jess, I am . . . I am thinking . . . I want you to know that I not doing this usually. I never, ever bring anyone here and . . ." He took a deep breath. "Will you still be here in morning?"

"What?" I started to laugh but then realised he was serious. His skin was looking paler than I'd seen it before and his fingertips, now brushing lightly against my cheeks, were ever so slightly trembling. He was serious.

"Mesut, of course I will be here in the morning. You'll have to kick me out of bed, you silly buggar."

He studied my face and my eyes and must have believed that I meant it because his shoulders dropped and the lines in his face smoothed. "I am sorry. I just . . . I not knowing how to do this. I not usually care so much. And definitely I not with anyone until morning. This is first time I am wanting to be with somebody in the morning."

"Mesut?" I said, with all the desperate courage and plain, ferocious truth I could muster, placing his hands flat and wide open on my breast so that he could feel its rising and falling, its heavy, burning impulse, "Before that morning comes? We have an evening to get through first."

And with those words he threw down his fears, pulled me in towards him so that every curve I had breathed fiercely into the hard, smooth lines of his body, and we kissed our way into oblivion.

28

MELIS

When I woke that morning, I was tangled in happiness. And him.

I lay in Mesut's bed, his arms and legs holding me in a knot that I didn't want to get out of. His breath, soft and heavy, indicated he was still sound asleep and his lips, lightly pressed against my forehead, held the shape of memories from the night before. I closed my eyes again.

His hands told the story of his desire . . . soft and gentle . . . then firm and forceful . . . a grip that all at once thrust my own passions out of me and into him, then just as swiftly stroked them, masterfully down, so that they were pleading to be let loose again. The fear he'd talked about earlier now was lost in the whiteness of my soft flesh and the contrasting dark, smooth contours of his . . . the slice of moonlight coming through the curtainless window had buckled only under the movement of our bodies, taking on a vulnerable, beautiful lucidity . . . his hair had splayed all over me as he'd trailed kisses into every dip, every mound, every curve he could find . . . lingering fingertips . . . one

moment light and tickling, the next firm and wanting and
working deep into the place where I led them . . . . My skirt lifted
gently, my legs parted slowly, while he found and devoured the
parts of me that held promise . . .

My memories were interrupted by a soft shiver running down
the length of Mesut's back as he opened his eyes and woke to
find me next to him. "My Gulazer", he whispered.

"Your what?" I asked, tying myself up ever tighter in his
embrace.

"Gulazer. Is mean, yellow rose. Is my new name for you."

"Yellow rose? Okay, I'll take that."

"But is only one thing . . ." It was those hands again, moving
up and down my back, waking up my flesh, crackling my soft
edges with the firmness of his touch.

"Oh yes? What's that then?"

"I need to know . . . you have any thorns or not?" His hands
were going further down now, rounding from my back to my
belly, brushing my thighs.

"Be careful," I breathed, "You might get scratched." I
pressed my nails into his shoulders and dragged them slowly
downwards.

"I am thinking is too late for that." He smiled.

———

It was wonderful to hear a north-eastern accent again. And
Beryl's was even stronger than mine, with her vowels long and
swooping, a friendly humour tingeing the edges of her words.
"Aw, Messy," she said, "I can't believe I missed your birthday!
But I'm only a day out mind, it's not that bad, is it?"

"No, sister. Not that bad." Mesut said and they bent their heads in towards each other, lighting up cigarettes using a Middlesbrough football team lighter she'd brought him back from England.

I'd been introduced to Beryl ten minutes ago, after Mesut and I had taken a long, lazy walk along the beach back to the bar, and we'd found her, sitting on the steps of Beerbelly with Gillie, waiting for her 'brother' to return.

She was a delightfully round woman with the most incredible head of jet-black tightly curled hair that bounced out to the sides at its own free will. Freckles dotted her cheeks but her skin was the creamy-white of a Northerner who preferred to be out of the sun. She had the slow, careful drawl of a woman who was not to be messed with, but the humour in her voice and the crow's feet by her eyes suggested she knew how to have fun with the right people. Evidently, Mesut was one of those.

"So, bloody hell Messy. I hear you took this one to the house?" She arched an eyebrow and nudged him in the side. "Must be serious, eh?"

"Sister." Mesut glanced at me shyly. "Really, I am not talking about this now."

Beryl turned to look at me. "Jess. I've never known, in the whole time I've had Messy as a friend, for him to even hold hands with a girl, never mind take her to the house. Now, I know he's not an angel. Lord knows, no man is an angel." She flicked a glance over at Esad who was counting up money at the bar. "But this one is at least a private man. Very private. So you must have done something to get him acting like this. I've never seen him like this before!" I opened my mouth to speak but Beryl was still on a roll. "It's bloody lovely to see though, Messy. I have to admit, it's bloody lovely to see." She patted him on the leg and they both, instinctively, inhaled deeply on their cigarettes, then looked out at the sea beyond the promenade and past the steady lull of strolling tourists.

In that slow, synchronised gaze, I could see the habitual comfort that comes from years of real friendship. Now what did the universe think it was doing, exactly, by arranging for my mysterious, other-worldly man from a remote part of Turkey that was steeped in ancient mysticism, to be best mates with a Geordie who lived down the road from me? Another omen? Another way to get me to see that everything is connected, we're all part of the same rich energy that turns the world, that slips through time and space and makes miracles happen? This called for a beer.

I was just about to suggest such a thing when Gillie pointed out at the promenade. "Aw, look." She said. She was pointing at Demir who was talking to a little girl of about four years old. The girl was holding tightly onto a man's hand while Demir was knelt down making a right fuss of her. She stood cutely in a frilly pink sundress, with brown curls hanging around her face. She looked terrified though. And the bloke she was holding hands with didn't look too keen either.

"Demir's so good with little ones. Oooh, it just makes my ovaries quiver." Gillie crooned.

Beryl chuckled and exchanged knowing glances with Mesut. "Well, he's trying at least. Even if it is a bit late."

"Late?" Gillie asked, checking her watch. "What do you mean?"

"Good god, pet. Has he not told you?"

"Told me what?" Gillie asked, her sun-kissed complexion starting to pale. "What should he have told me?"

Beryl sighed a huge, exhausted sigh and whispered something along the lines of '*fucking idiot*' under her breath before stubbing out her cigarette in the ashtray Mesut offered to her, lifting her chin up and looking Gillie square in the eyes.

"That, my girl, is Melis. Demir's daughter."

To Gilllie's credit, she hadn't gone completely off it.

While I might have expected her to march straight over there and drag the truth out of Demir in front of his daughter, she had seen fit instead, to drag it out of Beryl and Mesut.

Neither of them had been too willing to do this. Mesut, I'm guessing, didn't want to put his job at risk and Beryl, well to Beryl, it all seemed like such old news that she barely had the patience to go through it all with Gillie. She did it though. Between long, slow draws on cigarettes and plentiful eye-rolls, she told Gillie everything.

Melis was the result of a summer fling Demir had had with a tour rep a while back now. Apparently things had been quite serious with Tour Rep Girl. Demir had met the parents, put all other flings on hold and even started planning for the two of them to run Mega Tour together.

It was all going swimmingly until Tour Rep Girl got pregnant and jetted back to England to have the baby there. The prospect of paying hospital fees and going through labour with a Turkish-speaking midwife were simply not doing it for her and as far as Beryl knew, Demir had promised to apply for a visa to join her in the UK. Funnily enough, this never materialised. "These Turkish lads, they like their comfort zones you know," she drawled, "You can't take a fish out of water."

"So what's going on now?" Gillie asked, as Mesut placed a strong cocktail in her waiting hands. "Why's she here?"

"Well, Melis's mam drew a line under the whole relationship after Demir didn't sort himself out. He made every excuse in the book when it came to him going to England and she'd just had enough. So Melis doesn't even know her own Dad, you know? But we all know Demir and how he can turn on the charm whenever he bloody wants to . . . so every summer Melis's uncle comes to İpeklikum for his holidays and this year Demir got a hold of him one night and practically drank him under the table. Oh it was a right bloody show with the two of them laughing about old times and the like. Somewhere along the line he must have said the right thing because next thing we know he's here with his niece and apparently she's around somewhere too."

"Who?" I asked on Gillie's behalf. "Tour Rep Girl?"

"Yes. She's here."

"I'll bloody kill him!" Gillie muttered, then taking a massive swig of her cocktail. The colour was coming back to her cheeks. "Now I know why he was trying to palm off that flight ticket onto me. He wanted me out of the way! Honestly Beryl, honestly Mesut, just tell me straight. Is he getting back with her?"

"That, my girl," Beryl said, sympathetically, "is something you need to talk to him about."

Gillie downed her cocktail and threw the glass straight into Demir's empty office, so that it shattered loudly on the tiled floor.

"Don't worry," she said, "I will."

———

At the bar the next night, our penultimate night before going home, things were not good.

Gillie had spent the last twenty four hours either shacked up with Demir or in fitful, broken sleep by my side at Shit Class Hotel. She'd had it out with him good and proper, of course. In fact, the shouting had got so loud in the Mega Tour office that Esad had had a very uncharacteristic fit of authority and told them to close up shop and move their argument elsewhere. "Bloody hell," Beryl had drawled, "will wonders never cease?"

Now Gillie was staring moodily into her drink, glammed up to the nines and looking gorgeous in a green glittery dress, but with tell-tale signs of exhaustion around her eyes. Typically, she hadn't really shared many of her feelings with me, just the odd thing here and there about feeling let down and not wanting to be a walk-over. Demir had, predictably, told her that he wasn't interested in Tour Rep Girl, just in building a relationship with his daughter. This, I knew, would work right into Gillie's weak spots. All she'd ever wanted was a man who would adore her as much as the children they would have together. She'd spent a long time investing those hopes in Marcus and just because he was out of the picture, didn't mean that the hopes were too. The fact that Demir was trying hard with his daughter would be working a sinister magic on her.

So here we were, sitting in Beerbelly as always, me feeling peacefully connected to Mesut as he slinked his way around the bar, serving customers; Gillie tolerating Demir who was pawing at her and fetching her drinks and making her all kinds of promises; Kadafi leaping about us all, telling stories and posing his usual philosophical questions. Right now he was wafting a gigantic palm tree leaf over Beryl, who was finding the Turkish heat a little too much to bear. "That's it, Kadafi," she said, blissfully, "I bloody knew you were good for something!"

Kadafi laughed wildly and flashed us his gorgeous smile. "You know is my speciality, Mrs Beryl." He said. "I am the maker of comfort . . . the comfort maker!" And with that he leapt over to where Gillie and I were sitting and started wafting the leaf over us too, producing a cool, rhythmical breeze. Demir's phone started buzzing. He took one look at it, answered it with a "One minute please," planted a kiss on Gillie's cheek and disappeared into the Mega Tour office, closing the sliding door behind him. Gillie stared after him with a look that could have killed off the entire male race.

Kadafi was oblivious. "Mrs ladies, Mrs ladies, I am your comfort maker." He wafted the leaf in even bigger swoops over our heads, getting closer and closer to our faces. "Please be telling me what I can do to be making you ever-more comfortable."

"You can fuck right off, that's what you can do!" Gillie shouted as she thrashed the leaf out of her face, jumped to her feet and stared him down.

It was the first time I'd ever seen Kadafi speechless. There was a pause that stretched out in front of Gillie, a pause that wouldn't shift until she did. And in that pause I could see behind the intense fury of her stare, a vulnerability that fought to get out.

Eventually everything moved and breathed again as Gillie stormed off down Beerbelly's steps and into the night. Mesut's eyes found mine across the bar and he flicked his head in Gillie's direction. I nodded and he gave his tray of drinks to Bad Boy. He came over, grabbed my hand and off we went, leaving Beryl and Kadafi to get the night going again.

"Erm, I'm getting the vibes she doesn't want company." I said to Mesut, as we walked quickly along the promenade, chasing Gillie's shadow as it blended into the night ahead of us. She was walking out of the main resort, off to where the sea was fiercer, the waves were higher.

"Yes. You right." Mesut nodded. "But we will not be far away. Just if she need us."

I wasn't sure how chuffed Gillie would be to have me and Mesut in her wake. Just one look over her shoulder would be a reminder of how well things were working out for us and would surely be enough to piss her right off. I know it would piss me off. Was following her the right thing to do?

After a while Gillie came to a part of the promenade that stuck out onto an ugly, concrete pier. A few scruffy looking boats were moored here and they bobbed about quickly on the restless sea. She turned and started to walk down the pier, her pace slowing and her whole frame softening against the spray that formed a misty tunnel around her. After a while, she stopped and although I could only see the soft, blurred figure of my friend, the glitter of her dress now dampened and clinging, I could sense, almost feel, the deep, shaky breaths she was taking.

What now?

Mesut and I stood, hand-in-hand, just watching her for a few moments, unsure whether she knew we were there or not. Then, whether it was a change in his breathing, a shift in his energy or what, I just knew Mesut had resolved to do something. He led me over to a nearby bench and sat me down. "I back soon." He said, simply, and walked off in Gillie's direction.

As I watched him walk away, I had a great sense of peace. Weird. Absolutely nothing was peaceful. My best friend was in turmoil and tomorrow I was leaving a man who had changed my world. Yet I had a deep sense of peace running through me, shimmering through my muscles, strengthening my bones, and I felt the overwhelming perfection of the moment. The damp air settled on my skin and the freshness of it flowed into me, became part of me. Was this another Moment of God?

I wanted to fix things for Gillie, of course I did. And there was no denying that I felt her pain, I felt her confusion as if they were my own. But underneath all of that, shining madly like a forgotten jewel, there was the knowledge that everything was as it should be.

I looked out towards the pier and searched for the shapes of the people who both meant so much to me. Eventually I found them. Mesut's sleek, dark shape upright and strong and Gillie turned into him, her trembling breaths visible even through the constant grey spray of the waves and the blue-black sky. Mesut hadn't used words after all. He'd known what was needed.

I walked down the pier towards them, with every step wanting to feel the solid warmth of Gillie in my arms. When I got there, Mesut's eyes found mine over the top of Gillie's head, wisps of her hair leaping and curling freely into the damp air. He took my arms and folded them around both of them so that we were all together locked in a hug. Gillie moved quietly so that her cheek rested on my shoulder and she shuddered into me. "Jess . . . I just want to go home now."

"I know sweetheart," I said, looking up at Mesut, "and we are . . . soon."

29

PACKING UP

On my last day in İpeklikum I was woken by my phone bleeping. I had to lift Mesut's heavily draped arm off me to get to it and read the text:

Hello to you too stranger! Just got ur text coz been away a few days. Gud to hear from u. Let's hook up? Howz Jackie boy?

Jason Reeves.

Well who'd've thought it? It was still his number and he did remember me. Wait til I told Gillie about this. I'd reply to him later when I didn't have a heavy Mediterranean man curled around me.

Mesut stirred and I nestled back into his arms. The smooth, coffee colour of his skin never failed to move me. Maybe it was the way it contrasted so starkly with the bright white of my own skin, or maybe it was because I'd seen it so up close and personal. But now, as the sun wove its way in through the little window of his room, it gleamed like warm caramel, and melted over me like a dream.

Last night we'd taken Gillie to Shit Class and we'd all shared a nightcap of Raki and ice cold water on our tiny balcony. Not much had been said. Just comments about the moon and the beach and the things Gillie and I might miss about İpeklikum. Then Gillie had curled up on her bed and waved us out of the room. "Off you go lovebirds," she'd said, "fly away now. I need to sleep." So we'd trekked off to Beryl's empty house and found sanctuary there. Or rather in each other.

My eyes were closed now and just as I could feel my limbs growing heavier and I could have quite happily drifted off to sleep, drenched in the memory of last night, Mesut woke. He didn't speak though. His eyes just opened and he looked at me as if I was an apparition. He kissed me once, hard and full on the lips, as if checking to make sure I was really there. When he decided I was real, he pulled away and stood up.

He was naked and that lithe, brown body stood strong and tall, smooth and firm in front of me. I could scarcely believe it was mine for the taking. He looked down at me. "You are beautiful Gulazer." He said, with a fierceness that didn't really match the words. Then he grabbed me by the waist and gathered me up so that I was sitting on his hips, my legs wrapped round his waist and dangling, loosely over his bottom.

"Are we going somewhere?" I whispered into his ear and felt his skin erupt into goosebumps all down that side. To this he was silent but he walked with me, curved around him like that, out onto the landing.

He walked halfway down the stairs before placing me down onto a step that was so cold against my bare skin it made me squeal. He didn't flinch, though, when he laid himself down in front of me and dipped his head to my breasts. There was none of the tenderness or slowness of the night before because these weren't really kisses. More like hard, fast bites that brought the blood soaring to the surface of my skin and surprised gasps to my lips.

He worked quickly downwards and whilst clawing his fingertips into my back I arched myself suddenly so that he could take me in his mouth and I could get lost in the hard, impatient swell of his tongue. Even the gnawing of his teeth against the softest, most hidden part of me couldn't tame the heat that was growing, spreading from the inside out. He moaned loudly into me and his fingers gripped tighter into the flesh of my bottom, I grabbed his hair and knotted it around my fists and maybe that's what kept me grounded as I flew into my ecstasy, into my bliss.

After that, my legs still trembling from the shockwaves that had just ripped through my body, it was me leading him this time. I pulled him down the stairs and into the kitchen, pinning him up against the counter, grinding my hips against his. "Where do you want me?" I whispered and he flipped me round and bent me over the counter top in a way that said, *here, I want you right here.*

I was more than ready for him, and he moaned long and loud as he found me in that way. This position pushed the air out of my lungs as I gripped the sides of the counter almost as hard as he was gripping me. First my waist. Then my shoulders. Then my breasts and his hot, panting breath on my neck, in my hair, in my ear. "Gulazer. My Gulazer. Remember me like this." Then he shot his hands downwards and rubbed and stroked me in a way that, combined with the pounding of his pelvis hardened my senses to everything else but this . . .

Suddenly, as his need got more urgent, more forceful, I could feel pain prickling the edges of my rapture. I cried out and jolted away from him, springing to the other side of the kitchen. For a few seconds he stood, doubled-over and panting, me upright and breathless, our eyes locked and wanting. This wasn't over yet.

In three strides I was there, in front of him, pushing him down onto the floor with a force I didn't know I had. His head hit the tiles with a thud but he barely blinked, instead seizing the back of my head and kissing me feverishly. He stopped for breath and looked at me, his eyes brimming with a passion that I could feel burning throughout me. "You have to know, Gulazer," he said, "You have to know what it feels like."

"I fucking know what it feels like." I cried and straddled him so that I could push him into me quickly, so I could bring my hips down, grind and press and squeeze and thrust so that I could crush his world the way he'd crushed mine. I left streaks down his chest with my nails, I bit his neck and shoulders until the blood threatened to break through, blisters and ripples of my own pain right there on him. He clawed my bottom and scored hard, pink ridges in the snowy flesh, he pushed my hips forcefully up and down until the skin of my inner thighs felt bruised and raw. Then he rose up and whipped my legs behind him, locked his arms around me, his face right in front of mine. My breath, his breath, fast and fevered and fusing together, snarled beyond coherence.

His heartbeat was right there, pulsing hard and clear into my breast as if it were my own, only our skin, sticky and sweet, separating the two. As we began to breathe more slowly, I felt my arousal grow ever deeper, him still inside me, every muscle of my body claiming him and wanting him and owning him more than I could have thought possible. He kept his arms locked tight around me and I began to move gradually, slowly, so that there was barely an inch of us that wasn't touching, sticking, pressing. I noticed he had tears in his eyes and that my cheeks were hot and flushed, tears having already traced their way down and dropped onto my breasts, funneling down and clinging silently to the hairs on his chest.

"Oh, Gulazer." He sighed, a tremble running down the length of his spine and he pressed his cheek next to mine, holding me even tighter, even closer. We rocked together like this, all the madness at having found each other soothed, dissipated, and dispelled into a rhythmical tenderness and we lulled each other, inevitably towards an ecstasy that was age old.

————

"Don't forget your black and white stone thingies" Gillie said, as she squished scarf upon scarf from her İstanbul shopping expedition into her already bursting suitcase.

"Thanks, I've got them." I said, patting my jeans pocket where Urim and Thummim nestled together. I looked out of the window of our room at Shit Class. Rain. A lot of it. Drumming down onto the green swell of the waves. "And have you got Ella's present?"

"Yup," Gillie said, "here it is." She held up the package we'd been out to buy that afternoon from İpeklikum's shopping arcade. We'd seen all manner of ridiculous gifts that Ella would have practically wet her pants over. I mean, it's not every day you see a lilo shaped like a pint of lager or a bottle of perfume joyfully labelled 'Tat'. But we'd opted instead to buy her a beautiful purple patchwork cushion embroidered in gold threads and purple sequins. It was similar to those in Village Corner and we were certain she'd like a real-life prop to accompany all the stories we'd be telling her when we got home.

Gillie was quiet whilst we packed. I could sense how much she ached for home, but her withdrawn mood told me she still had unfinished business with Demir. I'd really tried to talk to her about it now we were alone in our little room in Shit Class, but she was having none of it. I knew by now when to leave well enough alone.

"So," she sighed, sitting on top of her finally zipped up suitcase and drawing her knees up to her chest, "What are you and Mesut going to do?"

"Isn't that the million dollar question?" I grumbled, "I don't know Gillie. I can't quite picture having a long-distance relationship, but then again I can't imagine forgetting him." I shuddered. "Nope. That's not going to happen."

"Have you talked about it?"

"Not really . . . we did have a kind of argument this morning though."

"Really?" Gillie raised an eyebrow.

"Well, it was . . . I've never known anything like it. It was a sex argument. A sexument."

" A sexument. Okay."

"No, no, don't look at me like that. Oh God, it was weird!"

"Yes, Jess. That certainly counts as weird."

"I know, I know. But think about it, right? Nothing with me and Mesut makes any sense whatsoever apart from what I feel in here." I pointed my finger to my heart. Gillie nodded in agreement. "So, whatever went on with us two this morning, I think, was a kind of anger that neither of us can figure it out. I was so furious with him, like mid-orgasm practically, that he'd swept in and changed everything. I never bloody well asked for that. And I wanted to show him how mad I was and maybe, just maybe, give him a reason to back out."

"Did it work?" Gillie asked.

I shook my head, shivering at the memory of how he'd held onto me, tight and strong, until those final, euphoric moments. "Nope. He just held on tighter."

"Do *you* want to back out?" She asked, gently.

I sat down on my own suitcase and, as was becoming my new special skill, allowed the answer to rise up, slowly, surely, with clarity and honesty, "No".

"Well, there you go then." Gillie smiled as she stood up and dragged her suitcase to the door. "What will be, will be. Now let's get to Beerbelly for our last visit. We've got a bill to settle."

30

İNŞALLAH

Luckily, this was one of Beerbelly's cheerful, upbeat kind of nights.

The music was good, the company was good, and the cocktails were (very) good. Everybody was there who we had met along our way on this crazy holiday – everybody who had touched our hearts or entertained us without even knowing it.

For once, Bad Boy was free of teenage stragglers and sat with us chatting and joking and shaking his head at the fact that we were leaving. He wore a grey trilby trimmed in a black ribbon along with his usual vest and baggy pants and strangely managed to carry it off. It must have been the arrogance. Works wonders in the fashion stakes. He kept removing the trilby and offering it to random customers, revealing a little nest of boiled sweets in there. They'd take one, confused but too polite to decline and he'd slip it back on, tapping his nose in a *'let's keep it a secret'* kind of gesture.

Kadafi had forgiven Gillie's outburst from the night before in a split second, as soon as he'd seen her walk into the bar. Something along the lines of, *"I not remembering anything bad about you Mrs Gillie. You follow the goodness! You follow the goodness!"* and all was well. Now he was performing some kind of dance mash-up with Esad over on the dance floor, which was going overwhelmingly in Kadafi's favour.

Not that Esad seemed to care. His shut-tight eyes and hands pulsing up to the heavens indicated he was having some other-worldly dance experience. Beryl held her head in her hands and a fag in her mouth and just sighed at the floor, "God, give me strength!"

Demir sat by Gillie in a stiffly starched suit, purple shirt and grey tie. He'd clearly made an effort for Gillie's last night at least in terms of his appearance. I'd never seen a head of hair that looked more like it had been glued on. We'd smelled him before we'd seen him, he was wearing so much aftershave. It reminded me of Ekrem and his many bottles of 'Black Heaven'.

Aw, Ekrem. I wondered what mischief he was getting up to at English Rose these days. The texts had died a death round about the time I was in İstanbul. I guess he'd got the picture in the end. I thought of him now with nothing but immense relief that I'd ducked out of that when I'd had the impulse. My impulses were shaping up to be pretty good for me. That was something I could certainly take home.

I glanced over my delicious cocktail at something, or some-one, I couldn't take home with me. There he was. My black shadow, moving with that grace, that ease, with that space around him that had somehow drawn me into it. Even in his scruffy, faded jeans and torn Harry Potter T-shirt combo, he had me practically drooling. I chuckled at myself. This was going to be a difficult one to explain at home. *Yeah Mam, yeah Dad, I've fallen heads over heels for this Turkish barman. What does he look like? Well, you know, kind of like a rocker / biker / hobo / druggie type. Nothing to be alarmed about.*

Mesut noticed me looking and smiled. He slunk over to me. He sat in the chair opposite and leaned forward, elbows on knees. Without even saying a word, Beryl stuck a cigarette in his fingers and a lighter in his hand. "Here brother. You're going to need a few of these tonight," and she smiled at both of us, those wonderful crow's feet creasing around her eyes. Then she tutted and flicked her eyes and chin upwards as seemed to be custom among the locals, "I never thought I'd see the day . . ."

Gillie chirped, "Jess, there's only an hour before we get on our transfer bus. I'm just, you know, saying." She gave Mesut a wink and turned back to Demir, who was trying to give her details of a cheap international calls deal for her phone. Mesut took a deep draw of his cigarette and then gave it back to Beryl.

"Thank you sister." He stood up and held his hand out for mine. I took it and we walked out of the bar and down the steps. *This,* I thought to myself, *is our last walk along the beach.*

———

The beach had been damp and clammy. The sand heavy and difficult to trudge through. The rain that afternoon had soaked İpeklikum to its core. Now there was that lovely, fresh smell to the earth as if everything could begin again, or at least choose to carry on in a different way. A fresh, wild, new moment.

Mesut and I had passed the rocks in the sea where we'd originally sat together. They were barely visible under the gently rolling waters now, just little grey peaks peeping out and glinting under the moon. There for another time, perhaps.

Now we were sitting on a ramshackle wooden pier, our feet dangling in the smooth, dark water. Earlier in the season, even just a few weeks ago, this pier had been packed with parasols, sunbeds, sun-streaked tourists and flip-flopping waiters. Now everything had been packed up and stored away in some other place, leaving the pier bare and prone to the elements.

I liked it this way though. It was shuddering gently above

the gentle roll of the glassy sea, creaking and whispering if you listened hard enough. I bet it had some stories to tell. And now it had us. Just us. Right at the end of it.

"You feeling okay, Gulazer?" Mesut asked. We sat side by side, brushing shoulders.

"Strangely, yes." I said. "I am having a perfect moment here."

He took a deep breath and looked out at the horizon, where the sea disappeared into a smoky-black sky. "I am going to spoil your moment now. I am thinking we should be talking. Talking about what we doing. You going home. Tonight."

"Tonight . . ." I echoed. "Yes, well . . . Look. What do you think? Do you want to keep this going? Can you manage a long-distance relationship?"

"I am not thinking like this Jess. I am just thinking of you. I am thinking, what you want?"

"Okay, okay," I said, suddenly feeling very practical. "I think we have a couple of choices. We could, you know, agree to stay together . . ."

"But apart" he smiled.

"Yes, but apart. And I could come visit you again soon and we could just see how things go."

"Or?"

I remembered to stay silent for a beat, to allow those words to come up from a true, genuine place. I owed that to myself and to Mesut. "If I'm totally honest, Mesut, I think we could just end this here. We could just take it for an incredible experience and say goodbye and wish each other well and get on with our lives. It would be a lot simpler."

"A lot simpler." Mesut laughed but his eyes were intent on mine, waiting to hear what else I had to say.

"But if I close my eyes", I grabbed his hand and closed my eyes, really visualising what life could be like without him, "I can imagine that I'd build a really exciting life, that I'd do fine, and so would you and we would, eventually, get over each other. And I do think, because of different types of love I've felt before, I could fall in love and marry someone and have kids and that would all be great. But I know," I opened my eyes now and looked at him, "I know that you would always have a huge part of me. Anybody I meet in the future wouldn't have all of me. I don't know if it's right to do that. You know, to them."

He nodded in that wise way of his and I swear if he had a beard he would have been stroking it sagely. "I am knowing what you mean." He said. "If I have wife, in future, I can not, will not, marry her before I am talking with her, about you."

"What would you say?" I asked, softly.

"I am telling her there is this woman who I never, never forget. Who I am thinking is part of me. And she need to know that if this woman ever come to me in this life again, I not let her go this time. I not marry anyone without them knowing about you, and knowing they might lose me to you, İnşallah."

"What does that mean? İnşallah?"

He brought my hands to his lips and kissed them hard. "God willing." Then he drew me in and we sat in quiet for a while, contemplating the apparent martyrdom of our future husband and wife.

We hadn't made a decision. At least, not out loud. But I knew that the choice was clear. The universe hadn't thrown us together for nothing. We owed it to every rapid heartbeat, every strange omen, every blast of magic we'd felt in each other's presence, to see what happened next.

We'd be together.

But apart.

31

NEW DIRECTION

Lindy had been lost in the sky and the story.

The swelling, deep indigo swathes of the night had wrapped her up during the entire thing. Her back was pressed into the sand now, and her heels dug snugly in. The dying embers of the fire were still just enough to throw out the warmth she needed to stay put. For now.

Together. But apart.

What did that even mean? She turned onto her side and looked over at Jess on the other side of the fire, who was also lying on her back, eyes turned to the sky. "So did you do it then? Did you get on the plane and go home?"

Jess glanced at her over the flaking red remains of burnt driftwood. "Yeah. Of course. I had stuff to get back to."

"But what about Mesut? And what the fuck did you tell your parents? I know mine would go mental." Lindy sat up to pour them both another glass of wine but found the bottle was empty. *Well, that was easy*, she thought.

"Yup. Everyone went mental in their own way. Understandable." Jess shrugged.

"Yeah," Lindy said, "I suppose." She watched as Jess stretched out then stood up, looking taller than Lindy remembered from earlier in the evening. That wine must be doing the trick. "Shall we get some more wine?" She suggested.

"Could do." Jess agreed. "Shall we walk?"

Lindy was reluctant to leave the snug little spot she had all marked out in the sand, but she also knew that the night was drawing in and it was only going to get colder. So she stood up to dust herself off, and watched the grains of sand bounce into the brittle, blushing driftwood below. Then she started walking along the shoreline with Jess, so that the very edges of each lapping wave came close enough to stroke her toes, sending refreshing ripples up her legs.

Jess's month in Turkey had Lindy thinking. It wasn't exactly a happily-ever-after kind of story, but it did seem there had been so much change for Jess during those four weeks, that a transformation of some kind had occurred. That was clear to see, even though Lindy hadn't known Jess before this night. Jess hadn't meant to go out and find a bloke, in fact it seemed that she meant for the very opposite of that. But the interesting thing was, that dark, handsome and brooding or not, the finding of the bloke was hardly the point. The point was that Jess had found herself. Or, more accurately, she had remembered herself.

And at what point had that actually happened? Lindy could really do with knowing so that she could unashamedly pilfer it and sort her own mess out. Although, come to think of it, that mess, that had dominated and defined her for far too long now, actually seemed a little less important right at this moment. Could it be the wine? The beach? The stars? Or was it how much she saw of herself in Jess?

After all this wasn't Lindy's story, it was Jess's. The weird challenges from Marcus that had opened her up and pushed her out of her comfort zone. The emerging friendship with Oliver that had given

Jess new insights, new learnings. The book called The Alchemist, the mountainside epiphany thing, the omens springing up left, right and centre and, of course the way she'd seen her own soul echoed in Mesut's over a coffee cup.

All achingly personal to Jess. So where did that leave Lindy?

Jess turned her pace away from the shore and towards the promenade. "Shall we have a walk through town?" she asked.

"Okay." Lindy said, following her up some wooden steps and onto the pavement. They both stopped and sat on a bench, bending to brush the sand off their feet, and put their shoes back on. Lindy looked out across the beach to where they'd both been sitting and she could see the pink glow still clinging to the sand like the remnants of Jess's story. "Jess, what was it like when you got home?"

Jess finished brushing her feet and slipped on her sandals, then looked up at Lindy. A smile glimmered over her lips. "Well, home was home, nothing had changed. But I had. So actually, it was all desperately different."

"Okay . . ." Lindy said slowly, "Elaborate?"

"I could do," Jess said, looking at her watch, "But are you sure you want to hear the rest? It's getting late."

"I do want to hear the rest, but I am starving." Lindy decided to be bold. Life was hers. "Know anywhere nice we could eat?"

"Yeah. Totally." Said Jess, and sprang up. "Come on, let's do it." So Lindy followed Jess onto the busy promenade, into the soft, warm light of New Year's Eve and amongst the gently vibrating energies of everyone around them.

Each person they passed strolling, dancing, eating or chatting, would have their own story to tell, their own discoveries to share. Lindy could practically feel those stories hanging in the air, following their owners around like faithful daemons. Her own was starting to linger, ever-unfolding, ever-growing. She could feel it as she walked.

It was stroking her cheeks, draping itself around her and nestling in her heart. And there was that growing, reassuring knowledge that perhaps hadn't been there before, that her story could change. It could and would take a new direction.

So, she followed Jess.

EPILOGUE

"Jess! Mam says you have to come home right now."

It's my brother, Max. He's rounded the corner and found me. He's very much out of breath. Pink cheeks. Freckles quivering all over them.

"Did you run all the way here. And what do you mean? Is Mam back from work already?"

"Yeah. She trusted me just this once to come and get you. I said I knew where you'd be. And I was right."

I shrugged. It didn't take a genius. "Why does she need me right now? Is Sandra still . . ?"

"No. Sandra's gone. Mam made her go. I don't know what happened but they've both gone."

"You mean . . .?"

"Yeah, he's not there anymore. There was a bit of shouting. That's why I came out of my room. Anyway, hurry up! Mam wants to show you something."

"Am I in trouble?" I ask, as we both begin the climb back up the road. "I didn't go past the crossroads."

"It's okay Jess. I think you're going to be happy." Max smiles and his freckles follow. I love how his whole face knows how to feel a smile.

Suddenly a jolt of lightning strikes a happy place in my chest. I think I know what it is. I turn to Max as we make huge strides over pavement cracks and old crisp packets, dog poo and chewing gum. "Is it what I think it is Max? Did Mam bring the thing home that she said she would? The thing from work?"

"I'm not telling, I'm not telling." He winks. When did he learn to do that?

It doesn't matter though because my strides are getting faster and faster and now I'm leaving Max and his little legs behind. It's okay. We can see our house now and he knows where he's going. The wind whips over my whole body and pushes me towards a joy I'm certain I'm going to feel in just a few minutes' time.

Because I know he's not there I burst through our front door and crash onto the carpet, yelling in whoops for my Mam. "Did you get it Mam? Is it here? Where are you?"

"Alright love." Her voice lands in my ears. "I'm in your room. Come on in."

I don't even take my shoes off. This is just too exciting. My room is downstairs, through my dad's little office. I skid through it and then through the already open door to my room. My Little Ponies are prancing across the walls in pastel-coloured bursts, looking almost as excited as me. My mam is bent over my ancient drop-down desk that came from her side of the family and she isn't even bothered that I've written poems all over it in my new paint pens.

She lifts her curly red head and shoots a sparkly smile right at me. "Come on then. Come and have a look. It's all yours now."

I look at it sitting there on the desk. It's got a faded, greenish plastic surrounding the mechanics but the keys stand out proud and strong all white and shiny as if nobody's ever touched them before. My mam has already wound a completely blank bit of paper into the roller-thingy. There's a shiny metal bit that sticks out of one side that I know, because I've watched my mam typing before, that when you hear the bell ding, you use it to move the paper along to start another line. I can't wait to hear the bell. "Does the bell work?"

"Och, well it does now. Thanks to the wee lads in the office we got it working just fine for you. They fixed it up all good and proper. Would have gone to the tip otherwise Jessica, now that we're getting computers to do all our work in the office. Well, aren't you going to have a go?"

I totally am going to have a go.

I sit down and lift my hands. I let them hover over this amazing beast of a thing until I think of something to write. I know. I definitely know. I point out my finger and press it against the letter 'T' until the long, graceful arm hammers upwards towards the paper and the waiting ink ribbon.

Where is the click? Where is the mark on the paper?

"Och, Jessica, you just need a bit more fire in your wee finger. Try again. Push it a bit harder love." My mam is gazing down on me with all the thrills I'm feeling too. "Go on. You'll get used to it soon enough."

I try again. This time a brilliant click sounds through my room and the 'T' is there, indigo and merry on the white, white paper. I keep going, taking care not to let my pointed fingers slip through the gaps between the keys.

"What are you going to write? Have you got an idea already you clever girl?" I might be wrong but my mam now seems a little sad. She's got her hands on my shoulders and is looking down as I type. She sniffs. It's okay. The click-clacking of the keys is so fantastic I can't imagine she'll be sad for long. And wait til she sees the title of my new story.

The Girl with the Dandeelyon Wishes, a storie by Jessica Parker.

Ping! The bell sounds and I think I might burst. This is the most brilliant feeling ever.

"What's she typing? Is it working? I can't believe she didn't wait for me!" My brother whines out loud as he explodes into my room – snot and fresh air clinging willfully to him. My mam lifts her hands from my shoulders and transfers them to Max's. She slowly turns his whole tiny body back towards my bedroom door.

"Right Max, time for us to leave Jessica well alone. She's making magic happen."

And right now, as Max moans for sweets and Mam sighs her tiredness away into the depths of our messy home, I don't care how long they leave me alone for. Because suddenly I'm lost and found all at once. Lost in stories and found in stories – and I'm staying here.

MORE BY ABIGAIL YARDIMCI

Life Is Yours (Book 1)

Destiny Is Yours (Book 2)

Everything Is Yours (Book 3)

My Little Ramadan - Coming soon

Lockdown Love Letters - Coming soon

ACKNOWLEDGEMENTS

I'm going to admit something to you, reader. Writing the acknowledgements at the end of a book is way scarier than writing the actual book.

But apparently, this is what proper authors do, so here goes . . .

Let's start with Pam Sweeting, a fellow Northerner who babysat my first son when he was nought but a babe in arms and we lived in Turkey. Without having that time to tip-tap away on my laptop in the sweltering heat sans enfant, I may never have got to the point of publishing this, the second book.

To all of the people who advised and / or mopped up my tears during the process of writing the Life Is Yours trilogy (and some of whom watched the love story unfold for real) – Susan Appleby, Tracy Brown, Louize Cattermole, Michaela Dicker, Gareth Farr, Joolz and Julie Form, Gary and Kathleen Heads, Peter and Lucy Maguire, Paul McArthur, Faith Miller, Jenny Rutter, Scott and Michaela Tennant, Lynn Wilson, Tony and Maria Wright.

To those of you who might recognise some of the characters in the book – I can promise you that you are far lovelier, brighter and more three-dimensional than anyone you will find in these pages, and for that I thank you . . . Gemma Cumming, Emma Boor, James Lowell, Brenda Brown, Muammer Ernez and Devrim Deniz. Mark Labrow – I'm forever indebted to you and your real-life 'Experiments in the Art of Living'.

Massive thanks to all of the literary pros who have watched me (probably quite amusingly) hurl myself into the publishing world. As you know, it's a learning curve . . . Kelly & Zoey Allen, Sandy Barker, Chris D'Lacey, Susan Hampson, Lynn Huggins-Cooper, Karen Huxtable, Lucy Keeling, Kriti Khare, Ian McLaughlin, Hayley McLean, Clare Nasir, Chrissie Parker, Matt Rogan, David Snape, Suzy K Quinn, Sarah Seed, Tracey Shults, Julie Spiller, Vikkie Wakeham and Shelley Wilson.

Thank you to all of the brilliant people who organise authors' groups on social media – especially Anita Faulkner and her Chick Lit & Prosecco Chat Group on Facebook. It really is the most friendly and supportive place for a romance author to be.

To Team Yardımcı . . . thank you for taking the time out to read and edit this version of Destiny Is Yours. You spotted things that went right over my stressed-out head (and Jill Cowan – you are now in charge of vetting the sex scenes).

Thank you to Bailey McGinn for the most awesome cover designs and your unwavering patience with me and my big ideas. You're bloody brilliant at what you do.

Paulo Coelho – I know I'm not alone in thanking you for writing a book such as The Alchemist. You certainly changed my world all those years ago and I hope that now, with my little story, I can point even more people towards the powerful tale of Santiago.

READERS . . . you are what make my heart sing (headed by Kirsty Walsh and Sue Baker of course – official super-fans). I LOVE when you send me messages, when you share your thoughts in reviews and when you tell your friends about my books – you are the final piece in my jigsaw of writer's ambition and without you the picture would be sorely incomplete.

Dad – I know you're aware of what's going down and I can feel the glimmer of your beardy smile when I'm writing. You know I'm forever grateful.

Mam – Thank you for all the edits and the encouragement. Editing and encouraging me in life has also worked out pretty well so cheers for that too.

Matty – You're more of an inspiration than you know and I'm forever held to your epic standard of writing at secondary school. I know I'll never reach it but a girl's got to dream.

Baran and Azad – If nothing else, I hope this book leaves you with something that hints at the breath-taking connection I have with your Baba and how special you are to have sprung from that.

Mustafa – This is *our* book in the trilogy really, isn't it? Who am I kidding, I know you'll never read it – but I hope you read this. Bird Poo. I love you. Don't ever stop bringing me yellow roses.

ABOUT THE AUTHOR

ABIGAIL YARDIMCI is an author, painter and mindfulness practitioner. She is a Geordie girl living by the sea in South Devon with her Turkish husband and two terrifying kids. She loves to blog and gets her kicks through mindful parenting styles, creative living and chocolate.

Abigail's writing inspiration comes from scratching the surface of everyday life to find the underlying magic that connects us all. The fire beneath the frustration, the creativity beneath the boredom, the stillness beneath the chaos.

The Life Is Yours Trilogy is published by Soft Rebel Publishing and there are more books by Abigail on the way.

Abigail LOVES connecting with her readers so check her out on social media and sign up to her mailing list now to get a FREE poetry e-book called 'What About Now?'

———

www.abigailyardimci.com

 facebook.com/AbigailYardimci

twitter.com/AbigailYardimci

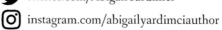 instagram.com/abigailyardimciauthor

Printed in Great Britain
by Amazon

42564867R00179